finding

her

edge

ALSO BY JENNIFER IACOPELLI

Break the Fall

finding her edge

JENNIFER IACOPELLI

RAZORBILL

RAZORBILL

An imprint of Penguin Random House LLC, New York

First published in the United States of America by Razorbill,
an imprint of Penguin Random House LLC, 2022

Visit us online at penguinrandomhouse.com.

Library of Congress Cataloging-in-Publication Data is available.

ISBN 9780593350362

Manufactured in Canada

1 3 5 7 9 10 8 6 4 2

FRI

Design by Rebecca Aidlin
Text set in Iowan Old Style

*To my family, who are absolutely
nothing like the family in this book.*

finding

her

edge

Chapter 1

$\mathcal{T}$HE PAIR FLOATS across the ice, hands clasped together, skates scraping against the surface in perfect synchronicity.

Or, at least, they're trying to.

"Okay!" I shout, my voice hoarse after a long day of lessons. Despite my aching legs, I'm circling around them on my own skates with a smooth, natural glide that, hopefully, they'll be able to mimic one day. "Keep your grip firm, but not too tight. Don't pull her with you, Jackson. Remember, she's smaller than you. You need to adjust your stride to match hers." The two eight-year-olds I'm coaching are getting used to holding hands and skating together, one of the foundational basics of ice dance.

My voice echoes up into the rafters of Kellynch Rink of Greater Boston, the place I've spent more time in than my own home. It practically is home. My sisters and I were on skates before we could see over the boards surrounding the ice, because that's what you do when you're born a Russo.

"He's not pulling you along anymore, Sadie, so you have to stay with him," I remind her after he stops yanking at her arm and she drifts behind.

Finally, they fall into step, her shorter legs stretching a little longer, his longer legs striding a little shorter, and from my vantage point, it looks like perfection.

"That's it!" They beam up at me, still holding hands. "Great job."

Sadie barely comes up to my hip, and she casts her eyes longingly at my legs. "I wish I was as tall as you, Adriana. I wouldn't have to stride so long."

"You're perfect exactly the way you are. Make sure you stretch tonight, especially your feet and ankles. Gotta keep them nice and strong for when I see you two again."

"Ugh, that's so long from now," Jackson whines as I lead them off the ice.

"Not too long," I say, clicking my skate guards on as soon as I pass through the gate. "Just until after Worlds."

"That's forever," Sadie says, probably because when you're eight years old, two months is an eternity.

To be fair, even at sixteen, it feels like forever for me, too, because by then Junior World Championships, the biggest competition of my life, will be over. It can't get here soon enough. My ice dance partner and I qualified for the second year in a row, but this year, we finally have a great shot of winning gold. So two months from now, I'll either be a World Champion . . . or not.

Right now, though, I'm a coach. I've been picking up more and more lessons in the last couple of years, trying to do my part to keep the lights on.

I wave to Sadie's and Jackson's moms as we approach them outside the rink. They're sitting in the parents' viewing area adjacent to the lobby. Banners cover the walls, citing the successes of the skating club in the half century it's been open.

"Ah, Adriana!" Sadie's mom says, racing up to me, her strides way faster than the ones her daughter can produce on the ice. "I'm so glad I got to see you before you left!"

"Oh," I say with a small smile.

"Please tell Elisa I said good luck! We'll all be watching her!"

I don't let my smile slide at all, but instead let it grow. "Of course, I will."

"You must be so proud of her. Your big sister going to the Olympics, what an accomplishment. Your father must be ecstatic."

"He is." I hold that smile, big and tight across my face. It's not the first time this has happened, and it won't be the last. Olympic Games trumps Junior World Championships, obviously. Elisa is a ladies' singles skater, and their careers tend to peak way younger than ice dancers. Four years from now, if everything goes as planned, I'll be headed to my first Olympics.

"Well, we don't want to keep you," Sadie's mom says, her eyes darting around the lobby, probably to make sure she didn't miss Elisa or Dad. Jackson and his mom are already gone.

"Sadie, great job today. I'll see you when I get back."

I lock the doors to the rink behind them, the last lesson we'll have for a while. It's sad, but necessary. I flick off the lobby lights before turning the COME IN, WE'RE OPEN sign hanging on the door to SORRY, WE'RE CLOSED.

While Dad and Elisa head to Beijing for the Olympics, we're hosting the other athletes and their coaches in the lead-up to Junior Worlds. Dad's always been able to charm people, especially anyone who understands our family's legacy. We've had elite camps here for years, and before Mom died, she ran summer camp intensives that were famous for getting athletes ready for the next level. The lure of training at our legendary rink was just too much to resist.

The fees Dad negotiated with each individual coach are nearly double what we usually make in skating lessons and birthday parties and hockey leagues. And as much as I hate it, hate letting down our students and all the people who've supported Kellynch over the years, there was no way we could afford to turn down that kind of money. Because as famous and successful our family has been, we have this nasty habit of spending way more money than we bring in. Like, *way* more.

Kellynch was opened by my great-grandparents back before even my dad first started skating. In the last fifty years, it's become the most prestigious club in the country. We've won more World and Olympic medals—most of which belong to my parents—than some countries, and it's a state-of-the-art facility. Dad won't stand for anything less.

It would be *impossible* for him to work in a place that was anything less than what someone would expect for an Olympic gold medalist, the patriarch of the most famous family in figure skating. That would be okay if it wasn't *also* impossible for Walter Russo to drive anything less than what someone would expect an Olympic gold medalist to drive or live in a house that was anything less than what someone would expect an Olympic gold medalist from figure skating's first family to live in.

No amount of rink rentals and skating lessons can make up for that kind of spending, and it's only gotten worse as we grow closer to Elisa's Olympic year. Figure skating is an expensive sport no matter what level you're on, but the Olympics is a whole other thing. Trainers and choreographers and consultants on wardrobe and makeup, not to mention the publicity firm Dad hired to really make the most of it. It all adds up to a hell of a lot of money we don't have. No matter how much we bring in, it gets spent.

The business is in massive debt and we needed creative solutions, and even I can admit that letting all the junior skaters and their coaches invade was one of the better ideas Dad came up with.

Our home is set on Kellynch's property, steps from the rink itself, but it was there long before that. It started as a small house my great-grandparents moved into when they saved enough money after emigrating from Italy, but every generation has expanded it, adding on bedrooms and bathrooms and a massive swimming pool in the backyard and a gym in the basement and an entertainment room on the top floor. There's even a rooftop deck where you can see all of our small hamlet of Kellynch up against the Charles River and then across it, the massive Boston skyline in the distance.

The original part of the house is old-school traditional with brick walls and dark shutters lining the windows, but the rest of it is a mishmash of styles and trends, ultramodern on one side from the renovation my grandparents did in the nineties and then farmhouse chic on the other side when my mom and dad added on to it before my sisters and I were born. It's a little wild to look at, but I love it.

What I don't love is that as soon as I walk in the front door, I'm hit with a wall of noise that rivals the loudest crowds I've ever skated in front of. There are at least a dozen people hovering in the foyer, two holding fluffy gray boom mics up over the heads of the others, another two with cameras braced on their shoulders, aimed at my dad from different angles.

Renting the rink was one thing. This circus, no matter how well it pays, is something else entirely. The camera crews have been with us for months leading up to the Games. When Tamara Jackson, the head of the United States Olympic Federation, approached Dad with the offer of a reality TV series starring him and Elisa, he didn't hesitate. The money was okay, not enough to really get us out of debt, but the sheer amount of publicity was too much for either my dad or my sister to turn down. They *live* for publicity.

It's made life completely insane, though. There's always someone watching, and that makes my dad and sister even more conscious of what they're wearing and how they look on camera. I'm pretty sure neither of them has repeated an outfit in the last six months.

I weave my way through the bustling catering staff moving our furniture around and setting up tables and chairs and a bar in the far corner where our dining room table normally sits. They are preparing for Elisa's going-away party tonight, and between catering and the camera crew, it's a complete zoo. Dad's directing traffic while also studying his reflection in the mirror above the fireplace.

"Which side do you think?" Dad says, his blond hair slicked back, as he dabs a silk handkerchief across his forehead. It takes me a moment before I realize he's talking to me. I tilt my head, considering, as he turns his head back and forth so I can judge.

"The right," I say, gesturing toward that side of his face before sliding past the group and making a beeline for the stairs.

He nods and then blinks at me with my hair up in a messy bun and my sweaty skating clothes. "What are you wearing, Adriana? You *are* coming to the party tonight, aren't you?"

"Of course. I just finished up my last lesson."

"Ice dance?" he clarifies with what I'm sure he thinks is a purely neutral voice, but Dad's never neutral, not about what counts as real figure skating, anyway, and ice dancing definitely doesn't. It never has.

"Yeah. Anyway, I was gonna take a nap and then shower and get ready," I say, not in the mood to rehash that old argument. I'm too exhausted.

"Ugh! Where is Adriana? I need her!" Elisa's voice carries over the din before she pushes through the crowd.

Elisa is my opposite in every way. Even though she's a year older than me, at five foot eight I tower over her by more than half a foot. Her hair falls in honey-blonde waves over her shoulders, a stark contrast to my dark curls. The only thing we have in common are our eyes, hazel, exactly like Mom's were.

"I'm here," I say, stepping out from behind one of the burly cameramen, who swings around to get us both into the shot.

My sister grabs me by the wrist and tugs with insistence toward the stairs, and even with the advantage of my longer legs, I have to hurry to keep up with her.

"I need you to look at my luggage. I don't know how I can be expected to pack my things for the Olympics *and* prepare for the party tonight. Like, there's no way I'm going to remember what I need. This list they sent us is so overwhelming," she says as we pass through her bedroom door. She swipes the list off her dresser and shoves it back at me before shutting the door in the face of the cameraman who was struggling to follow us. I guess she doesn't want this on camera.

I take the list and then look around her bedroom. It's a total wreck. There are clothes everywhere, across the floor and her bed and her furniture. Every drawer in her dresser is empty, and hangers hang in her closet with nothing hung on them.

"Um, how much did you get done?" I ask, but I can answer my own question. Her two suitcases are in the center of her bed and completely empty. Nothing. She got nothing done.

"I took everything out," she says, flopping back onto the chaise lounge in the corner of her bedroom.

With a sigh, I glance at the list. It's nothing crazy. Just an itinerary of their training plans leading up to the Games and the events they'll need nice clothes for along the way. Mom used to always sit with us to pack for our competitions, but after she got sick, and then after she was gone, we started to sit with each other. For Elisa, though, it usually turns into me packing while she supervises.

I place the list down in a free bit of space on her bed. "Okay, I'll help, but you're sitting on a pile of leggings."

Giggling, she reaches underneath and pulls out a ball of black fabric and tosses it to me. Before I catch it, her phone is out and she's tapping away at the screen.

"Has Brayden said anything?" she asks, not looking up as I detangle the leggings and roll them neatly into a corner of her suitcase.

"About what?" I ask, wrinkling my nose. Brayden Elliot is my ice dance partner. He's eighteen, and he and Elisa had a *thing* back when he and I started skating together two years ago.

It did not end well.

Not that any of the *things* Brayden has ever had with any girl end well. I don't know the exact details—and never, ever want to know them, thank you very much—but I do know he was the one who ended it. He's always the one who ends those *things*. Yet somehow, despite that, my sister, who could probably have any guy she wants, never seems to give up hope that he might change his mind.

Personally, I don't get it. Brayden's a great partner, a cool guy and undeniably hot, but when the word *fuckboy* gets into the dictionary, his picture will be right there next to it.

"Did he ask about me?"

"I haven't seen him since training this morning." That's not really an answer, and I hope she doesn't notice. I don't want to tell her no, Brayden hadn't said anything, because Brayden isn't interested anymore. "You shouldn't worry about Brayden. You're going to the Olympics."

"Yes, and I'm currently trying not to think about how our entire family's legacy is on my shoulders now, thanks. So . . . Brayden, did he ask about me?"

Ah, so she did notice, and yeah, that's fair. Okay, distractions.

"He didn't say anything," I tell her. "Sadie Mortenson's mom wishes you good luck, though."

Yeah, that's probably not that helpful.

Elisa sniffs and continues to scroll through her phone. "He never said whether or not he was coming tonight. Did he mention the party at training?"

"He said he was going to try to stop by."

What I don't say is that Brayden said he'd try to stop by after he met up with the girl he's having his most recent *thing* with. There's no way I can tell Elisa that without a total implosion, though.

9

"We've been training really hard. He might want to crash to-night."

"He at least owes me a 'good luck.' I'm going to the Olympics." She sighs heavily, but then pivots, clearly remembering she doesn't want to think about that. "Don't you wish you hadn't switched to ice dance? You won't get the chance for another four years at least."

It's a very old conversation that always comes back to one im-portant point.

"You know I'm too tall for anything other than ice dance," I say dully, like I have every time anyone has brought this up in the last decade.

Elisa's gaze flicks up from her screen. "Whatever. If he doesn't come tonight, tell Brayden that—"

Whatever I'm supposed to tell Brayden is cut off by the bed-room door swinging open. Our younger sister Maria flies through it, flinging it shut behind her so hard the walls shudder.

"Charlie is the worst, and I am so sick of him," she whines, marching straight for Elisa and throwing herself into the empty space on the chaise beside her. Maria is only two years younger than me, but sometimes those two years feel like twenty. Charlie is Charles Monroe Jr., her skating partner.

She skates pairs, which is nearly as acceptable as singles skat-ing, according to Dad, at least. My sisters both inherited our dad's blond hair, our mom's tiny stature, and the firm belief that ice dance doesn't really belong in the sport of figure skating. Ap-parently, it's only a real sport if you hurl your body through the air while spinning like a top. Unlike Dad, however, they're both totally fine with my chosen discipline, since it conveniently never puts any of us in direct competition. Mom loved that part of it, that she never had to worry about who to cheer for on the ice, that if her girls all went out there and did their best, then she knew we'd come home with three gold medals.

"What now?" Elisa asks as Maria curls into her side, but she meets my eyes over her head and rolls them dramatically. Elisa doesn't usually have patience for our youngest sister's drama, but apparently, it's a decent enough distraction for her right now.

"He's just there and hot and so nice and . . . why does he have to be gay?"

"I know it's tough," Elisa says, squeezing our little sister's shoulders. "Maybe it's better, though. Mixing a partnership with romance can be tricky. That never really works, right, Adriana?"

I freeze. My stomach lurches and the air prickles around me. Elisa stares, waiting for me to agree and tell Maria she's better off not dating her skating partner because it is actually good advice. There's no innuendo in her voice. She's not talking about . . . *him*. She probably doesn't even remember the crush I had on him before he left, before I made him leave. In fact, knowing Elisa, she probably doesn't remember him at all.

He is Freddie O'Connell, my former partner, former best friend, and first crush.

Two years ago, I sprouted up to my current height, and he barely matched it, with no guarantee he'd ever grow enough for us to be successful together. So I had to decide.

It was the toughest choice I've ever made in my life, to leave Freddie and partner up with Brayden Elliot.

Now he skates with a good friend of mine, Riley Monroe, and

they've been pretty successful. So much so that they'll be headed to Junior World Championships too, after training here at Kellynch, starting tomorrow.

I push that thought away, like I have since Dad told us about the arrangement with the rest of the Junior Worlds team, ignoring the fact Freddie will be here soon, at the same rink as me. The ice dancing world is small. I haven't been able to avoid him completely, but we aren't friends anymore. I can probably count on one hand the number of words we've exchanged since his last day training at Kellynch.

The last time I saw him was at Nationals, when Brayden and I beat him and Riley out for gold. He'd done what you're supposed to do, shook my hand and mumbled congratulations before I stepped up onto the podium to get my medal. He didn't even look me in the eye. Not that I can blame him, really.

"What do you think?" Maria's voice cuts into my thoughts. Only seconds have passed. I blink away the memories and focus on her.

I pick up a dress from Elisa's bed, a red sequined minidress that I'm pretty sure actually belongs to me. Folding it into a neat square, I place it in my older sister's suitcase and then turn to my little sister.

"You deserve someone who wants to be with you as much as you want to be with them."

Maria blinks at me once, then twice before her face crumples and tears start to gather at the corners of her eyes, her cheeks flushing bright. "But I can't help it. I love him." She launches herself off the chaise and starts pacing the room.

Elisa stands, moving by me with the grace of the Olympic figure skater she is. She reaches into her suitcase to pick up the dress I put there. "Here," she says, holding it out to Maria. "Wear this to the party tonight. I'm wearing white, and the dress I got for Adriana is blue. It'll be so perfect for pictures. I'll do your hair and makeup and we'll find someone who will appreciate how absolutely gorgeous you are."

Maria drags Elisa out of the room and across the hall into hers, leaving me with two nearly empty suitcases. Glancing around at the stuff that needs to be in them before tomorrow morning still strewn everywhere, I sigh before getting to work.

Chapter 2

THE PARTY IS in full swing by the time I make it back down the stairs, showered and changed from my skating gear into the blue dress Elisa picked out. My sister's taste is too expensive, but it is good. The silky fabric swishes pleasantly about halfway down my thighs, and my hair is up in a ballet bun since I didn't have enough time to blow-dry it.

A yawn takes over my face and I try to hide it behind my hand. Didn't have enough time for a nap either.

There are tons of faces I recognize: Elisa's friends, Dad's friends, sponsors, agents, officials from the National Figure Skating Coalition and the United States Olympic Federation and the film crew, their cameras taking in the dizzying spectacle of an Olympic send-off fit for a queen. Music pumps through the speakers of the sound system, an instrumental jazz compilation that seems familiar, but I can't name.

Servers are loaded down with trays of drinks and appetizers that look way fancier than the usual mozzarella sticks and chicken fingers we sell at the rink's concession stand. Puff pastry probably stuffed with lobster and drizzled with truffle oil and whatever expensive things Elisa and Dad thought were necessary.

I'm about to take the final step and enter the fray when two hushed voices drift up into the stairwell. I can't see them—they're off to the side of the stairs and definitely can't see me. One voice is almost as familiar as my own, though.

"And a mortgage won't be hard to get?" Dad asks, though it doesn't really sound like much of a question.

"The property itself is worth quite a bit, plus a house in this area, considering the school district and its proximity to Boston? If you ever had to sell, you'd more than recoup the cost."

A mortgage. The place we live. The place we train. My *home*.

That was the one comfort of the last few years as the bills kept piling up. We owned the house and the rink and the property free and clear.

Have things gotten so bad that we have to risk that?

My skin prickles and a wave of uncomfortable warmth slides through me. I swipe my palms over the silk of my skirt, but then clench them, my fingernails digging into my palms. This stupid dress. This ridiculous party. All of it completely unnecessary, and meanwhile, we could lose everything. The blood is roaring in my ears.

Their voices fade as I try desperately to calm down. I need a glass of water, cold water. Spotting the bar on the other end of the room, I make a beeline for it, and the bartender raises his eyebrows when I only ask for ice water, but he puts it in front of me and I chug it down and ask for another. The bartender snorts this time. He's probably used to people throwing back tequila and vodka like this. I finish the second glass and then take a long, deep breath and let it out slowly.

I need to get myself under control. There are cameras everywhere and even more eyes. People who know me well enough to know with one look that something is very wrong.

"I have to tell you to smile on the ice enough, do I have to do it off the ice too?"

I turn to my left, where my coach, Camille Radinski, is standing beside me, a drink that definitely isn't water in her hand. There's a bright pink umbrella stuck through the orange slice sitting on the lip of the glass with a fizzy pink concoction inside. Camille's been my coach forever, but she's been in my life even longer than that. She and my mom were best friends. She's my godmother, Elisa and Maria's too, but they've never been as close.

"This is one hell of a party," I say through gritted teeth.

"Your mom would have loved it."

I huff in disbelief. Mom wouldn't have loved how insanely expensive it was, but then again, if Mom had planned this, it wouldn't have ever gotten to that point.

"You forget, Adriana, I knew her better than anyone, even you. She loved a good party."

"Shouldn't they save it until they get back? You know, maybe after she actually wins something."

Camille purses her lips, a sure sign that she agrees with me but doesn't want to say something bad about my dad in front of me. Elisa's got a good chance to medal in Beijing. It would make way more sense to have a party once she does, and maybe then we could actually afford it. Olympic medals mean sponsorships, big companies with money to throw around. And that's what could finally get us out of this crunch. Dad wouldn't have to mortgage the house and—

"Think, though," Camille says, pulling me out of my thought spiral, a skill she's honed in the decade we've worked together. "Four years from now, we'll be having a send-off party for you."

"No." I shake my head. Parties like this one are not my thing. I'm not even sure I'd want one if I won a medal. The very idea makes me nervous, and I wipe off a sweaty palm on the skirt of my dress.

"Celebrating is important, Adriana, especially something as huge and life altering as your first Olympic Games. If Elisa wasn't headed to Beijing, I would have insisted on a party like this one for you and your teammates going to Paris."

"Paris," I repeat, unable to keep the smile off my face. "It will be, by far, the biggest and coolest place I've traveled to for skating."

"Indeed," Camille says, and takes a sip of her drink, humming in appreciation of whatever the pink fizz tastes like, and her pause sends my mind veering back toward where it was before.

"Did you know Dad is thinking about mortgaging the house?"

Camille coughs, a hand flying to her nose, where I suspect some of the fizz ended up. "He told you that?"

"I heard him say it," I hedge, not really needing a lecture about eavesdropping to derail this conversation.

"That's really not something you should be worrying about," she says, but her brow is furrowed, and her mouth sets itself into a thin line. Confusion.

She didn't know. That means Dad didn't tell her, which means he doesn't want her opinion because he knows it's a shitty idea.

"We can't let him do this," I say, my panic rising again. "We could lose the house, the rink, everything."

"Adriana, breathe. None of this is your responsibility. I'll talk to him, okay?"

A knot in my chest loosens. Camille can always get through to Dad. She's really the only one he listens to anymore.

"Now smile, your sister is coming over," Camille warns, her eyes focused over my shoulder, and I turn to see the crowd parting as Elisa slides toward us in her bright winter white jumpsuit, blonde hair shining over her shoulders.

She flashes a smile at Camille before turning to me. "Is Brayden here yet?"

"I haven't seen him."

"Ugh, I wanted to make sure he was here for the toast, so the cameras could get a shot of him. Be a peach and go to the kitchen and tell them to hold off for another hour or at least until Brayden shows up?"

Her tone rises at the end of her sentence, but it's not a question.

"I'll . . ." Camille starts, but I shake my head.

"Thanks," Elisa says before her eyes catch on something over my shoulder. "Oh! Those are the reps from Nike! I should go talk to them."

She's gone before either of us can respond.

I roll my eyes at Camille before placing my empty glass on the tray of a passing server and make my way through the throngs of people toward the kitchen, at the back of the house. Servers in black pants and matching button-down shirts are practically sprinting back and forth through the archway, emptying their trays and filling them again while a frenzied caterer barks orders.

"Hi," I say, trying to get her attention, but she clearly doesn't hear me as she rearranges a platter of stuffed mushrooms before offering it to me without looking. "Uh, no, sorry," I say, not taking the tray, and she turns, blinking at me in confusion. "I'm Adriana, Elisa's sister. She said to hold off on the champagne flutes for now. She's still waiting for a few people to show up."

The caterer goes red in the face. "We poured the flutes already. The drinks will go flat. How am I supposed to . . ." She trails off, staring into the distance like I've destroyed all hope that her night will go smoothly.

"I'm so sorry," I say, biting my lip, trying to figure out a solution that won't send Elisa into apoplexy. "It shouldn't be much longer."

Pulling out my phone, I tap out a message and hit send, hoping against hope that the recipient will see it soon.

A buzzing sound almost immediately responds. I whirl around, and across the room there's Brayden leaning against our kitchen table, a charming grin spread across his face, a champagne flute already dangling from his fingers. He's tall, easy to see in the crowd of servers bustling around the room, with a head of shaggy sandy-blond hair, broad shoulders, and a frame of lithe muscle, strong enough to lift me as we travel across the ice. One curl is falling charmingly over his forehead, the only thing marring his clear olive skin, as his blue eyes twinkle at one of the servers. She's a blonde too, with a French braid holding back her hair, and she's hanging on his every word. And then he smiles, and I swear I can hear the girl's sigh all the way across the kitchen.

"Forget it," I say, turning back to the caterer. "You can start now."

"Get those flutes on trays and get them circulated," the caterer orders, and the servers, even the one who was giggling at Brayden, snap to it.

"Hey," I say, moving toward my partner, on the ice, anyway. "You made it."

"I said I'd try."

"You said you had a thing, and that usually means you're busy . . . till breakfast."

His eyes twinkle at me while he shrugs, unbothered. "Her sorority had a party, something with the pledges. No boys allowed."

"BC? BU? Emerson?"

"MIT, actually," he says with a smirk. "Even the genius girls love me."

"Or MIT's academic standards are slipping."

"Ooh, harsh," he says, but can't help laughing, which makes me laugh too. He pushes up off the table and offers me a champagne flute from the tray beside him. "Dom Perignon Rosé. You know this stuff is like three hundred fifty dollars a bottle?"

My eyes fly over the entire counter filled with bottles, too many to count.

"Of course you know that and of course it is," I say, and the anger and panic from earlier are gone, overwhelmed by sheer exhaustion. "We are never going to get out from under this debt if they keep living like this."

"Hey," he says, "it's gonna be okay. You'll all be flush once they get back from Beijing."

I nod, not in the mood to go over point by point exactly why that's probably not true. His eyes look concerned, but he's also shifting back and forth uncomfortably. Brayden doesn't have the patience for long serious conversations and honestly, right now, neither do I.

"C'mon, Elisa was holding off the toast until you got here and nearly gave the caterer a heart attack."

"She was waiting for me?" he asks, eyebrows shooting up. "Why?"

"You know why," I say, and grab the flute he's still holding out for me and take his free hand in mine. "Let's go before we miss it."

We follow a line of servers back into the living room, including the one Brayden was flirting with. She glances back toward us and then scowls when she sees his hand in mine. Poor girl. It's not me she has to worry about. Brayden is totally oblivious, though, as usual, and he tugs me over to the back wall as soon as everyone has a glass and the clinking of a fork against crystal brings the din to a low hum.

At the center of it all, Dad and Elisa stand together, smiling brightly, glasses held out toward our guests.

"Ladies and gentlemen," Dad says, his smile somehow widening as the eyes of everyone in the room focus on him. He loves a spotlight now as much as he did back during his glory days. Actually, he might love it more now. "I want to thank each and every one of you for coming out tonight to celebrate a hallmark day in the Russo family's storied history. A second-generation Olympian. I only wish Guilia could have been here to see this day. I know she's looking down on us right now." He puts an arm around Elisa's shoulders and kisses the top of her head. The guests let out a soft collective *aww* before quieting so he can continue. "As many of you can attest to, our family's legacy is something I'm tremendously proud of, and I cannot think of anyone more worthy than Elisa to carry on the legacy in Beijing and bring honor and perhaps another medal or two home to Kellynch." He raises his glass. "To Elisa."

"To Elisa," the crowd says, taking a sip together before applauding, which quickly morphs back into conversation.

"To Elisa," I say, softly touching my glass to Brayden's, but I don't drink mine.

Brayden snorts, but follows suit. "To Elisa. You know it's bad luck not to drink after a toast."

"Would you rather have us on camera drinking underage when Elisa's show airs?"

There's a soft noise beside us, a camera's zoom focusing. I turn and there's a cameraman barely an arm's length away, his lens pointed right at us. I nod my head toward him and Brayden laughs softly.

"Good call," Brayden says. "You know, four years from now, it'll be us they're following around, and I'll be twenty-one by then."

"Good luck getting me to sign off on that."

He raises his eyebrows. "Really? You know we're going to be marketable as shit, and think about it, the money we'll be able to bring in, you won't have worry how much the champagne costs at our victory party. Picture it with me," he says, positioning himself behind me, leaning his chin on my shoulder. "All these people here for us, gold medals around our necks. Nike and Adidas in a bidding war for us to wear their warm-up gear."

I can picture it. Clear as day. I know we're good. We're better than good, actually. We competed in the senior division at Nationals this year and nearly won. Four more years of training together, four more years of perfecting our connection on the ice, four more years and this could be ours. This and so much more. Olympic gold. That's the dream.

"Four years is a long time," I say.

"Not that long," he responds, his breath ghosting against my neck, and despite myself, I shiver.

There's a tiny part of me, very small, that wonders about that. We've always had amazing chemistry on the ice, and sometimes I can't help but think it would be the same off it, but curiosity doesn't outweigh how bad an idea getting involved with Brayden would be on so many levels.

"Hey, guys," I say, shifting away from him even more as Maria approaches with Charlie in tow. Charlie's sixteen and Black, his hair braided close to his head in rows, his light brown eyes always darting from one thing to the next, eager to take in everything. He's about my height, making him the perfect partner for my tiny sister, at least on the ice. Maria's brows are pulled together, her lips in a tight, thin line, while Charlie's usually pleasant expression is twisted in clear frustration. "Everything okay?"

"Fine," Maria says. "They'd be better if Charlie would talk to his dad."

"I told you that I did, but he doesn't have time right now, not with the Olympics so soon. He said he'd consider it when we all got back from Paris."

Charles Monroe Sr. is a sports agent and one of the best in the business. He represents Dad and Elisa. Technically, he also represents the rest of us, but as junior athletes no one is really interested in sponsoring us. Yet. But tonight has really brought the world into sharp focus—sponsorships are where the real money is, the kind of money that could help us keep the house or, if worse comes to worst, could fund my training once I'm old enough to go out on my own.

"See," Brayden says, nudging my shoulder with his, "it's not too early to think about it."

"Thank you," Maria says, smiling at him, but then turning to Charlie. "Even Brayden thinks so."

Charlie's face clears a bit as he turns to Brayden. He has the most massively obvious crush on my partner, which Brayden, being Brayden, doesn't discourage at all, despite being super straight.

"You really think so, Brayden?" Charlie asks.

"What's the harm in exploring our options early?" Brayden says with a casual shrug, smiling at the other boy.

I'm pretty sure if he were capable of spontaneously combusting, little pieces of Charlie would be splattered all over the ceiling.

The crowd starts to thin around us, and the servers have begun to clear the plates, napkins, and glasses left strewn on every free surface in the room. Soon enough it's only a few stragglers milling around. Dad and Camille are talking in the corner. Elisa is standing with them, her eyes starting to glaze over, and then her attention is drawn toward me.

Or Brayden, actually.

Letting out a squeal, she leaves Dad and Camille to their conversation and struts over to our group.

"Brayden, you made it," she says, somehow slipping her slim form into the space between us. I slide over a bit and meet Brayden's eyes over her head, commiserating in being cornered. "Were you here for the toast? Adriana was supposed to hold it off until you got here." She turns to me with a glare.

"As soon as I saw he was here, I told them to go ahead with it," I say, but I'm ignored.

"I can't believe I leave for the Olympics tomorrow. I'm going to be an *Olympian*," Elisa says, her arm winding around Brayden's.

"That's usually how it works," he says, sending her a tight smile that doesn't quite reach his eyes.

"Aren't you going to wish me luck?" she asks, her eyes wide.

"You don't need luck," Brayden responds with a shrug.

"You're right," she agrees with a bright smile, but it fades when Brayden's phone buzzes and he extracts himself long enough to glance at the screen.

"Sorry, guys, I gotta run. Safe travels, Elisa," and then he leans around her to me. "Think about what I said. I'll see you tomorrow."

Before I can answer, he's gone.

"What did he say? What are you supposed to think about?" Elisa asks as we all watch him wave to Camille and Dad before disappearing through the front door.

I shake my head. "Nothing important. C'mon, we should help clean up."

It's late by the time the living room looks even close to how it normally does, and it's past two in the morning, long after Elisa and Maria went to bed, when the last of the servers and the camera crew finally pull out of our driveway and disappear into the night.

Camille and I are grabbing the last of the garbage bags to bring out to the curb.

"Give me those," she says. "You're dead on your feet. I'll push back tomorrow's training session. Text Brayden and tell him I don't want to see either of you before noon."

I shake my head. "No, I don't want to cut it that close. Everyone else is supposed to be here at one."

"Fine," she says, giving in, with clear disapproval in her eyes, but she refocuses quickly. "Speaking of *everyone*—"

"Camille," I warn. I'd managed to put it out of my head for a hot second, but now there's nothing to distract me. No lessons to teach. No family drama to solve. No ridiculously expensive party to attend. Even as freaked out as I am about our finances, there's nothing I can do about it tonight. So there's nothing separating me from the reality of Freddie O'Connell arriving at Kellynch tomorrow morning.

"It's perfectly natural to be nervous about him training here. You two were close once and I know there's some awkwardness."

"Awkwardness? I guess you can call being perfectly polite and looking through me awkward."

Camille sighs. "You made the best decision you could make with the information you had at the time. Skating partnerships aren't school dances. They're career choices. I'm sorry if I . . ."

"No, I don't blame you. You gave me advice and I took it. That doesn't mean he's not totally justified in how he feels."

"He had something of a crush on you back then, and if I remember right, it was reciprocated."

"I was fourteen and we were friends. We dreamed about going to the Olympics together and I ended that."

"You couldn't help a growth spurt."

"It doesn't matter anymore. He's with Riley and I'm with Brayden and that's the way it is."

"Well, that's a very mature way to look at it," Camille says, her voice wary, like she doesn't quite believe I'm really that mature. She's not wrong.

"We're going to Junior World Championships. Everything worked out. How else am I supposed to look at it?"

"You're entitled to your feelings, Adriana. You're allowed to feel however you want about Freddie O'Connell."

"Exactly," I agree, "and he's allowed to feel however he wants about me."

"Have you tried talking to him about it? It's been years."

I shake my head. "I don't even know what I would say. The only thing I plan to focus on is winning gold. Everything else is just noise."

Camille smiles. "That's what I like to hear."

Chapter 3

I'S FREEZING OUTSIDE. Of course it is. This is Boston in the middle of winter. Piles of dirty slush line the street at the end of our driveway, and every breath I take is echoed out into the air, freezing as soon as it passes my lips. The sun is barely a glimmer on the horizon, and the early morning has that surreal quality to it that never goes away, even if you're normally up at this hour.

Which I am.

Except usually, I'm already at the rink, warming up for our first training session of the day. Instead, I'm on the sidewalk, rocking back and forth from toe to heel, trying to keep my legs from freezing beneath the thin leggings I pulled on this morning, not realizing how long this would take.

Dad and Elisa are leaving for Beijing.

If it were any other competition, they'd simply get in a car and go to the airport, but things aren't that simple, not when it's the Olympics and not when there's a camera crew around. A bunch of fans are across the street holding signs and stuffed animals, the same kind they throw on the ice after a successful routine, and some local news crews are set up near them. The cameraman is directing the driver of the biggest limousine I've ever seen on how he wants the car to pull up into his shot. Dad and Elisa are still back

28

in the house because apparently they need to emerge out the door precisely when the car pulls up.

"How much longer?" Maria whines next to me, feverishly rubbing her hands over her arms. "I'm going to get sick standing out here for so long. My throat is already sore."

I don't answer her. It's maybe the tenth time she's asked, and I still have no idea, though I kind of want to ask how she makes it through training if the cold makes her sick.

Then, finally, things seem to be moving in the right direction. The limo driver circles back to the end of the street. The director stands out of the shot and signals the crowd to start cheering, then he gives a thumbs-up toward the house. Right on cue, Elisa and Dad come out the door, each rolling a suitcase behind them with one hand and waving to the fans and the cameras with the other, smiles plastered wide and white across their faces.

"Looks like I got here just in time," a voice mutters, coming up beside me. "I went to the rink and you weren't there."

"Please do not ruin this shot," I grind out from between my teeth, clenched together in a smile, not looking up at Brayden. I lift a hand to my mouth, trying to blow some warmth into it. "We've been out here for an hour already."

"An hour?" he says, louder than I'd like, while he grabs one of my hands and rubs it between his, the feeling in it returning after a few seconds.

Elisa and Dad have made it to the end of the driveway now, but walk right by us, like they're supposed to, across the street to the fans, where they'll pose for pictures for a minute while the documentary crew gets the shots they need of their adoring public.

Brayden switches to my other hand as the car pulls up and the limo driver hops out and loads up the suitcases, half of which are already in his trunk.

"So this is total bullshit?" Brayden asks, huffing out a laugh.

There's finally feeling in all my fingers, so I pull my hand away. "Yep."

"I can't believe so many people showed up!" Elisa says, jogging back across the street to us, her arms full of stuffed animals. "Brayden, you got out of bed early just to say goodbye?" He opens his mouth to say that he's *always* up at this hour to train, but she doesn't give him the chance. "Adriana, can you take these?" She shoves the toys into my arms. "I promised I'd send them all autographed pictures, so could you get their info after we leave?"

"Sure," I say, shifting my grip on a pastel pink elephant that's threatening to topple out of my arms and into the slushy mess at my feet.

"Give me those," Brayden says, taking them from me, while Elisa turns to wave at the fans who are cheering Dad as he retreats toward us.

A man with a steady cam on his shoulder accompanied by another with a boom mic held high over our heads approaches from the same angle the other camera is filming.

"This is it," Elisa says. "Wish me luck!"

"You're gonna kick ass," Maria says as they hug, her potential sore throat completely forgotten now that Elisa is in front of her. "I'm going to miss you so much. Bring me back something from China."

Elisa laughs, pulling away. "I'll bring you back a gold medal, how's that?"

"Good luck," I say as she turns to me, and we hug tightly. "We'll be watching."

I squeeze her one more time before I let go and sniff, trying to pretend it's because of how cold it is outside. We might not be that close anymore, but I am really proud of what she's accomplished. Mom would have been too. I kind of want to tell her that, but I can't quite find the words.

"And what about you, Brayden, will you be watching?" Elisa asks as Dad and Maria hug quickly, but I don't hear what he says, and Dad shifts his attention to me. I want to ask him about what I heard last night. I want to know just how bad it's gotten. But the words stick in my throat.

"Take care of this place and your sister," he says, "and listen to Camille."

"I will, I promise," I say, and then they're in the car, like the director wanted, with the fans still cheering and waving, leaving us at the curb as the limo disappears into the distance.

The crowd is still hovering around, probably to make sure I get their contact info, but the camera crew is packing up around us and it suddenly hits me that they're leaving too.

Kellynch has been a zoo of activity for months with our usual lessons and the show and all the Olympic hype, but now it'll just be Maria and me at the house, with Camille checking in to make sure we don't burn the place down.

It won't last. By this afternoon we'll be invaded by the NFSC's Junior World Championships team and their coaches. That's this afternoon, though—for now, I want to relish the quiet.

"Um, where should I put these?" Brayden asks, and when I turn to him, he's still holding about a dozen stuffed animals, and the unfortunate pink elephant is on the ground. There's also a gigantic red lipstick stain on his cheek that extends, barely, to the corner of his mouth. I bend down, pick up the elephant, and balance it at the top of the pile.

"Go put them inside. I'm gonna go get contact info from those people and then maybe, if Camille doesn't kill us for being late, we can actually train."

"Sounds like a plan to me."

"ONE MORE LAP," Camille commands from her spot up against the boards. "Thirty minutes late, thirty laps."

Thirty laps of the rink wouldn't be so bad, normally, but it's thirty laps where Brayden and I have to be perfectly in sync, and this early in the morning after a party last night and standing outside in the cold for so long, it's been a struggle.

Camille's one of the people I'm closest to in this world, but when we get on the ice, she goes into a different mode, morphing from my sweet, understanding godmother into the best coach in the world of ice dance.

"Well, at least we're warm now," Brayden says under his breath, our strides matching perfectly as we make the final turn in our last lap.

"For sure," I agree, and we come to a stop in front of Camille, who nods in approval.

"What time was the flight?" she asks as we both grab for our water bottles and try to steady our breathing.

My gaze flies up toward the far wall of the rink, past the rows of banners that proclaim in bold lettering all the champions who have trained at Kellynch for the last thirty years. The clock reads after eight.

"They should be taking off in a little bit."

"At least our Olympics will be in Milan," Brayden says. "No twenty-hour flight for us. And Italy's only a six-hour time difference, like Paris."

"One competition at a time, Mr. Elliot," Camille admonishes. "Let's not jinx it."

"C'mon, Camille, you don't believe in jinxes."

"Maybe not, but that doesn't mean we should take anything for granted. You two have come a long way in the last two years, but you have even further to go before you stand on top of that Olympic podium, and the first step there is winning these World Championships. To get started today, I want a full run-through of both programs so we can identify any trouble spots before the rest of the team arrives, especially Freddie O'Connell and Riley Monroe. They may be your teammates, but they are also your competition, and I don't want to give them a confidence boost by picking apart your weak spots while they're here to see it."

We stare at her silently.

"What?"

"So inspiring, Camille," I say, shaking my head but grinning.

"Truly," Brayden quips. "A speech worthy of a Super Bowl locker room or, you know, at least a training montage set to rousing music."

Rolling her eyes, she matches my grin. "Shut up, the both of you, and get going."

Brayden slides his hand into mine and grips it firmly as we turn and skate out to the center of the ice.

"Ready?" he asks.

"Let's do this."

Less than an hour later my breath comes hard and fast as our music cuts off in the rink's speakers. It's our third run-through and by far our best free dance of the morning. The key for the next month is to make our first attempt our best, because that's what it's going to take to win gold in Paris and put us on track for the Olympics.

"Better, much better. You're both still losing steam at the end of the twizzles," Camille calls out from a few yards away. "You're losing steam in unison, so there's at least that, but if only one of you fixes it, it'll be a mess. And, Adriana, *expression.*"

I nod, slowing to a stop at the center of the ice as Brayden drifts toward the edge of the rink for a drink of water. I blow a wayward curl out of my eyes and then tilt my head back to redo my ponytail. It's the correction she's been giving me since I started skating. I don't think there's been one practice where Camille hasn't reminded me that I'm not doing enough to really sell the routine. It's so common now that all she has to do is say the word *expression* to let me know I'm skating stone-faced when I should be emoting.

"I've gotta get going," I say, skating over to Brayden. He hands the water bottle over to me before wiping at his mouth.

"Let's go one more time," he suggests.

"The beds in the guest rooms still haven't been made. I asked Maria to do it yesterday, but I'm pretty sure she didn't, and I want everything to be ready to go once they get here."

"Yeah, about that . . ." he begins.

"If you two aren't going to vacate the ice, I'd like to see those twizzles again, and remember, Adriana—" Camille demands, which makes the decision to go again for us, and then nods her head toward the door where Charlie and Maria are coming in, chatting. They have the ice next.

"Expression!" I fill in for her, and then turn to Brayden. "Let's go one more time." I echo his words with a smile.

After I take a quick sip of water, we skate together to where our twizzle sequence is supposed to begin.

"Let's push it," I say, and I count us in. "One and two and three."

We push off together, spinning in sync over the ice. It's important to get this right, to build momentum through the rotations, because the sequence comes right before the music swells into a crashing crescendo that's supposed to get the crowd riled and pull them into the second half of the dance. Our free dance is set to a *Game of Thrones* medley—it's Brayden's all-time favorite TV show— and it never fails to get the crowd excited as we act out the tragic romance of Jon Snow and Daenerys Targaryen.

Personally, that particular love story kind of grosses me out, but the fans and, most importantly, the judges eat up the routine every time, especially when I manage to make it look like it *doesn't* gross me out, which I think I'm doing a pretty good job of right now.

After five *one more*s, Camille is finally satisfied both with the speed and the unity of our twizzles.

"There's a party tonight in Fenway. You wanna come?" Brayden asks as we glide off the ice.

"Whose party?"

"Does it matter?" he asks, laughing. "Some people I know."

"I'm good."

"You are," he agrees. "Too good."

"Good work today, both of you," Camille says, coming over and saving me from having to respond.

"A compliment!" Brayden says, leaning in close to our coach, eyes narrowed. "Were you body snatched?"

Camille rolls her eyes with affection, a smile creeping over her mouth. Once we're off the ice, the stern taskmaster disappears and it's back to the woman who practically raised me.

"Last chance," Brayden says. "You'll have to come home with me so I can get ready, though. My mom would love to see you. She likes you more than me."

I laugh, mostly because it's probably a little bit true. "I have too much to do here. Have fun, though."

With a nod he's gone, headed toward the locker room, already swiping through his phone, probably finding a date for tonight.

"Is there a practice schedule yet?" Camille asks.

"If you ever checked your emails, you'd know we finalized it yesterday."

"I don't know my password," she protests.

"How do you not know your own email password?" I ask, shaking my head. "We have the second session."

"You'd think as the only favorites to win gold, you'd give yourself the first practice session," Camille mutters.

"I didn't want to make it seem like we were giving ourselves priority just because we own the place."

"But you do."

"Yeah, but who knows for how much longer?"

That makes Camille stop and grimace. "It's a shame that you didn't have any other options." She knows better than anyone how much we need the money. "I spoke to your father last night. You're right, he is thinking about mortgaging the property. He seemed pretty set on it, especially if Elisa doesn't medal."

"Did he say that to her?"

"No, of course not," Camille says, and then sighs heavily. "Your mother never would have let things get this bad."

"I know," I say, resigned to it. I have to be, I guess. I can't control what my dad does with his money. No one can and no one ever could, except Mom.

I miss her pretty much all the time. She's always in the back of my mind, even after four years, but it's impossible not to think about her when the subject of money comes up.

When she was alive, she handled all the finances and always managed to come up with some awesome compromise where no one felt like they were being deprived of anything, but the bills were still being paid. Now? Not so much. Not that Dad ever gets into the specifics or details, but I do enough of our paperwork to know things aren't good.

After a long pause, my godmother tries a different tack. "Are you going to be okay? After what you said last night, I'm worried about you . . ." Camille trails off and bites her lip, a rare expression. It means she's literally holding back something she wants to say, and Camille almost never holds back. And if it's not about money, which it's not because she clearly doesn't have a problem talking about that, it can only be about one other thing.

"Are you really still worried about the Freddie thing? I told you, it's fine. I'm fine."

She lifts one eyebrow in complete disbelief. "Having him back here after all these years, and the last time he was here you were going through so much; I wonder if agreeing to this was the best idea."

"The money is too good. This plus whatever Elisa brings in from the sponsors after the Games? We might start to make up some ground. Like you said, we don't have any other choice. Just like I didn't really have any other choice two years ago."

She nods and sends me a tight smile before she leaves for the day.

I let myself linger in a long, hot shower back at home, maybe longer than I should have if I want to have everything ready, but it feels good on my muscles after our intense workout.

The NFSC was trying to organize something themselves this year, a team-building camp, but Dad beat them to it, contracts signed and finalized before their plans even got off the ground. It's amazing how fast Dad can move when he wants to use his legacy to piss off the NFSC and make some money while he's at it.

Everyone will be staying at Kellynch House. It's a massive old Victorian that sat adjacent to the rink's property for years before my grandpa bought it, just before my dad took over running the family business. Some people in the figure skating world call it the Kellynch Estate because we basically own the entire block. My dad wanted it to look like something out of the Historical Society's magazine, so after a total renovation I only have vague memories of that preserved the outward look but completely modernized the interior, Kellynch House was born.

It's able to house more than a dozen people. Each room has two full-size beds with memory foam mattresses, two dressers, and an attached bathroom, plus we've got new linens for every bed. It's not a five-star hotel, but from what I can tell it's at least on par with a Hilton or Marriott. Almost everyone on the team will be at Kellynch, but Freddie's sister—and coach—Georgia O'Connell-Croft and her husband are going to take over the guest room in our house for the time being, so that's mission one, and then the rest of the beds at Kellynch need to be made up.

Usually there's a full staff, but since everyone's coaches are coming with them, Dad decided to let people fend for themselves once they get here, and it felt like a waste to have them in just to set everything up. I can do it, and we won't have to pay them and cut into the profit we're making.

"Some help would be great," I say to Maria after changing the sheets in the guest room and putting fresh toiletries in the bathroom.

"Charlie and I are going shopping in a bit."

"Shopping?" I ask, raising an eyebrow at her. We do *not* have any money for shopping right now.

"Don't look at me like that. He wants to get a Gucci belt and his dad finally gave in, and I have a few gift cards that I didn't use from Christmas."

"Okay, we need five rooms ready to go for this afternoon, and if you help me, I have a Visa gift card in the top drawer of my dresser you can take with you. There's at least a hundred dollars on it."

Her eyes light up immediately. "Really? Because I've been looking at these amazing shoes that I'd love to take to Paris. Like, can you imagine how people are going to dress at the parties after the competition? It's *Paris*."

"Make up two of the rooms, and the gift card is yours."

She pulls the sheets and towels out of the closet so fast that the rest spill out onto the floor at my feet.

It's not hard to get the rooms ready, but halfway through the third room, it hits me. By tonight one of these rooms is going to half belong to Freddie O'Connell. I bet he'll room with Ben Woo, one of the singles skaters. They've been close friends for a long time. And one of these beds might be Freddie's.

Ugh. I'm being such a creeper. Who cares where Freddie sleeps? I shouldn't, and he'd be so freaked out if he knew I was thinking about it. This shouldn't be anything new. We've been around each other before.

Not this close, though, and not for this long, I remind myself.

But we can be mature about it, right? Or maybe not mature, but we can ignore each other, just like we have at every competition and event we've crossed paths at in the last two years.

Maybe it'll be like that. He stays in his lane and I stay in mine. That's probably best, because there's no way we're ever going back to the way we were before. We were partners, but more than that, we were best friends. We skated together for four years. He was there for me when my mom died. And then I turned my back on him and no matter how good a reason I had, it was still a betrayal, and it uprooted his entire life and so many others'. He moved down to Atlanta to live and train with his sister and started skating with Charlie Monroe's twin sister, Riley. Charlie's mom lives down there with her full time, while he and his dad live here in Boston. It's not the weirdest figure skating family living arrangement I've ever heard of, but it does suck.

And by this afternoon, every single one of them will be here.

Turning, I catch a glance of myself in the mirror hooked over the back of the door. So much upheaval, all because I grew before Freddie did. Because he did grow, eventually. Less than a year later, he shot up, not as tall as Brayden, but tall enough to be my partner and definitely strong enough.

What would have happened if I'd *waited*?

Back then, that didn't feel like an option. It could have meant sitting out an entire season, or more, for the both of us. We wouldn't have gone to Junior Worlds the next year. Who knows where we'd be now? Where I'd be.

The front door slams downstairs and brings me back to my surroundings. From the window I can see Maria skipping out the door toward Charlie Monroe's car.

How long have I been standing here?

I peek into the two rooms she got ready and roll my eyes at the totally wrinkled duvet covers before remaking all four beds neatly. I'm fluffing the last pillow when I hear the crunch of gravel and slush underneath tires.

They're here.

Chapter 4

I HEAR THEM BEFORE I see them.

Well, actually, I hear her.

"Adriana!" Riley Monroe shrieks from outside before bursting through the front door, dropping her luggage behind her, and sprinting across the room to me as I descend the final step. "We're going to Worlds together!"

There's no time to answer her as she launches herself the last few feet that separate us and jumps up, forcing me to drop the blanket I was carrying down the stairs to catch her. Riley's only a year younger than me, but she's so small it feels like way more. She's barely five feet tall, and I feel like an Amazon as she squeezes me tight in a hug. Over her shoulder, her dad, Charles, is lifting her bags from the pile she dropped them in when she came through the door.

She's a miniature version of Charlie, sparkling brown eyes and dark skin, her hair in tightly woven braids pulled back into a thick ponytail.

Riley and I grew up together here at Kellynch. She moved with her mom down to Atlanta two years ago so she could partner with Freddie. It's been hard to stay close, but it helps that Riley's one of those friends you might not talk to for a year, but you pick up right where you left off the next time you see each other.

If she's ever noticed that her partner barely acknowledges my existence, she's never said anything.

"Can you believe it? We're going to Worlds together!" she repeats, and I laugh.

"Just like we talked about when we were little. Or at least when I was little. When are you going to grow?"

She smiles and shakes her head. "Doctor says I'm all done."

"Ugh, lucky."

"Are you kidding?" she says, grabbing my hands and holding them out. "You should be walking fashion runways or something. Look at you. Well, okay, maybe like the Victoria's Secret Fashion Show, you know, because of the . . ." She motions at my chest, which, much like my height, is larger than pretty much any other figure skater I know.

"Enough." I laugh, dropping her down and pulling away. "C'mon, grab your bags. I put you in the main house with me and Maria. You can have Elisa's room."

"Actually, I was thinking I could stay here," she says, before biting her lip.

"Here?" I ask. "Why? The house is way more comfortable and closer to the rink. And the heat works better."

"I don't think it's about any of that," Charles jokes from behind her, and I blink in confusion. He's a little taller than me, and his hair is long gone, shaved off, the top of his head buffed to a shine. "A certain someone is staying here . . ." He trails off before turning away and heading back outside, presumably to get the rest of the luggage.

"Da-ad," Riley says to his back, but then her frown gives way to a bright smile. "It's not like that. I think since we're partners, Freddie and I should stay in the same place."

"That makes sense," I manage to say, holding back the tsunami of panic that immediately rages through me. They're partners, of course they should stay together, but that's not what it sounded like. It sounded like that was an excuse. It sounded liked Riley wants to be as close to Freddie as possible. It sounded like she likes him. You know, likes him, likes him.

Who even am I right now? Who talks like that? Likes him, likes him?

But why wouldn't she like him and why wouldn't he like her back? She's adorable and sweet and they'd probably make a great couple. They've trained together six days a week for the last two years. This shouldn't be shocking. In fact, I should have guessed it way before now. They look great on the ice. Why wouldn't that become more off it?

"I mean, nothing's happened," Riley's saying, but I only catch the end of it. "But I don't know. Is it stupid to go there? What do you think?"

"I think . . . we shouldn't talk about this right now when every-one else is probably going to be here any second."

"Yeah, Dad knew the fastest way from Logan, but they had to wait for cabs . . ." she says, gesturing back behind her. Car doors slamming and voices chattering over each other start to draw closer from behind the door.

"We'll talk later, okay?" I assure her, and she nods as her dad comes back inside with a woman behind him bundled up tight to fight against the Boston winter.

"How do you stand it?" Georgia O'Connell-Croft says, unwinding her scarf from around her face, her eyes, the same ones she shares with her brother, twinkling at me. Her hair is a bright red, not the chestnut brown that Freddie has, but the resemblance is almost uncanny, right down to the light green eyes. "Boston is a great place to visit, but my God, why would anyone subject themselves to this cold on purpose?"

I send her a small smile, a little unsure of myself. I've never actually spoken to Georgia before. There was never any reason to. She always lived and trained down in Atlanta, even when Freddie and I skated together. She retired from ice dancing the same year Freddie and I stopped skating together, and when he moved down there, she and her husband, Harry, started coaching. They must be pretty good at it. Freddie and Riley's improvement in the last year has been amazing.

The next four years should be interesting. We all have the Olympics in our sights, and there's only one gold medal.

"The cold builds character," I say softly, and she laughs out loud.

"That must be it," she says, and comes forward with her hand extended. "I'm Georgia, and you are Adriana Russo. It's so nice to actually meet you after hearing so much about you for so many years."

My smile falters, half terrified. Whatever she heard from Riley was probably fine, but I can't imagine Freddie spent any time singing my praises to his big sister after what I did.

"It's nice to meet you too," I say. "Don't take off all your gear, though. I set you and your husband up in the main house. I figured you'd be more comfortable sharing a room with one big bed instead of two smaller ones."

"Well, lead the way," Georgia says. "Harry and the rest are still getting the luggage out of the taxis, but I need to get off my feet." Her hand comes up to rest against her stomach, which is kind of protruding even through the coat. She's having a baby.

"Follow me," I say, leading her out the front door. In the distance, her husband is lining up bags on the sidewalk, talking to a few of the other skaters and coaches. I think I see the top of Freddie's head sticking out of the crowd.

Yeah, that's him, bouncing up and down on his toes against the cold. Then he wheels around and in one motion scoops up a handful of slush, turning and firing it behind him. I can't see the intended targets, but it's probably one of his friends, and sure enough a second later a snowball pelts him in the shoulder as he tries to spin out of the way. He throws his head back with an infectious laugh that echoes up into the winter air.

He's always like that, unable to sit still, vibrating against his own skin to do something, usually something outrageous and fun and completely unexpected.

I might have played it cool with Camille, but I can't handle this right now, not if my suspicions about him and Riley are correct. So, I duck my head and lead Georgia away without looking back.

God, I'm such a coward.

"I can't tell you how excited we were when we found out that training camp was going to be at Kellynch. When I was growing up,

I dreamed of training here," Georgia says as we reach the house, but as we climb the steps of the porch, she turns and faces the rink next door. "I came to a summer camp once when I was very little. It was the highlight of my career up until I went to Nationals for the first time."

I lead her into the house and then straight back toward the largest guest bedroom. "You guys will be in here. Bathroom is attached."

"Wow," she says, coming in behind me. "This is . . . that's . . . a lot of mirrors."

I glance over to the far wall of the room, which is entirely covered in mirrors and another freestanding mirror reflects them back. We don't have a lot of guests at the main house, so Dad usually uses it as a dressing room.

"Yeah, my dad likes to make sure he looks just right before he goes out in the world."

Georgia laughs and then shrugs. "I guess I'll make sure not to look up when I drag myself out of bed in the morning."

"Adriana!" Maria's voice carries from somewhere in the house.

"We're in here," I call, sticking my head out into the hallway. "What are you doing back so soon?"

"Charlie got a text from his sister that they got here, and his dad said we had to come back. We're going to have a team party at the Kellynch House tonight . . . oh . . . hi," she says to Georgia, recognizing her immediately. "I don't mean like a real party, just hanging out."

"You must be Maria," she says, and extends her hand, which Maria shakes quickly.

"Anyway," my sister says, refocusing on me. "I really want to go, but I got a text from Julian Tarasi's mom confirming for later and I totally forgot to cancel his last lesson and you know what a total bitch she is. Don't say it, I know you told me to cancel all my lessons. I'm not as responsible as you, but, like, I really want to hang out with everyone, especially Charlie, and you're really good with parents like that . . ."

"Go," I say, cutting her off. "I'll take the lesson."

"Ah!" she shrieks, and then gives me a fierce hug before pulling away and bounding up and down on her toes. "Thank you, thank you, thank you! I'll totally make it up to you, I promise."

"Go, before I change my mind," I warn, and she's off like a shot, totally unaware there's zero chance I'll be changing my mind. This is the perfect excuse. I can go give this lesson and then come back to the house, and for at least one more night I can avoid Freddie.

I turn back to Georgia, who is eyeing me curiously. "I'll leave you to get settled in."

"Yes, a nap is calling my name," she says, pressing her palms against the mattress, and when the memory foam conforms around them, she moans. "I think I'm going to like it here."

By the time I grab the keys to the rink and my skates, Mrs. Tarasi and her son Julian, a nine-year-old who would much rather be playing hockey than figure skating, are already waiting for me out in the cold.

"I'm so sorry for the oversight," I say as she glares at me while Julian chucks icy snowballs at the building. "All the lessons this week and going forward were supposed to be canceled, but obviously I'd be more than happy to give Julian his lesson now, no charge."

Mrs. Tarasi sniffs her agreement, possibly because her mouth has frozen shut standing out in this weather, and when we walk inside, I motion to the coffee machine in the far corner.

"There's change at the front desk," I say. "Please have a hot drink on us. Julian, this way."

The lesson is a total nightmare. The kid doesn't want to be here, but his mom refuses to let him play hockey, which I totally get. He's undersized for his age, and hockey in Boston is no joke. Kids around here leave the maternity ward with little hockey sticks and skate before they can walk. Once they start to grow, there's no stopping them on the ice. There are technically rules against checking in the lower levels, but it's still rough, and even if Mrs. Tarasi is kind of a jerk, she understandably doesn't want to see her little boy get decapitated by some peewee hockey goon.

We run through some standard skating drills, working on long, smooth strokes across the ice, but Julian is super bored and we're only halfway through when he's complaining about wanting to jump.

"Maria said I'd be able to do a waltz jump this week."

"Oh, did she?" I ask in total disbelief. This kid is nowhere near ready for a waltz jump. He's not terrible, but sometimes he still randomly loses his balance just skating. "I don't think that's such a good idea, Julian."

But it's too late. He's streaking across the ice backward before swinging his leg out to leap into the air, but instead his toe pick gets caught underneath him and down he goes, face-first into the ice.

The rink is silent and then his mom, who looked up from her

phone at exactly the wrong moment, screams in terror. I skate up to him frantically before falling to my knees beside him. There's blood coming out of his nose and leaking onto the ice in tiny rivulets. His mom's screams finally seem to register for him and that's what makes him start to cry. His hands come up and clutch his face, probably making it way worse, and I try to pry his hands away. The blood running from his nose starts to leak into his mouth and he coughs against it, splattering the ice, which sets his mom off again, but I can't worry about her right now.

"Julian," I say softly, my hands over his. "Julian, you have to let me see, okay? I promise I won't touch it, but I need to see how bad it is, okay? I need you to be brave."

His eyes are filled with tears and they're streaking down his cheeks, mixing with the blood that's already slowing. His hands come down and I hold his face gently in my hands, turning his head back and forth. The blood has completely stopped now.

"You look okay," I say. "How does it feel?"

He sniffs and then reaches up to touch it. "All right, I think." His fingers press against his nose and he doesn't even flinch. "I think I just got scared."

"Okay, we're gonna get you up," I say, and take his hands. "On three—one . . . two . . . three." I lift him, and he's back up on his skates, holding my hands tightly as he finds his balance. Together, hand in hand, we make our way to the edge of the rink.

"Julian!" his mom shouts, her voice echoing up into the rafters of the empty rink. "Get off the ice right this instant."

I can't hear whatever bullshit Mrs. Tarasi is spewing at me and I'm about to scream in this woman's face when the doors to the rink open and Freddie O'Connell strides through them.

The air leaves my lungs and I can't seem to pull in another breath.

Mrs. Tarasi is still yelling, but my focus is drawn to Freddie and Ben Woo, who walks in behind him, as I fumble with grabbing the first aid kit. Ben is a Korean American singles skater who qualified to Junior Worlds too this year. They're both in skates and each has a hockey stick in his hand. They grew up playing hockey before swapping over to figure skating.

Freddie took a lot of heat from the kids we skated with when we were little when he made the choice. He's even sort of built for hockey, broad shoulders and really strong legs. I asked him once if he regretted giving it up, but he just scoffed at me, green eyes sparkling, like the answer was obvious. My heart had stuttered in my chest when his eyes met mine. That was the first time I wondered what it would be like to kiss a boy.

Then for a moment, as Ben turns to say something to him, my eyes meet Freddie's for real this time.

Oh God.

It's worse than I thought.

His eyes are the same, a soft green, but there's no sparkle, not for me. Not anymore.

I've seen him in the two years since we stopped skating together, obviously. We stood on the same medal podium at Nationals, went to the same events, but there's something about this moment, back at Kellynch, that's too much. And immediately, I know what it is.

We're only feet from where we were standing when I told him we couldn't skate together anymore. That I needed to find a new partner and so did he. In fact, Julian is sitting in the exact spot Freddie was on the bleachers while he stared back at me as I cried and tried to get the words out, tried to explain.

The feeling is wildly familiar to the blood rushing in my ears and the knot in my chest, climbing up into my throat, my eyes burning with the effort to just *not cry*. And now, of course, when I need it to most, my head won't let go of that memory, not fully.

It's Mrs. Tarasi's rant that finally pushes it to the back of my mind, tearing my gaze away from Freddie, trying to make all of this end. "Please, Mrs. Tarasi, I'm so sorry. I have some wipes and gauze for Julian. It looks like he's okay, but . . ."

"And how would you know if he's okay?" she shoots back. "Forget it. We're never coming back here after this disaster anyway."

"As I said earlier, Kellynch is closed to lessons for the next month and we've rescheduled all our usual students with other rinks, but please don't let this incident affect your future plans," I say, but she cuts me off with another tirade until . . .

"Mom!" Julian yells from behind me, which should be impossible because the rink is behind me. "Mom, look!"

"Julian?" Mrs. Tarasi asks, blinking over my shoulder, and I turn to take in whatever she's seeing.

"He shoots!" he yells with sheer joy, the laughter clear as a bell. Ben's skating alongside Julian as he pushes a hockey puck forward with Ben's stick, Freddie gliding backward in front of him as they approach two cones set out on the goal line. "He scores!"

And he's laughing and smiling, tears long gone, with a bunch of tissues stuffed into his nostrils.

"Well," Mrs. Tarasi says, "it looks like he's . . . okay."

"Yes, it seems that way. You should probably get him checked out anyway. Just in case."

She hums in approval and her rage seems to have faded. "Julian, let's go. I want to stop at urgent care on the way home and make sure you haven't broken your nose."

Freddie and Ben turn and bring him toward the door before swinging him between them and letting him land lightly through the gate and onto the floor outside the rink. Then Freddie corrals the puck Julian was using and takes off down the ice immediately without even glancing in my direction, and Ben shoots me an apologetic grin before following his friend.

I follow Mrs. Tarasi and Julian off the ice, locking up behind us and walking them to their car, carrying Julian's skate bag for them. Finally, they're gone, and I sigh in relief.

For a moment I turn back to the rink and think about going inside to thank Freddie and Ben for their help, but there's no way I can face Freddie.

I'll have to eventually, and getting it over with is probably the smart thing to do, the brave thing. But today, I can't. After two years of near total silence, and the first time he really saw me was in the middle of *that*—it's too much. Instead, I'll grab some food, and barricade myself in my room for the rest of the day.

I've had enough.

Chapter 5

*T*HE BLARING OF an ambulance siren jolts me out of a dead sleep. My hand shoots out from beneath the covers and slaps around on my nightstand before finding the right bit of phone screen to make it stop. That obnoxious sound is literally the only thing that will get me up and out of bed before the sun comes up every morning.

I'm not a morning person.

At all.

Figure skating is a morning sport, though. There's only one rink at Kellynch, and even though it's only the Junior Worlds team using it, ice time is still limited.

As I slide out from underneath the covers, the textbook I fell asleep reading falls to the carpeted floor, the thick hardcover barely missing my toes. With the amount of training we do, regular school isn't really an option. I've been homeschooled since the eighth grade and it's one of the only things that sucks about having an Olympic dream. Back then I thought it was cool to not have to go to class every day when all my friends did, but over the years I lost track of most of them. Now I'm that ice skating girl they used to go to school with. No junior prom for me this year or senior prom next year or homecoming court. Is that even a thing anymore? I wouldn't know. The one nice thing is not having to be in class super early after skating. Now it's just skating and then falling asleep in the middle of reading a chapter on the rise of industrial capitalism after the Civil War.

It's worth it, though. Completely and totally. There are some days I question that I'm even a Russo, and I barely recognize anything of myself in my dad or sisters, but when it comes to skating, I'm a Russo through and through. I can't imagine my life without it and I don't even want to try.

That being said, I'm barely human at this hour. I need coffee and to forget about how much of an idiot I made of myself yesterday and focus on the mission for today, perfecting the programs for Worlds.

Trudging down the stairs, I can already smell a pot brewing, which means Camille is here. Which means I don't have to cook breakfast today. Part of me is thrilled to not have to do it, but most of me is terrified of what my kitchen is going to look like afterward since she's not exactly a master chef.

Cooking was my mom's thing and we used to do it together before she died. I love it almost as much as skating. There's something so satisfying about putting a bunch of random ingredients together to make the perfect dish. And sometimes, when I'm really into a recipe and the time crunch of getting everything just right, I can hear her in my head talking me through the steps while we made her sauce or giambotta or pasticcio. When she got sick, I used to sneak food to her so she could avoid hospital food as much as possible.

A couple of years ago that memory would have hurt, but now it's warm and almost comfortable, knowing we still have this connection all these years later.

"Caffeine now, please," I say, going straight for the mug cabinet and then the coffeemaker on the big island at the center of kitchen. I've been running on caffeine and a prayer for days now.

"Made a fresh pot," Camille says from her spot at the stove. "Scrambled egg whites or," she says, glancing down at the pan, "scrambled egg whites?"

"Can you even make egg whites not scrambled? Like, all the ways you make eggs are about the way the yolk is, right?"

"You are so weird," Maria mutters as she takes a seat at the island, then folds her arms on it and rests her head against them.

The coffeepot is finally full, and I pour myself a cup, black. It's the closest I can get to injecting it right into my body. The second it passes my lips, my brain responds. I mean, it's impossible that the caffeine is already working, but my body knows it's coming.

"Where did you go after the lesson yesterday?" Maria manages to say through her arms. "Everyone was asking about you."

"Everyone?" I ask, taking a seat and smiling at Camille when she shoves a plate of egg whites and toast at me.

"When Freddie and Ben came back from the rink, they said you finished your lesson, but then you never showed up after. I was going to come and find you, but I didn't want to miss anything. Also, I didn't remember Freddie being that hot."

"You were like twelve when he left, Maria; *hot* wasn't in your vocabulary yet."

"Uh, yes, it was, but he definitely was *not* this hot."

She's right.

He wasn't.

The last two years had been very, very good to Freddie O'Connell. He's grown, sure, but it's not just that he's broader at the shoulders and narrower at the hips. Or that his forearms are muscular and defined, strong enough to lift my five feet, eight inches on the ice if he had to. It's that he looks grown-up, his skin clear of the spots we'd both had a couple of years ago, and his jawline carved sharp instead of a soft baby face. Maria's right. He got hot.

It's not that I haven't seen him in the last two years; of course I have. I just haven't really let myself look. It hurt too much, and it was too damn awkward.

The last time I really looked at him and he looked at me was the day he left. The day I told him to leave. He showed up for practice like normal, ready to run through our routine, a routine without any lifts that would make us competitive at Nationals the next year. The night before I'd cried myself to sleep. My eyes were still red and raw when I found him lacing up his skates on the bleachers just outside the rink, the same spot he found me in yesterday. And the memory comes back full force, and this time there's nothing to distract me from remembering every little detail.

He'd stood, only one skate on, hands reaching for mine. He'd asked if I was okay, squeezing my hands gently and listening while I stumbled and stuttered through the speech I'd rehearsed over and over again the night before. We had to call it. I was too tall. He was too short. We couldn't skate together anymore. We couldn't be partners anymore. It was the only way. He had to find another partner. I did too.

He dropped my hands and without another word, still only one skate on, he walked away, taking years of friendship and . . . well, the dream of anything more than that with him, on the ice or off it.

There's a lot of that boy still left in him now. He's just *more* now, and he became more without me.

And it still hurts, less now than it did then, but also . . . he really is wildly and unfairly hot.

My stomach flips and it has nothing to do with the slightly charred egg whites Camille tried to pass off as breakfast.

Oh. This is not good.

I cannot crush on Freddie. There is nothing good down that road. It would be even worse than crushing on Brayden. Riley clearly likes him, and it almost sounds like Maria is ready to give up her completely hopeless crush on Charlie in favor of my former partner.

Crap. This is very, very not good.

"Anyway," Maria's still talking, and she breaks into my thoughts, "he was kind of rough on you."

"What did he say?" I ask a little too quickly, suddenly very awake, but Maria doesn't notice.

"He said that you looked tired."

"Well, he's not wrong."

Here I am thinking about how he grew up to look like a Greek god and he thinks I look tired.

Wow. That stings.

Camille turns to me and twists her mouth into a frown. "You do look a little tired," she says. "Are you getting enough sleep?"

"Eight hours every night," I say, shrugging, pushing the egg whites around the plate.

That's a lie, but she hums her approval. "Well, I hate to break up this party, but you and I have the ice in less than an hour."

"When do Charlie and I have it?" Maria asks.

"Noon," Camille says.

Almost instantly, Maria is out of her chair, across the kitchen, and headed toward the stairs and I assume back to bed.

"I'm gonna go shower and I'll meet you at the rink," I say, taking one last bite of the egg whites, making a mental note that I should cook breakfast tomorrow.

THE POP BEAT of the Weeknd's "Blinding Lights" pounds through Kellynch's speakers, but not loud enough to drown out Georgia O'Connell-Croft's directions from the edge of the ice while Riley and Freddie skate through their free dance.

Every ice dance couple has two routines. The rhythm dance is the shorter of the two, where the dance style and the beat of the music are picked out for us by the sport's governing body before the season even starts, though we do get to choose the actual song. This year we have to skate a Westminster Waltz. It sounds super stuffy—because it is—but as long as you're doing the right choreography and formations, it's easy enough to disguise that with your musical choices. The second program is the free dance, where we can really let our personalities and strengths shine through, both in the choice of music and choreography.

This program is exactly why Riley and Freddie work together so well on the ice. They're both so high energy, constantly bouncing off the walls, they need something the crowd can clap along to, and it's a little bit retro with the synthesizers playing in the back-ground, almost like it sampled a song from the eighties.

"Watch your footwork there, Riley!" Georgia calls out. "Another millimeter and your skate would have tangled with Freddie's and *splat.*"

I make my way over to some of the empty space beside the rink to start stretching and warming up. They should be finishing up soon and Brayden should be here any second. He's never late, but never early, either.

My eyes follow Riley and Freddie as they crisscross the ice. They're good. I mean, of course they're good, they qualified for Worlds too, but they're not as good as we are. Their lifts and the overall complexity of their routines just aren't where they need to be in order to really challenge us.

Not yet, at least.

One day soon, though—maybe even later this year if some of the things I've seen them working on in the videos Riley's always posting work out—they'll be nipping at our heels.

I make myself stop watching and start jogging back and forth, swinging my arms around in circles to get my blood pumping against the cold of the rink.

We'll be working on our rhythm dance today, so I turn the vol-ume all the way up on my earbuds and let the sounds of Billy Joel's "Vienna" totally overpower everything around me.

It's kind of an old-school choice, but Brayden got to pick the song for our free dance, so it was only fair that I got to choose the rhythm dance music. "Vienna" was my mom's favorite song, and it was barely out of my mouth before Camille agreed to it. Skating to it is like having Mom at practice every day, sitting in the bleachers silently and then smiling widely afterward, asking me if I had fun, because that was the most important thing about skating, even when you dream about gold medals.

As my muscles loosen and my body feels ready to put in a full workout, I start running through some of our choreography, arms held out as if Brayden is standing opposite me, one hand across the middle of my back, the other holding mine in his firm grasp as we waltz together over our frozen stage. I'm halfway through the section when my imaginary partner becomes flesh and bone, and I don't even open my eyes when he falls into step with me and I let him lead me through the last bit of choreography. Dancing with Brayden, on the ice or the solid ground, is as natural as breathing. He's the kind of partner who knows how to bring out the best in whoever he's skating with. I'm lucky to have him.

I spin under his arm one final time before he draws me close for our final pose and I bend back over his arm. He follows, his forehead resting against my neck, his face buried in my shoulder. Then as the music cuts, he pulls me right back up. I finally open my eyes, and his gaze meets mine immediately and holds.

These are the moments on the ice when I don't struggle with expression, when we look at each other. It's easy to look into Brayden's eyes and react, reflect the emotions I see playing across his face. And this one is easy to identify. Want.

Something in my chest twists pleasantly at that thought, especially after thinking about what Freddie told Maria. Even if he's playing it up for the performance, it's nice to be looked at like this, like someone wants me.

"Good, you're both here," Camille says, coming over and breaking the moment. I pull out of Brayden's grasp and turn to face her, hoping she didn't notice what she interrupted, but Camille, being Camille, misses nothing. She only raises an eyebrow at me and continues talking. "Finish warming up. I don't want to waste a minute of ice time. You should consider *today* the beginning of World Championships. You'll be skating against your fiercest competition every day from now through the final skate in Paris. That's the level of focus I expect of you each and every time you're out on the ice between now and then, am I understood?"

"Loud and clear," I say. It's what I want to hear. I want to throw myself into training for the next few weeks. I want to block everything and everyone else out and keep my sights set on one thing, a Junior World Championship gold medal, the perfect jumping-off point for a four-year run to the Olympic Games.

Brayden nods and salutes, but without the usual accompanying smirk spreading over his face, which is about as serious as he ever gets.

Freddie and Riley are leaving the ice and Camille motions for us to follow her.

"Twizzles today," Camille says, and Brayden groans.

We're a great ice dancing pair, but if we do have a weakness, it's in our twizzle sequence. Ask us to do a complex lift that even some of the senior ice dancing pairs would shake their heads at, no problem. Brayden and I have this sort of innate trust and we've had it from almost the first moment we started skating together. He's not going to drop me.

Twizzles, though? It might sound like a ridiculous made-up

word, maybe a candy or a kid's TV show, but when we first started skating together, twizzles were the bane of our existence. They're multiple turns done across the ice with your partner, but unlike most of the rest of the program, there's no contact between us, so it's easy to lose rhythm and fall out of sync. We've improved vastly over the last two years, but every once in a while, problems still crop up and it's always super obvious when it does. You can't fake a good twizzle sequence.

"Hey," Riley says, leaning over to put on her skate guards. Freddie and Georgia are already out the door. "You're coming tonight, right?"

"Tonight?"

"Yeah, team dinner at the Kellynch House. We're gonna eat and then watch the first episode of Elisa's show."

I blink in surprise. "I forgot that was airing tonight."

It's funny that almost as soon as Elisa and Dad left, all my attention centered on the people surrounding me instead. I stopped focusing on everything they talked about for months: sponsorships and Beijing and what exactly would have to go right for her and wrong for everyone else in order to medal. It was all replaced by Paris and Brayden and our chances at Worlds and Freddie O'Connell's reentrance into my life. I guess tonight those two worlds are going to converge.

Riley rolls her eyes at me and giggles. "It'll be fun, and you didn't come last night, so you cannot say no. Besides, I need you there as my eyes."

"Your eyes?"

"You're so good at reading people. I need you to observe Freddie with me and see if there's any hope."

"You can't tell if he likes you? Freddie's not exactly a subtle guy."

What you see is what you get with Freddie. He wears his heart on his sleeve, so open and free and, yeah, a little bit wild. Willing to try anything once and always down for an adventure, like giving up hockey for a one-in-a-million chance at going to the Olympics.

Riley's eyebrows furrow and her head tilts. "Freddie? Freddie O'Connell? My partner? He's the least obvious person in the world. We spend almost all our time together and I can *never* guess what he's thinking."

"Really?"

The Freddie I know wasn't like that at all. He always shared what was on his mind, even if it was the most random thing, like the time he spent an entire training session thinking out loud about how whenever people talk about their past lives, they always talk about famous people, but that it wasn't possible for everyone to have been famous in a past life, which turned into a weeklong debate about whether or not either of us believed in reincarnation.

I thought no.

He thought yes.

I wonder what he thinks now.

"See? This is why I need you there tonight. You've known him a long time. You'll be able to tell. Please say you'll come. Six o'clock!"

"Adriana!" Camille calls out.

"No excuses!" Riley says.

"Okay, okay," I finally agree as Riley disappears through the doors and I turn toward the ice.

Joining Brayden at the far end of the rink, we wait for Camille to count us in to the steps.

"What was that about?"

"Apparently tonight's dinner at Kellynch House is mandatory attendance."

"Huh," he says, "I guess my invite got lost in the mail."

"If I'm invited, then you're invited. Come with me?"

"Ah, how the tables have turned! I'm *always* inviting you places, and you never say yes."

"Because you're always going to keggers and clubs and that's so not my thing."

"And team bonding night seems like something that's *my* kind of thing?"

"Please? I don't want to go to this thing alone," I say, and then press my lips together, widening my eyes at him in a silent plea, sticking out my bottom lip, just for effect.

"How can I say no to that?" he asks with a laugh as Camille's voice echoes out to us.

Pushing off together, we spin over the ice. Keeping no more than arm's length apart the entire time, less if we can manage it, we rotate one way and then the other, arm positions firm and sharp, our footwork matching exactly for a dozen rotations across the rink.

"Excellent!" Camille skates over and applauds. "That was the best I've ever seen you two do the first time out. You feel good about it?"

I nod, hands falling to my hips as Brayden and I circle her, waiting for our next instructions.

"You know what? If you're both feeling it like this today, let's start with a run-through of 'Vienna.' Don't want to waste the good vibes."

She skates to the gate and we head for the center of the ice while she cues up the music.

Brayden holds out his hand to me and I stand a few feet away with my back to him. Then, as the tinkling of the piano signals the start of the song, I drift farther away while he follows, easily catching up, grabbing my hand and leading me into the first steps of our program, as Billy Joel's voice implores us to slow down and he calls us crazy, ambitious children. He's not wrong, but we're definitely not going to slow down. Not now. Not ever.

THE SHOWER AFTER a great practice is always the most rewarding one, and I'll usually let myself linger there for a while, but I don't have time. A full day of training, even one as good as today's, is exhausting, and I'd like to fit in a quick nap, but I got a text from Riley a few hours ago that she wants to bake a cake for tonight before we get started on dinner, and I am definitely not letting her loose in my kitchen without supervision.

With my makeup already done and my damp hair wrapped in an old T-shirt (no terry cloth towels on the curls!), I stare into my closet, wondering what the hell to wear.

This isn't fancy. There are a lot of us, but it's only a team dinner in the huge Kellynch House kitchen. It's not a sweet sixteen or a party or whatever . . . it's dinner next door. Still, I want to look nice.

I want to make a good impression on my teammates. And, yeah, I might as well admit it to myself, I want to replace that last image Freddie has of me in his head.

I push hanger after hanger of workout clothes out of view and finally reach the portion of my closet usually reserved for skating events beyond the actual skating part, the ceremonies and parties, like the other night when we sent off my dad and Elisa. My eyes catch on an oversize cropped sweater, which I totally made fun of when I saw it at the store, because what exactly is the point of cropping a sweater? But when Elisa made me try it on and I saw myself in the mirror, I loved how it looked. It shows a sliver of skin when I pair it with high-rise jeans, which make my legs look, somehow, even longer than they actually are. A disadvantage on the ice, for sure. Longer limbs make it harder to spin and twirl and be lifted into the air, but off the ice? That's a different story.

Outfit in place, I turn toward the mirror in the corner of my room. The T-shirt hair wrap looks ridiculous, obviously, but the rest of me? The rest looks pretty good. I pull the cotton fabric out of my hair and let the curls shake free. Okay, that's even better. They're a wild, shiny mess. Perfect.

"Adriana, are you ready?" Maria asks, not even bothering to knock as she comes into the room. "Whoa."

"What?" I whirl around, panicked.

She shakes her head. "Not a bad whoa, A good whoa."

"Yeah?"

Nodding, she reaches out for my hand. "Come on. Charlie is already downstairs waiting."

"You're going early too?"

"Well, if Riley's cooking, then Charlie's going to want to help his sister, which means I'm going to go too, obviously."

"Obviously," I repeat with a little bit of exasperation. I thought she was moving on.

"I know, I know, but I can't help it," she says, tugging on my arm, and I let myself get dragged out of the room, managing to snag my phone off my dresser.

Maria stops dead in her tracks when we make it down the stairs. "Selfie," she says, leaning into me, and I quickly snap a picture of us, her blonde locks tangling with my brown curls as we smile for the camera.

I lower the phone and see Charlie waiting in the front hall, along with Brayden.

"Hey," he says.

"I said six."

He acknowledges it with a nod. "You did, but then Charles here"—Charlie practically swoons when Brayden says his given name—"texted me that he and Maria were going early, and so here I am."

"You've never been early a day in your life," I say, narrowing my eyes at him while I grab my coat. Kellynch House is only a few yards away, but it's still below freezing outside. "Something's up."

"Nothing's up. Why would anything be up?" he asks, stepping forward and holding out my scarf for me when I turn to face him. His eyes are alight with mischief.

The next few hours are going to be very interesting.

Chapter 6

$\mathcal{F}$IRE.

That's my only thought when I step into Kellynch House and the acrid smell of smoke fills my nose and makes my eyes sting and water.

"No!" a desperate voice shouts somewhere inside the house. Panic floods through me. I take off at a sprint toward the kitchen, Maria right behind me. With every step, the scent gets stronger, but as soon as I make it through the archway, I let out a sigh of relief.

There's no fire, at least not one I can see. There is, however, a gigantic mess. Bowls and ingredients everywhere, flour and eggs and sugar in splotches on the countertops and a massively burned *something* in a pan on the counter. Riley has a streak of flour in her dark hair and is staring at the thing like it insulted her skating technique.

"Um, Riley?" I ask, biting my lip. "What is that?"

"I was making us a cake for after dinner and . . ." She gestures at the mess as pounding footsteps from upstairs get closer and closer.

Most of the team spills into the kitchen, led by Ben Woo, Freddie, and the other male singles skater, Jimmy Harville, hot on his heels.

69

Jimmy, with his straw-blond hair and light brown eyes, looks like he's been imported directly from a cornfield, but he's from suburban Detroit, and like most male singles skaters, he's about Ben's height. He's almost toppled over by Katya Belikova and Gillian Azarian, the two ladies' singles skaters, both of whom barely reach the boys' shoulders, and for the first time since everyone arrived, the entire US Junior World Championships team is in one room.

Silence reigns and no one knows what to say to Riley. Her eyes are wide and she's frozen in horror.

"Last I checked, being able to make a cake isn't a category on the judge's scorecard, so I think we're still good, Riles," Freddie jokes, coming around the counter to stand next to his partner and give the charred cake a closer examination. "Yeah, it's dead."

Riley laughs at that before leaning toward Freddie and bumping her shoulder against his bicep. It's a sweet moment and the tension in the room disappears almost entirely.

"Yeah," Katya says. Her mousy brown hair is in a tight bun, like she wears it at training, and she has huge ice packs wrapped around the lower parts of her legs. Her pale skin stands out even more starkly against the beige wraps. "It's fine. Let's get this cleaned up and get dinner going. I'm starving. Practice was rough today."

"For sure," Gillian agrees, pulling back her frizzy, jet-black hair into a ponytail. "But I ate so much ice on my triple axel today, I'm not sure if I can stomach anything for dinner."

We all laugh, but Katya winces as she shifts her weight from one leg to the other. She's been nursing injuries to her ankles all year long even though she made it onto the team after a second-place finish at Nationals to Gillian.

I set to work wiping down the counters and for once, Maria helps without being asked, probably because Charlie and the rest of the group did. A few minutes later with the kitchen windows wide open to let out the smell of charbroiled cake, the room is clean and ready for dinner prep.

"What are we having?" Ben asks, taking a seat at one of the stools and leaning against the stained hardwood of the massive butcher-block island.

"Besides flambéed chocolate rock cake?" Jimmy jokes, poking at it with his finger, but stops when Freddie shoots him a withering glare.

"We always have massive amounts of food in the pantry," Maria says, grabbing Charlie's hand and pulling him toward the huge sliding door that leads to where everything is kept. The pantry normally has to hold food for an entire camp's worth of kids for a week, which is about the same amount of food as feeding the ten of us and our coaches until we leave. "How about zucchini pasta? I know we have a ton of it."

"We could do an assembly line," Brayden chimes in, rolling up the sleeves of his shirt, "and I bet if we all ask really nicely, Adriana would make us some of her famous sauce."

"Your mom's sauce?" Freddie asks, and my eyes fly to him. Those are the first real words he's said to me since he got here, and for the briefest moment our eyes meet, but then he looks away, frowning at something. Me, I guess? He used to come over for dinner every Sunday when we were little. My mom and I did the whole Italian thing, sauce and pasta and meatballs and sausage. At some point, when he became a semipermanent fixture at our house, Freddie and I were put in charge of the sauce, adding the spices and herbs, letting it simmer and stirring it when necessary, and most importantly, taste testing. It was a sacred responsibility.

The entire group turns to me, and my cheeks flush at their focus.

"Yeah, but it takes too long," I say. "It has to simmer for hours."

"You can shorten it though, can't you?" Gillian asks. "It doesn't have to be perfect. We need something to make zucchini taste like . . . not zucchini."

Everyone chuckles at this and I nod. "Yeah, sure, I can pull together something like that, I guess."

"Perfect!" Brayden says. "We've got pasta—sort of—and sauce. What else?"

"Garlic bread?" Jimmy suggests, hopefully.

"There's some bread in the pantry," I say, with a nod toward it.

"Sweet!" Jimmy heads in that direction as Charlie and Maria emerge with armloads of zucchini, and a few moments later Jimmy reappears with four loaves of bread.

I quickly take stock of the kitchen and our supplies, sliding around everyone to get out the ingredients and tools we'll need while they get to work. And after I'm sure Riley isn't looking, I dump her failed attempt at dessert into the garbage.

"We need music," Riley suggests while she and Freddie set up the spiralizer to make the zucchini into something at least resembling pasta. Everyone else hums in agreement.

"I got this," Ben says, pairing his phone with the speaker in the corner of the kitchen.

Soft, mournful music starts to play, like the kind of instrumental that would accompany a tragic death on a TV show, and I wrinkle my nose.

"Anything more cheerful?" I ask. "We're celebrating."

"What? This is *relaxing*," Ben protests, but everyone else groans.

"Yeah, it'd be great for, like, a really relaxing funeral procession," Freddie says.

"I'll have you know this playlist got me through my recovery from knee surgery and an abandoned broken heart." Everyone stares at him. That's exactly what the music sounds like. "Ugh, fine!" he concedes, and flips to another song, which sounds almost exactly like the one before it.

"Ben. C'mon," Jimmy says from where he's slicing up the bread. "I know you're still moping over Sawyer, and I'll admit, my brother is awesome, but it's been six months since you guys broke up. He's at Michigan State, not dead. And your knee is *fine* now. No more whiny music."

I knew Jimmy and Ben trained together at a rink in Michigan, but I had no idea that Ben dated Jimmy's older brother. Sawyer's a hockey player. Jimmy's a figure skater. Ben's bi, Sawyer's gay, and Jimmy's straight. So much for stereotypes.

"Let me see," Charlie says, patting Ben on the shoulder and taking the phone from him, his thumb swiping over the screen. "Okay, here we go."

The peppy sounds of a song I recognize from the radio station we play at the rink, but that I couldn't name to save my life, filter through the kitchen, and a murmur of approval follows from almost everyone.

Ben rolls his eyes but settles at the counter again, crushing up the garlic cloves I put in front of him.

It's not exactly a gourmet meal, but it's not bad for a bunch of teenagers who mostly don't actually cook for themselves, ever, Riley's ruined cake notwithstanding. As we finish up the prep work, the kitchen starts to smell way better and my stomach growls in response.

"Hungry?" Brayden asks, checking over my shoulder as I sprinkle a handful of basil into the sauce and turn down the heat on the stove.

"Yep," I say, stirring the pot and then putting the lid over it so it can simmer.

I lean back against the counter, watching the rest of the team bustling around the room, and I grin. I've never been on a real *team* before. I mean, me and Brayden and Camille are a kind of team, I guess. And even if it sometimes feels like I'm dragging them kicking and screaming into it, my family is a team too.

But this feels different. This is sort of cool. We've been to Junior Worlds before, and while we were always technically a team, it never really felt nice like this. It's still a little bit weird, to be honest. But by the time we leave for Paris, nights like this one will hopefully feel normal.

"I'm gonna go set the table," I say, pushing off the counter and sliding by Brayden, who moves out of the way to let me by, but I can still feel him there. I don't actually mind it. At all. It's nice, having him close. Comforting and soothing and easy.

"I'll help," he says as I open a cabinet and reach toward the top shelf. I'm tall, but these cabinets are huge, and the drinking glasses are actually out of my reach. Before I can move out of the way, his hand is on my hip as he balances against me to reach over my head and grab the stack of glasses. It's not as if his hand has never been there before. In fact, his hand might have touched my hip more than anyone else's in the world, including my own, but there's something about it right now, with everyone else in the room—oh, who am I kidding?—with Freddie in the room, that makes it matter.

I hold my breath until he lets go and steps away and then exhale slowly before I turn and glance back at the rest of the room.

And yeah, he saw. Most of them did, if the eye rolls are any indication, but I can't control my gaze settling on him. Freddie's face is entirely passive, nothing in his eyes, not one flicker of jealousy or, really, anything at all.

He doesn't care.

Of course he doesn't care. Why would he? How self-centered am I that I think anyone in this room cares whether or not Brayden Elliot touches my hip, especially Freddie? I need to stop obsessing and being constantly aware of him. It's not healthy.

Giving myself a small shake, I take down a stack of ten plates and walk into the dining room to lay them out. There are two massive wooden tables, but we'll all fit at one.

"Leave them on the table, I'll put them out," I say to Brayden coming in behind me, who probably grabbed more glasses.

"Sure," Not-Brayden's voice answers.

I turn and Freddie's behind me, not more than a foot away, actually less, and I catch a scent vaguely like cinnamon. Is there cinnamon soap or cologne, is that a thing? It's spicy and warm and really, really nice.

"Oh." I blink at him, stupidly, trying to refocus my brain. "Hi."

He raises an eyebrow but doesn't say anything as he puts a handful of napkins and silverware on the table.

"Thanks," I manage to choke out.

Nodding, he bites his lip, opening his mouth to say something, but then a moment later he just shakes his head, before turning and leaving through the archway to the kitchen.

I exhale.

Shit.

Okay, it's over. That wasn't so bad. Now I've spoken to him, for real, sort of, and he very clearly has nothing to say to me, which is fine. I think I can deal with silence better than a complete recitation of all the reasons he has to not be anything more than just civil. How I didn't stand up to Camille and Dad. How I should have waited it out, even if it meant we had to give up that competition season. Just like he would have for me after Mom died. How we were starting to figure out, even then, that our friendship was deeper than most. Or at least I was. That it was special. And that I ruined that too.

He doesn't have to say any of it. I've said it to myself more than enough. Maybe he knows that. After all, for a long time, no one knew me better than he did. So maybe he knows, and he's decided to leave it alone. That's something he'd do.

Freddie, at his core, is a good guy. He always has been and probably always will be. He even helped with Mrs. Tarasi yesterday, whether he knows it or not. He's the kind of guy who sees an upset kid and figures out a way to fix that. The kind of guy who forgives and, if not forgets, at least moves on. So maybe he has moved on and knows how much I regret what I did and now he's happy and skating with Riley and probably, eventually, doing other not-skating things with Riley, and if not Riley, someone else. Someone who is not me.

My hands shake as I reach out for the silverware he left. This is ridiculous. I need to calm down. Clearly, he's not affected like this. He's moved on. I thought I had, but apparently not. Whatever. I can do it now.

There. It's decided.

It's time to move on.

I'm moving on.

I circle the table quickly, getting the rest of the flatware into place as everyone else files in, dishes full of food for us to eat.

We all go to sit down, but Riley yells, "Wait! Okay, so I read about this team building exercise, and I want to try it." Several people, me included, groan, but she just talks over us. "We pick names out of a hat and put them on the table, and that's the order we sit in. Oh! And you can't sit next to your partner or anyone you train with because that defeats the purpose." She runs back into the kitchen and returns seconds later, brandishing a baseball cap with folded pieces of paper in it.

Those rules don't leave me with a lot of options; I try to do the math in my head quickly, but probability was never really my strong suit.

"Okay, Brayden here," Riley says, motioning to the head of the table and then placing cards for Jimmy and then herself, followed by Katya and Maria.

My odds are looking worse as she places Gillian at the foot of the table and turns. Charlie's name is next, and then she picks my name but drops it back in because we train together. There's only one arrangement left that doesn't break her rules. I glance at Ben, who plops down next to Charlie with a smile and a shrug. I fall into the seat beside him, and then Freddie slides into the last open seat, between me and Brayden.

I could kill Riley for suggesting this.

It's fine, though, actually. Everyone spends the meal chatting lightly, especially with the people beside them who they don't know well. Even Brayden and Freddie talk a bit, but *I'm* not fine because while the table can hold us, it's a bit of a tight squeeze. I've spent the entire meal making sure my right leg doesn't come anywhere near the orbit of Freddie's left leg. My entire body is hyperaware that he's sitting inches away, entirely ignoring me, but still *right there*. His shoulders are wider than the chair's back, and every time he turns from talking to Brayden toward the rest of the table, I swear I can feel the cotton of his shirt brushing against my sweater. Was that me not so long ago putting together an outfit to impress this guy?

That girl would roll her eyes and scoff at the ridiculous bundle of nerves I am right now, but I've never felt like this before.

I hate it.

"You know what we should do?" Freddie says, and the entire table quiets down. "We should play Odds."

I tense beside him and suddenly the air between us feels supercharged. That's . . . that's the game we played together, constantly, for years. It started out as just silly things kids do, like blending fast-food leftovers and drinking it like a smoothie or doing something embarrassing in public like wearing your red, white, and blue

spandex costume from a Fourth of July skating tribute out to dinner in January. Or—

"What's 'Odds'?" Maria asks, cutting off my thoughts.

"It's the *best* game," Riley says, giggling, and of course they've
played it together. They both love shit like that, being crazy and
living life in the moment. That doesn't make it hurt any less.

"It's like playing truth or dare, or actually, mostly dare if you're
playing it right," Freddie says, a wide grin spreading over his face,
and I recognize that wicked gleam in his eye. "You just sort of play
it forever. You ask someone what the odds are they'll do something, like one out of three or five or ten. Then you shoot with your
fingers to see if they have to do it. So like, I say one out of three
odds that Ben does a naked lap around the house right now."

"And I say one out of ten, not three," Ben shoots back, snickering
from the other side of the table.

"Fine," Freddie agrees, his eyes sparkling like I remember them.
"Then we shoot to see if our numbers match. One . . . two . . ."

On three they both put out their hands. Freddie with six fingers.
Ben with just three.

"And since they don't match, I don't have to do it," Ben says with
obvious relief.

"Should we go around the table?" Brayden asks, clearly thrilled
with this game.

"Nah," Freddie says, "we're all gonna be together for weeks. You
do it when something good comes up or something that feels right
for another person. Everyone in?"

It's unanimous, or at least it sounds that way to them, since I
definitely didn't agree. A game of Odds for the time we're together.

Fantastic.

"Leave your plates on the island, guys. I'll clean up," I say to a chorus of protests when we all start to get up from the table. "Trust me, it'll be easier for me to do it. I know where everything goes. Go get everything ready to watch Elisa's reality TV debut. It starts soon."

I flee into the kitchen, and once they've all left their plates, I exhale for the first time in what feels like nearly an hour. The place is a total mess, but I've worked enough summer camp kitchen duties to get everything in order pretty quickly. Pots and pans go from soaking in the sink to the industrial-size dishwasher, and then the plates with the flatware follow suit.

Using the hair tie I always keep on my wrist, I pull the curls I was so proud of earlier up to the top of my head in a messy bun and roll up my sleeves as I put away whatever ingredients we left out while we were eating.

"Your hair looks good like that," Brayden says, coming into the kitchen.

"Thanks," I say, wrapping up the bread that's left over and putting it in the freezer.

"I'm glad you made me come to this tonight."

"Yeah?" I ask, finally turning to him as I push a curl I missed out of my eyes.

Oh.

He's very close. He hums a positive response and takes a step closer. He doesn't smell like cinnamon. Brayden, off the ice, always smells the same: a clean soap scent and Creed Aventus, a ridiculously expensive cologne that mixes citrus and woodsy fragrances together to make something intoxicating, especially since he doesn't wear too much like so many guys do. What is with the guys around me smelling so good?

I put out a hand and it lands on his chest, but I'm not sure if I'm doing it to push him away or brace against him for what's coming. What am I doing? He reaches up, his fingers twisting into the curl before tucking it back over my ear.

"Oh, sorry!"

We don't jump away from each other, but my eyes fly toward the door. Brayden turns and glances over his shoulder. When my gaze follows his, I want to vomit.

It's Freddie and Riley. Together. He's carrying her, piggyback style, into the kitchen while she giggles nervously, looking back and forth between me and Brayden like they interrupted something.

Something that wasn't what it looks like. Mostly.

"We wanted some drinks," Freddie says, looking directly at Brayden and not at me. Riley jumps down from his back, still laughing.

"There's—" I clear my throat and take a step back from Brayden, my hand dropping from his chest. "There's a whole thing of lemonade in the fridge."

"Perfect!" Riley says, giggling nervously. "We'll grab it and leave you guys to, you know . . . whatever it was you were doing."

Every single millisecond of Freddie standing there while Riley hands him a sleeve of Solo cups is too long. His eyes haven't left Brayden the entire time, which is a relief because I think if he looked at me right now, I would spontaneously combust.

They're gone moments later, and Brayden turns back to me with a sigh.

"So, they probably think . . ." He trails off and I groan.

"Not probably. Definitely. Ugh, this is a nightmare."

Brayden lets out a heavy breath. "A nightmare, really? Isn't Maria the dramatic sister?"

He almost sounds hurt and I wrinkle my nose. "It's not that. You know what I mean."

"Yeah," he says, tilting his head at me, his mouth ticking up in a grin. "I do."

Does he, though? "Brayden, I—"

"It's starting!" Katya's voice carries into the kitchen, interrupting me, even though I'm not sure what I'm going to say.

"Come on, let's go," I say, relieved at the interruption. "We're about to be reality TV background characters."

He laughs and his smile becomes a real one. "Can't wait."

Chapter 7

THE COMMON AREA of the Kellynch House has a huge U-shaped sectional sofa in front of a big TV. Our camps are built around group activities, so a viewing room to watch training footage and, of course, movie night for the campers was a must, at least according to Dad.

Brayden and I slide into the last empty seats at the end of one of the couches and it feels like everyone is looking at us, which, maybe they are. Maybe Freddie and Riley came back in here and told everyone what they walked in on . . . or what it looked like they walked in on. Katya and Gillian are whispering to each other and glancing over at us.

Ugh, why do I even care?

Brayden seems totally unaffected by it, sitting back on the couch. I try to do the same, but my eyes keep flickering from him to Freddie, who is chatting with Ben, completely unaware of my discomfort. Obviously. If neither of them is bothered, I shouldn't be either. Right?

But then Maria leans over and Katya and Gillian are giggling and yeah, they definitely know.

The best distraction is when the opening credits start to flash on the screen. Dramatic music plays over black-and-white footage of Dad and Mom and then finally Elisa skating, and a quick flash to Maria and me, both with our partners gliding along the ice and then a black screen where the words *KELLYNCH: The First Family of Figure Skating* flash in graphic letters that look like they were made of ice shavings.

The show is pretty standard to start. It gives an overview of our family history. Mom and Dad's success, their marriage, the arrival of the three of us, and then Mom's death. The room around me becomes tense for a moment, but thankfully the screen shifts to some training footage almost immediately. A lot of it is background stuff anyone could google about Kellynch and how the NFSC has struggled to put out gold-medal-winning performances at Worlds and the Olympics in recent history. Then an interview with Elisa where they ask about her own lack of international success, especially compared to our parents.

"Well, I plan on surprising a lot of people," she says to an interviewer off-screen, and then it cuts to her training her triple axel and falling.

Oh, she is not gonna like that.

The rest of the room seems to agree with my thoughts. There are a couple of groans, and Brayden, sitting next to me, actually lets out a laugh. I turn to glare at him and he manages to cover it up with a cough.

"What?" he asks, smiling down at me, and I shake my head.

There's an interview with Dad where he's his usual charming self, but then the episode takes a sharp turn.

"What do you say to the people who believe that Kellynch isn't what it once was?" an interviewer asks.

Dad scoffs at the question. "It is still the finest rink in the country, and we've housed more champions in the last twenty years than some nations have *ever* produced."

"None in the last five years, aside from the junior titles your middle daughter, Adriana, and her ice dance partner, Brayden Elliot, have brought in, beyond that . . ."

"We'll see what happens in Beijing, shall we?" Dad says, downplaying our ice dancing wins, as usual.

I can feel every eye in the room turn to me, but I keep my gaze trained on the screen and swallow down the lump in my throat as the footage shifts again. Elisa is in the foreground of the shot working on some choreography, but the camera slides over her shoulder, her image out of focus as it clearly narrows in on Brayden and me all the way across the ice. I'm in his arms, legs wrapped around his waist while his hands support me in the center of my back. I'm leaning out, arms stretched back over my head. Camille's off to the side coaching us through how we'll disentangle ourselves from the move and continue to skate. I remember that day clearly.

I fell.

A lot.

This isn't one of those moments, though. This was when we finally nailed it. There's nothing in the world like that feeling, when you're achy and sore and on the edge of giving up and then you hit and it's perfect. Once I'm standing firmly on my feet again, Brayden and I high-five and he slings an arm around my shoulder for a celebratory squeeze.

Real-life Brayden chuckles and does the same thing, pulling me closer to him.

"And what's your relationship like with Brayden Elliot?" the interviewer asks as the screen flashes to Elisa again.

She shrugs coyly. "I don't kiss and tell," she says, the smile following it all that needs to be said.

Brayden snorts, and then from across the couch Maria says, "What are the odds *you* do?"

Shrugging with his usual nonchalance, Brayden pulls away from me, sits forward on the couch, and says, "Three."

"Oh!" Ben and Jimmy yell together. One out of three. The odds are very good we're about to get details of something I've never, ever wanted to know. I begged Elisa back then to not mess around with Brayden, but Elisa does what she wants, so I settled for just asking them to keep me the hell out of it.

One. Two. Three. Maria puts out a one, he puts out a three. "Better luck next time, Little Russo."

And then the footage is back and it's Brayden and me working through some choreography, our bodies pressed against each other, one of my legs sliding over his as he dips me low toward the ice.

I swallow and I can feel where this is going before the next question is even asked.

"And your sister doesn't mind? They seem *very close*."

"Adriana?" Elisa says, laughing at the implication. "No, they're definitely just partners. He thinks of her like a little sister."

Beside me, Brayden stiffens, his arm tensing against mine, and I'm guessing he might have said that to her at some point, but maybe it wasn't entirely true. My mind flicks back to just a few minutes ago. No, definitely not entirely true. Brayden and I are partners and we're friends, but we are *not* siblings.

The footage flickers back again. Brayden and I are leaving the ice, his arm around my shoulder again. The cameras aren't close enough to pick up what we're saying, but we're laughing, and he plants a kiss on the top of my head before we step through the gate. I go first and head straight for the locker room, but the camera catches him standing there, watching me go.

The show breaks for commercial, and silence reigns in the room, somehow suffocating even the obnoxious detergent ad blaring from the speakers. Their eyes are still all on me . . . on us. I can feel their stares, and finally I work up enough courage to look away from the screen.

"Elisa is going to *freak*," Maria says, the one to break the silence.

"It's not that bad," Jimmy tries to insist, but no one backs him up.

"I can't believe they did that," I say, anger bursting out of me and totally overpowering the embarrassment I was feeling seconds ago. "What? They didn't think they had an interesting figure skating angle, so they what? Decide to come up with a bullshit love triangle? Are they serious? Ugh."

"It's fine," Charlie says. "No one takes what happens on these shows seriously anyway. Like, everyone knows it's fake."

"Uh, do they?" Jimmy says, swiping through his phone. "Brayden is starting to trend in Boston."

"What?" Brayden asks, and shifts beside me as he digs in his back pocket for his phone.

I glance over at his screen as he pulls up his account and yep, there it is, except his is set to show trending topics in the United States, and there's his name, and below it there's Elisa's, and then below hers . . . my name.

"How many people do you think saw this?" I mumble, but it's a dumb question. Enough to get us trending. Enough for the vast majority of them to believe what they saw.

More than enough.

"So, what are the odds Elisa saw this?" Brayden mutters.

"I SAW SOMEONE compare us to the Kardashians. It's awesome!" A blurry version of Elisa squeals through video chat. "This is definitely going to get Nike on board."

I didn't really sleep last night, and now it's five in the morning, five in the evening Beijing time, and Maria and I are in her bedroom, on a call with my older sister and my dad. Actually, it's mostly Elisa. Dad's in the background, wandering in and out, checking different ties against the suit he's wearing in a mirror.

"It was really cool to see our family on TV like that," Maria says. "Charlie and I had a whole featurette!" And they had, toward the end of the episode, when they recapped how our family did at Nationals, before they started filming. "And obviously Adriana and Brayden too."

"I mean it mostly focused on you," I add hastily, not needing to rehash it, since she's very clearly ignoring what actually happened on-screen in favor of how much publicity we're getting from it, "but I think they were trying to give a lot of background for the audience so they'll be able to know who everyone is in the next episodes."

"Yeah, and social media has completely blown up," Maria squeaks. "We're all verified now too, just like you. I have nearly five thousand followers and Adriana has even more and Brayden is at like fifty thousand. The stans are going wild, they're completely obsessed with him and—"

"How's training going?" I cut off Maria. Time to not talk about how I now have the same number of followers as her, closing in on twenty thousand and growing. I had to turn off my notifications last night just to get some sleep.

"Amazing!" she says. "And not to name any names, but *a lot* of falls have been happening during the Russian training sessions. I think you're going to see yours truly on the top of that podium."

Maria squeals beside me, and I smile. I love my sister and I want her to succeed, but those Russian girls almost never fall in competition. They're like little jumping machines that also manage to have incredible artistry and balletic form.

"Listen, I've gotta run, but give Dad a hug for me."

"And give one to Brayden for me!" she says. My eyes widen in panic, but her face is completely free of irony and her tone has no sarcasm laced through it. "Tell him I miss him!"

"Sure!" I say, and end the call when I see Maria opening her mouth to respond.

"Hey!" she protests. "I didn't get to say goodbye."

"You weren't going to say goodbye."

"You have to deal with it eventually. Might as well be now."

"I'm hoping that by the next episode they move on from that ridiculous storyline."

Maria clearly disagrees. "You guys trended like all night. You probably still are. There's no way they're going to move on from it. You should see some of the edits people are making, like legit tribute videos."

I push off the bed and grab my skate bag. "Ugh, enough, I really do have to get to training."

"Not me," she says, setting her computer on the floor and snuggling back into her covers. "I need at least three more hours."

"Night," I say, flicking the light off as I leave her to her sleep.

"I BEAT YOU here," Brayden says as I hustle out of the locker room, looking around for Camille and sighing in relief that I'm not actually late.

"I had a video call to Beijing this morning and it ran over a little."

"Oh?" he asks, unable to keep the tension out of that one word.

"She's just sort of ignoring it." I answer what he was really asking. "You know Elisa, anything she doesn't like she pretends like it doesn't exist. She's talking about Nike instead."

"Well, that's good money-wise, right?"

"Yeah, it's very good money-wise," I agree. "I still can't believe the show went there, though. Like, what was even the point? It's not like anything is happening between us or you and Elisa."

Brayden cringes. "You're still upset."

"Yeah, I am. It feels so cheap. You're my partner and Elisa's my sister and those two things are so much more important than some stupid fake drama for a reality TV series that isn't even about us. We're not in Beijing. We're not even senior skaters yet. And we don't need this distraction before Paris. It's not the Olympics, but it's the most important competition of our careers and I don't want to finish off that podium again. So enough of that, let's train."

"You're right," he agrees as we skate out onto the ice.

Last year we finished fourth. There's nothing worse than a fourth-place finish. I'd rather finish last. That would have stung less than to come so close to a medal and leave empty-handed. To be fair, no one had expected us to finish that high, and all three couples that outscored us are competing as seniors now, but *still*, I'll never forget the sting of seeing our names out of the medal standings. I have to try to focus on that and nothing else.

We don't have the rink entirely to ourselves this morning. Riley and Freddie, along with their coaches, Georgia and Harry, have laid claim to one half of the ice and left us the other.

Camille comes in and smiles at the both of us waiting for her.

"Ah, the It Couple," she jokes.

I roll my eyes. Camille loves reality TV, especially dating shows and all the drama. She raises her eyebrows suggestively and Brayden laughs, so I join him, but it's totally forced and I'm guessing she can probably tell.

"Okay, well, since your chemistry is apparently an internet phenomenon, let's not disappoint your adoring public. We'll start off today with some choreography work—let's make sure that connection to the music and each other shines through for the judges too. We'll work on *Thrones* first. Remember, forbidden love, the fate of the entire world rests on both your shoulders, and one false step, even taken together, will bring it all collapsing from under your skates. I need to see that on your faces." She says it to both of us, but that last bit was definitely directed at me.

"No pressure," I mumble. Maybe the stakes are a little less life-and-death for us, but the ideas resonate. Something about all of this feels fragile this morning in a way it didn't a few short days ago. Maybe I can use that, *feel* that as we skate. Maybe that'll help.

I reach out for Brayden's hand and he takes it gently, before I spin away from him and we get into our starting pose, back-to-back, both hands linked together. A cello that starts off the *Game of Thrones* medley our rhythm dance is set to sings out slowly in the brief "Rains of Castamere" intro section of the music. I spin to face Brayden, and his hands withdraw from mine before stroking up over my arms to my face, one landing at the base of my neck, the other falling to my waist as we spin in place and then fall into our first dance hold.

Camille stops us there. "Okay, Brayden, a little less 'I'd like to rip her clothes off' and a little more 'we're about to fight a war.'"

Brayden laughs. Camille doesn't mince words and she's said stuff like that to us before. It's definitely a thing he does when he looks at me, enough for everyone watching that show last night to notice. And it's not like it's not nice, to be looked at like that, but immediately my gaze flashes over to the other side of the rink.

Did Freddie hear her?

No, of course he didn't. He and Riley are working through a complicated lift sequence, one I haven't seen them do before in competition. It's really difficult and it kind of looks like crap, but his attention is completely focused on her, obviously.

I need to stop this.

I'm never going to get through the next few weeks if I don't stop it right now. I'm a professional athlete. I am one of the best figure skaters in the world. I can stop worrying about the boy I used to have a crush on to concentrate on the biggest competition of my life. Right? Of course I can. I'm a Russo. That's what we do. We win.

And then it occurs to me that I didn't get a correction for my expressions from Camille.

Huh. It worked. Okay, then.

"Let's do this," I say to Brayden, and he grins as we move back to center ice to start all over again.

From that moment on, training is business as usual and we are on fire.

"Yes! Fire. Ice. Forbidden love. War. Sex. Tragedy!" Camille yells from the other side of the boards as we skate through our free dance and the music builds and builds before finally crashing to an end as Brayden mock stabs me while we're in an embrace and then lowers me to the ice to finish, with his forehead pressing against my neck. "That's it!"

With every breath I take, his lips brush my pulse point. We hold for another moment before he rises and pulls me with him. I smile and laugh at the way we killed that run-through.

"Awesome," Brayden says, his arm falling over my shoulder like he did last night in that video clip. I never really noticed before, but I guess it's something he does a lot, now that I think about it.

Camille's applauding as we skate off the ice, and so is the small crowd that had gathered without me noticing. Most of the team is here now, warming up for their own practice sessions. I can feel a flush burning in my cheeks at the attention. It's weird, I don't mind a huge crowd full of nameless faces, but considering what we all watched last night, this feels like their applause means something else entirely.

Standing off the ice while Katya and Gillian skate onto it for the ladies' singles practice session, we take in some of Camille's corrections, because even when we nail a performance, there are always corrections, and that's it for morning practice. A sliver of panic brushes against my mind. Katya and Gillian are junior skaters, like me, but they came up through the ranks with Elisa. They're way closer to her than they are to me. What if they say something to her? I try to ignore them and focus on Camille instead. I'm being paranoid, and honestly, what are they going to say? Brayden and I are training together and it's going great?

"What are you up to tonight? Hot date?" I ask Brayden as we head toward the locker rooms.

"Nah, I think I'm just gonna chill."

I blink at him, stunned. "But it's Thursday. You always go out on Thursday."

He shrugs. "Not always. Besides, maybe it's time to cool it a bit with Worlds so close."

"Ah! Brayden, Adriana, I'm glad I caught you," Charles Monroe calls, climbing down from a spot on the bleachers and cutting off my complete disbelief in Brayden's ability to cool it.

"Hi, Mr. Monroe," I say, adjusting my bag. "What's up?"

"I wanted to let you know that I've been getting calls about you two this morning. Mostly brands who'd like to partner up and have you feature them on social media a bit."

"Seriously?" Brayden asks, his eyes widening.

"Seriously," Mr. Monroe says. "One of my social media kids at the agency took some initiative and set up a joint social media account for you two."

"Wow, that's . . . something," I say, furrowing my eyebrows. "There's actual interest?"

"Like I said, nothing huge, a few ad requests, mostly product placements, but still, far more than most junior athletes would expect. I'll have the products sent over with what you're supposed to post written up. They requested that you're in the picture together. Apparently, your appearance in that show last night really made an impact. They love you two together. Sponsors love a marketable couple."

"Oh, we're not—"

Brayden nods, though, cutting me off. "Sure, sounds good. Thanks, Mr. Monroe."

Mr. Monroe leaves us with a smile and heads toward Charlie and Maria, who are sitting on the bleachers surrounding the rink, waiting for their practice time in about an hour.

I turn to Brayden and send him a disbelieving smile, but he scoops me up and spins me around and I let out a squeak that draws everyone else's attention.

"Do you believe this?" he asks after setting me on my feet.

I shake my head. "It's crazy."

"They love us together. I mean, who wouldn't?"

"We do make a good team."

He stares at me for a second and then a tick longer. Long enough for it to feel a little uncomfortable. "What?" I ask.

Glancing around, he takes my hand and pulls me toward a trainer's room just off the rink. When the door swings shut behind us, he turns to me and looks me dead in the eye. "What if we were more than that?"

Oh.

Is that what he wants? Like, for real? I mean, he's always flirted, but that's Brayden being Brayden. He can't actually mean . . .

"Brayden . . ." I say, starting there and trying to figure out what to say next, how to untangle the panic swirling in my mind.

He must see the confusion playing across my face, because he shakes his head. "No, not for real. I mean, just, you know, for social media, play it up for the fans and the sponsors. We're great together and you heard Charles, they want us as a couple, so that's what we give them. *We* could be the next big thing in US Figure Skating, and you know the money that comes along with that is pretty good."

He's right. Damn it. He's very right.

"I . . ." His eyes light up. "I have to think about it."

The light fades a bit, but he nods, stepping closer and taking my hands, squeezing gently, and God help me, that makes me feel a little better about this. This is Brayden, my partner, the guy I trust to lift me in the air as we skate full speed across the ice. "Think about it and let me know, but promise me to *really* consider it. Give us a chance."

"I will. I promise."

Chapter 8

"WE ARE SUCH good sisters," Maria says.

"What?" I ask distractedly. I heard her, but my brain is a second late processing her words. My brain has been a second late for the last week or so. Ever since that conversation with Brayden, my mind has been working in overdrive. Sponsorships. Money that would make the next four years a little bit easier, setting us up for an even bigger payday after the Olympics. And all for keeping my head down, skating my best, and not telling anyone that Brayden and I *aren't* a couple.

The second episode of *KELLYNCH: The First Family of Figure Skating* aired the other night and they haven't exactly dropped the love triangle plotline. The way they edited it, anyone watching would easily assume that Brayden and I were together despite Elisa's obvious feelings for him as we all train at the same rink. And since we hadn't exactly gone out of our way to contradict it yet, the viewers are eating it up—at least I think they are, based on my now nearly hundred thousand followers and their constant messages about how much they love us.

"I said that we are such good sisters."

"Yeah, we really are." I use my elbow to lever the glass door open and Maria, who has a hand free, opens the door behind it.

We're up at five in the morning to make sure we see Elisa's first Olympic skate live. The Games kicked off less than a week ago now, and tonight—Beijing is twelve hours ahead of us—is the final night of the team figure skating competition. She'll be on the ice for Team USA in the ladies' free skate. The rest of the team wanted to watch too, so we asked our coaches to push back our training times, which was easy enough to do since no one else has access to the rink.

It's nice and almost feels like a routine now to come to Kellynch House and hang out with everyone. Even being around Freddie is easier now. Sure, we barely talk, but I can also be in a room with him now without feeling every nerve ending in my body vibrating in anxiety.

And that's fine. It makes everything so much easier.

Inhaling the scent of breakfast wafting out from the kitchen, I call out, "Whoever decided today is a bacon day, I will love you forever."

I'm so glad someone else thought to get breakfast going while Maria and I picked up coffee. I think I'd probably burn anything I tried to cook this morning. I'm a nervous wreck. So much is hinging on Elisa's success at the Games. I can't imagine how nervous she must be right now. Then again, it's Elisa. She's probably not nervous at all.

Walking into the kitchen, Freddie's at the stove, staring at me, mouth slightly open and a spatula hovering over the frying pan. His eyebrows are up and practically disappearing underneath the lock of slightly too long hair falling over his forehead.

Oh, shit.

"Forever's a long time," he says softly, and I just blink at him stupidly, having no idea what else to say. His expression doesn't change, however, and then he's looking back at the bacon like it called his mother a dirty word.

"There's bacon?" Maria asks, following right behind me, nudging me out of the way so she can get through the kitchen archway and put the coffee down on the island.

"Turkey bacon," Freddie calls back over his shoulder, and then focuses on it again.

I unload my own cartons of coffee and pour myself another cup.

"Almost done?" Riley says, coming into the kitchen, still in her pj's and her hair wrapped in a pretty silk scarf that matches. She doesn't look like she just rolled out of bed, at all.

"Actually done," Freddie says, as she sidles up next to him and grabs a plate, holding it out to be filled. He smiles down at her while she gazes adoringly back up at him.

"Thank you," Riley says.

I have to look away. It feels like a private moment, something I shouldn't be seeing or hearing. Ah, and there they are again, all those nerve endings vibrating, and a stomach twist this time too.

Jealousy sucks.

"Uh, Adriana?" Ben asks from behind me.

"What?" I ask, maybe a little more sharply than necessary. He raises an eyebrow at me, then after a quick glance over my shoulder, his expression softens a touch.

Oh God. He knows. I mean, of course he knows that Freddie and I used to skate together. Everyone knows that, even though no one has said anything—but that look. That was the look of someone who understands exactly why I just snapped at him for seemingly no reason at all. Someone who knows why I'd be tense around Freddie and Riley. Why else would he be looking at me like that?

Ben grimaces and motions toward the door. "There's a camera crew here who seems to think they're filming us today."

That snaps me out of it. "Excuse me, what?"

He's right.

The film crew that left us a couple of weeks ago is back with their boom mics and their cameras and their ridiculous storyline about me and Brayden and Elisa. They're also back with a contract signed by my dad.

"Hey," Brayden says, arriving in the middle of the chaos that is the crew's setup. "I thought this was done?"

"Apparently not. They want our reactions to Elisa competing."

"Yeah," a guy wearing a headset with a radio clipped to his belt says, shoving a clipboard with a consent form at Brayden. He's eighteen and can sign for himself. "We need you to sign here, bro, if you want your face on camera."

"Sure," he says, signing it and handing it back.

Just like that. No hesitation.

"I don't know if this is a good idea," I say, biting my lip.

The headset-wearing man is approaching everyone else with consent forms, their coaches signing them for anyone who doesn't have a parent around.

"Hey," Brayden says, his hands landing on my arms, rubbing up and down, like he does before we go out to compete. "This is what we talked about, right? I know you haven't decided one way or another, but this is the kind of thing that will help us for the next four years."

He's right. Some more airtime now and maybe more companies will want us to do social media ads. Charles showed us the agreement with the first one and it's more than enough that I won't have to give lessons for weeks after we get back from Worlds. And that was for one pic with the company tagged in it. We haven't even done it yet and part of the payment is already in the bank. After practice we'll take some pictures with the stretch band the company that contacted Charles sent us and we'll post. It'll maybe take ten minutes and then another month's worth of lessons will be in my account.

Maria is already signing her consent form. It's sort of moot because Dad already gave his permission, but it's nice that they pretend, I guess.

"Okay," I say, reaching for the clipboard my sister passes to me, and sign my name.

The crew arranges us on the couch and the seats are oddly close to how we sat a couple of nights ago to watch the most recent episode of the same show they're filming right now.

Riley, Katya, and Gillian file down the stairs definitely not looking like they all woke up less than an hour ago, and Maria begs Gillian to let her borrow some makeup. I don't bother. Maybe if I don't wear makeup everyone will think I'm not hot enough for Brayden and some of this stuff will stop. Do I really want that, though? I promised Brayden I'd think about it, really consider letting the world believe . . . well, whatever they've probably assumed about us up until now and use those assumptions to cash in. Would it really be so bad?

When I take a seat, my leg bounces up and down over and over again until Brayden reaches out and grabs my knee to make me stop. I don't want to hate this, but I do. It would be living a lie. A lie of omission, but still a lie.

I leap out from under his hand. "I'm going to grab another cup of coffee. Anyone want any?"

A chorus of yeses follows. Good. That'll keep me busy.

"I'll help!" Riley calls out, and follows me into the kitchen.

I pour out ten cups of coffee and then five more. It's now barely after seven in the morning, and who knows what time the crew got up to be here. They deserve caffeine too.

"This is so exciting," Riley says. "I can't believe I'm going to be on TV."

"You've been on TV before, for competitions."

"It's not the same thing," she says, her eyes bright and her smile wide. "Think, maybe all those people who are obsessed with you and Brayden will love me and Freddie too!"

"They for sure will. You guys are awesome together and speaking of, how *are* things with Freddie?" I kind of hate myself as I ask the question, but I can't help it.

"Good," she says. "He's so super sweet and supportive and he's so cute, but he *won't* make a move. I don't know what else to do except, like, throw myself at him at this point."

Grimacing, I shrug. "He knows you like him?"

"No! At least, I don't think so. I don't know. Maybe?" She bounces on her toes. "Help me. I don't know what to do."

Swallowing back the urge to tell her she should wait around for literally ever, even if Freddie O'Connell never, ever expresses interest, I suggest, "You could tell him? Though," and I hate myself as the words start to pour out of my mouth, "are you sure that's something you want to do? Mixing your partnership on the ice with romance? It's a lot. Things could go wrong."

"You're right," she says, and then seems to come to some kind of decision in her head. "I need to be sure he likes me first before I tell him, that way there's no way for things to get messy." I want to interrupt her there and tell her there's no guarantee they won't anyway, but she's still talking. "You've seen us together. Do you think he likes me?"

I have seen them together. Skating together, laughing and joking, hugging at the end of a successful routine. "Why wouldn't he? You're gorgeous, smart, and talented, and he trusts you not to impale your blade into his femoral artery every time you do a lift. I think that if he *doesn't* like you then he has a lot of explaining to do."

It's the truth, even if my stupid jealousy is raging over it. Why wouldn't Freddie like Riley? She's perfect for him and it isn't like I have any claim to him. Not anymore. Not that I ever really did. And who knows if what I feel for him is even real anymore? I've barely spoken a word to him since he's been here. Maybe I love the idea of childhood sweethearts falling in love? Clearly, I'm the only one hanging on to it, though. Freddie definitely isn't. I swore to myself I was going to get over him. It's time to live up to it.

"You're right," Riley says. "Who needs the guy to make the first move, right?"

"Right," I agree as we balance the coffee cups on two large trays and carry them out for the group.

Riley goes for the crew, so I turn to our group, passing the mugs around along with sugar, milk, and creamer, but one of the cables from the cameras gets caught around my ankle, and for a split second I'm falling and taking a tray of scalding hot coffee with me.

And then I'm not and the tray is steadied. A strong hand is at my elbow and an arm almost completely wrapped around my waist, its hand holding me in place.

I know who caught me without having to look, but I do anyway. Our eyes meet and hold, Freddie's touch somehow both familiar and foreign. How is that possible?

Then his hand flexes impatiently against me. The contact sends sparks flaring out over my entire body, a pleasant prickling over my skin, while I gently dislodge my foot from the thick tangle of wires. But it's like those sparks burn his fingers and he pulls away immediately, like he can't physically stand to be touching me. And that takes the breath out of me, like I landed chest-first on the ice. I barely mumble a thank-you before he's turning back to where Riley is offering him a mug.

Glancing around at the cameras, I wonder which one caught my stumble. Probably more than one. Who knows, maybe by next week it'll be a love parallelogram. You know, just to keep those ratings up.

"Nice catch," Jimmy says, holding out his fist for a bump to Freddie. I step away carefully and place the tray down on the coffee table at the center of the sectional, find my seat, and wait for the competition to begin. Brayden offers me the last mug of coffee on the tray. I take it, the cup warming my hands, before turning to the TV so my face doesn't give away that I am so not over Freddie O'Connell and I'm not sure how I ever will be.

The broadcast rescues me. "And here's Elisa Russo. She's looked solid in practice all week, but none of that matters until you get out on the ice," the commentator says as Elisa skates across the ice and her routine begins, almost as familiar to me as my own. She's so graceful, every fingertip, every tilt of her head perfectly placed. Every old video I've ever seen of Mom looks just like this. Flawless.

Putting my mug down on the coffee table, I clench my fingers together, not exactly praying, but you know, not exactly *not* praying. Out of the corner of my eye, I see the bright light of a camera focused on me, and even I have to admit that's a pretty good shot. Little sister praying for a good result for big sister, nearly seven thousand miles between them. Yeah, the story writes itself.

I pull in a deep breath as she goes for her first jump, close my eyes, and wait. The only sound is the music from Elisa's program and the quiet buzz as the cameras zoom in, probably on my face.

"Oh! Oh no. A major tumble from Elisa Russo on a triple loop that's supposed to simply get her into the routine."

"That's such a shame."

When I open my eyes again, Elisa is still skating, but there's a long wet mark down her leg, visible against her tights, evidence of her fall. I breathe out and drop my head, shoulders pushing up near my ears. Brayden's hand lands, warm and attempting comfort, on my shoulder, but it doesn't help.

Shit.

"And unfortunately, that's a complete disaster for the United States. They were relying on a hit routine from Russo to stay in medal contention."

The announcers aren't wrong; that fall is a big deal. The US team was fighting for bronze before Elisa went out there, but there's no way they're going to medal now.

The room stays silent. There's nothing for anyone to say. I look up and try to keep my face as neutral as I can for the cameras as Elisa skates through the rest of her routine, getting through it without another fall, but the damage is done. And when the scores come up, they confirm what I already knew.

"Don't forget, tonight we'll be airing another episode of *KELLYNCH: The First Family of Figure Skating*, where you can watch Elisa's journey to these Olympic Games," the announcer says as they wrap up the coverage for the night.

"Well," Maria says, sitting back. "At least they're not in last."

No, they're in fifth, so it might as well be last. There's one routine left in the team competition, ice dance, and after Elisa's performance there's no mathematical way for the US team to make up the points they'll need for a bronze, let alone a gold. But I can't say that out loud, not with the boom mics over my head picking up every word. Forget Russo and Elliot, the next trend would be about how I predicted an off-the-podium finish.

They won't even make the podium.

This is the program we're inheriting. A shadow of its former self, when Team USA contended for medals in all disciplines, regardless of the year. Four years from now we'll be the ones skating in front of thousands in the crowd and millions at home. Will we falter under that spotlight the way Elisa did or will we rise to the occasion?

"That's not going to be us," Freddie says from across the room, and I look up, straight at him, and his eyes meet mine. There's a fire there, one I used to see reflected back at me when we skated together; whenever he looked at me like that, I knew we were going to kill it on the ice.

I blink and the contact is gone. He's looking around the room, clocking the cameras, but shaking his head and ignoring them. "We're a stronger team than that and we have four years to make sure what's happening to them doesn't happen to us."

"Amen," Charlie says from his spot next to Ben.

He's right. He's *so* right and this matters so much more than anything else. It matters more than sponsorships and social media ad money. It matters more than whether Freddie likes Riley back or whatever the hell is going on with me and Brayden or if I'll ever be over my feelings for Freddie.

It's the only thing I've ever wanted, and I'm going to get it.

Four years sounds like a long time, and it is, but in a figure skating career it's not. Every ounce of experience we can squeeze out of the lead-up to the Games is important. And in order to do that, I'm going to need time. Time that can't be spent worrying about how our bills are going to get paid.

Once the crew packs up their equipment, promising to be back for Elisa's short program in two days, I turn to Brayden. "Can I talk to you for a second?"

We leave the rest of our team chatting about what we saw play out on TV. I slide out the front door with him just a step behind. We haven't exactly been subtle. The conversations have fallen almost silent and most of the eyes are on us, but they disappear from view as he shuts the door behind us.

"I've thought about what you said and you're right. I can't pass up these opportunities. There's no reason we can't let people believe whatever they want to believe about us and if companies want to pay us because of it, well, who the hell am I to say no?"

Brayden hesitates for a second and looks down at me with his brow furrowed. "Are you sure? I know it feels . . ."

"Shady?" I fill in for him and he laughs.

"Yeah, a little shady, but I know how much you worry about your family's finances, and if this can help, even a little . . ."

"It will," I say, thinking about that money already in our account and how much more will show up when he and I take some stupid picture later and post it for the world to see. "More than a little."

Looking up into his eyes, I bite my lip, wondering how much of my integrity I'm sacrificing for my dream.

"Hey," he says, reading the concern in my expression. He reaches up and cups my face in his hands. "We'll make sure it's worth it, okay? We're going to kick ass in Paris and then in four years, we'll do it again in Milan. And in between, we'll win Nationals and Grand Prix and Skate America and Skate Canada and Worlds a few times too. You and me, Russo. All the way, okay?"

I wrap my arms over his shoulders, holding him in a tight hug. His arms easily fall into place around me and squeeze. There's warmth in this embrace and a flair of heat I know could turn into an inferno if I let it, but I don't have time for that either. Instead, I pull him closer and agree. "All the way."

Chapter 9

"WHERE DO YOU want these?" a burly guy wearing a flannel shirt and a black skull cap asks as he and his partner move the massive space heater into the house, struggling to keep it up off the ground.

I cringe while holding the front door of the house open for them, still in my training clothes, gross and sweaty from early morning practice. "Um, up those stairs and then, um, up the second flight of stairs to the roof."

He gives me an incredulous look, but then with a grunt, he and his partner move past me, tracking slush and mud across the floor.

Tonight's the night. After the disaster of the team competition, Elisa is taking the ice in the individual ladies' free skate. Just two days ago she completely nailed her short program and she's sitting in second place, right between the two Russian girls. My older sister is one performance away from winning an Olympic medal and there was no way the show was going to let us watch it without their cameras there to catch our reactions.

It seems like that's what our lives have become in the last week, training and then sitting down to be filmed watching other people skate. Oh, and posting on social media to keep up the hype from the show, which still hasn't dropped that love triangle storyline.

There's something almost comforting about it, though, all of us together, focusing on skating, determined to make sure we do better than the people who came before us, a weird sort of semi-existence outside of reality, like a bubble where we're being held in suspense.

After Team USA's disappointing fifth-place finish, none of the individuals or couples have been able to secure a medal, but Elisa has a chance to change that tonight.

Hence, the space heaters being brought up to the rooftop of our house, where we're having a viewing party for the team, our coaches, and a few dozen other people, including some NFSC executives and sponsors who didn't make the trip to Beijing. The only reason my head isn't exploding is because the NFSC is footing the bill for this one, though that didn't stop Dad from calling all the way from China to make sure not a single detail was overlooked. He might be on the other side of the world, but the NFSC doesn't mess with Kellynch without Dad's say-so.

I grab a mop from the hall closet, wanting to get the congealed winter gunk off the entry's floor, and I'm just about to get started when Camille walks in and raises an eyebrow at me.

"No," she says.

"No?"

"No," she affirms and reaches out, taking the mop from me. "Last I heard the girls were coming over to get ready together."

"So?" I ask, shrugging. "I'll grab last shower. It's fine."

"No," she says again. "Go up there now. They should be here any minute and I swear you are going to sit back and enjoy yourself tonight. Nothing else. No hosting or cleaning up after everyone or dealing with—" She's cut off by the return of the space-heater movers, who leave even more gunk in their wake as they head out to their truck to retrieve another one.

"Camille."

"Adriana," she snaps, and then takes a deep breath. "Go, have fun. You deserve it. You know that, right?"

"Yeah," I say, eyeing that gunk.

"I worry about you. You do too much, take too much on yourself. Maybe part of that is my fault. You remind me so much of your mom, but I need to remember more that you're not her. You're sixteen years old."

"With a professional athletic career," I remind her, but the compliment isn't lost on me. Camille loved Mom like a sister.

Camille nods. "That's fair, but you still deserve to *feel* sixteen sometimes."

"Would you want to feel sixteen?"

"Oh, hell no, but that's the point. You want to look back when you're my age and know that for sure! So go upstairs, get dressed up, have fun tonight, and maybe even kiss a cute boy at some point?"

"Cam—"

"I'm just saying."

"THANKS FOR LETTING us raid your closets," Katya says, and Gillian nods, holding up one of Elisa's dresses against her. It came out of Maria's closet, but I recognize it immediately. My little sister giggles and shrugs when I turn to her with an eyebrow raised.

"Don't go too crazy," I say. "Even with the space heaters, it's still like barely above freezing outside."

Riley emerges from Maria's bathroom. "So?" She's got on a pair of black leather pants and a bandeau top that shows off how hard she works on her abs, with a short leopard-print winter coat on top of it.

"Freddie is going to *die* when he sees you like that," Gillian squeaks.

"Oh, and you and Adriana match!" Katya says, motioning to the leather leggings I'm wearing. I've got a black long-sleeved lace top on. It's the outfit Elisa put together for me when we shot our family Christmas card last year, all black outfits, which didn't quite match the holiday spirit, but apparently the style fit the aesthetic of the cards she'd picked out.

"Let's take a picture," Riley says, bounding toward me, and we pose quickly for her to snap a selfie she posts with a cute caption about how we're twinning. It's only a second or two later that she lets out a short shriek. "Freddie liked it. Like *immediately*. I think tonight is finally the night."

"You're going to tell him how you feel?" I ask, glancing around the room. Everyone else's eyes are trained on Riley, who is still staring at her phone.

"Yep! It's the perfect time to do it. It'll be so romantic with all those lights you have hung around the rooftop and Boston across the river all lit up in the dark."

"It'll be perfect," Gillian says, and the rest of them giggle in response. She's right. That would be perfect.

My phone buzzes and I glance at it quickly, a handy excuse to not react to what Riley said.

"Brayden's here," I murmur, and the room goes quiet. "What?"

"You and Brayden," Katya says.

Gillian lets out a giggle. "Yeah, are you *ever* going to spill? Like, I know you didn't want to talk in front of the boys, but it's just us now."

"It's not that . . . I . . . just . . ."

"It's okay if you don't want to talk about it," Riley says. "But I would like to discuss the way he looks at you because, *girl,* it is fire."

"Yeah," I admit, and it's not even a lie. Brayden does have a way of looking at you like you're the only girl in the world and he's completely uninterested in anything else in the universe. "He is very good at that."

"So, what else is he good at?" Katya asks, but I just roll my eyes and they burst into a fit of laughter, letting me off the hook.

It's not like I haven't thought about it, but I'd always shoved him into this box in my head—he's my partner and my friend, but anything else wasn't even the slightest bit possible.

Except, maybe the universe is pushing us together. I'm not sure if I believe in fate or signs or whatever, but lately it feels like I'm being pulled to him, the way the show has framed our relationship, the way the entire world seems to be reacting to us, and then him suggesting we pretend.

All of those things feel like I should just give in to the inevitable. But that's not how things like this are supposed to go, is it? Isn't love supposed to be a thing you know, a thing that feels right? You either want to be with someone or you don't.

My phone buzzes again. Brayden, getting impatient. I stride to my bedroom door, throw it open, and he's standing there, hand raised and ready to knock. The girls behind me let out another chorus of giggles.

"Ladies," he says, winking over my shoulder at them before looking down at me, a slow grin spreading across his face. "And you, you look—"

"Like Elisa picked my outfit."

He sends me a withering eye roll and I laugh, sliding past him, grabbing his hand as I go. "Let's go."

There's already a small crowd gathered on the rooftop when we make it up the stairs. Music is playing softly in the background, and strings of lights hang from post to post, brightening up the space. Without Dad here to direct traffic the party is way more low-key than almost any we've ever had at Kellynch, aside from the cameras moving around the space shooting footage of all the guests.

At the far end a large projection screen is set up for when the competition starts up in a few minutes, with a view of the river and Boston's skyline rising in the distance, the space in front of it lined with tables and chairs so everyone can sit, eat, and watch. The space heaters, pushed back against the brick half-walls surrounding the roof, are actually keeping the air comfortable.

Still, my sleeves are only thin lace, not enough to stop a chill running through me.

If I'd been in charge of everything, I would have moved the party inside, but that was the point Camille was trying to make earlier. I'm not in charge. This isn't my responsibility. I'm just supposed to have fun and cheer on my sister tonight. And that's what I plan on doing.

The group around us has swelled to include the other boys, all of whom have scrounged semiformal outfits together, button-downs and dress pants, but they look underdressed compared to the girls. I wonder if this is what a high school dance feels like. I've always figured they're awkward as hell, completely nerve-racking, and that maybe girls took them a little more seriously than the guys. I guess some things are universal.

There's a bartender in the corner and I spy what looks like a coffee machine. "Anyone want drinks?" I ask, but no one seems to hear me, so I slip away, wanting something hot to stave off the cold.

The cup is warm in my hands and I hold it close, inhaling the scent. My addiction is real, because my entire body buzzes a little at the incoming caffeine.

"What are the odds," Brayden says when I make my way back toward the group that's formed a small circle near one of the massive heaters, "that you let me add a little something to that drink?"

He's in all black, even the crisp shirt blending in with the night sky. I wrinkle my nose as he pats at the pocket of his suit jacket. That's probably where he's hiding a flask of whatever he'd like to spike my drink with tonight. Take the edge off, or whatever.

Riley lets out a short giggle while Katya and Gillian look on with their eyes wide. Jimmy snickers and Charlie raises an eyebrow at me while Freddie leans over and whispers something to Ben, who shrugs, shaking his head.

What did he ask? I'm suddenly desperate to know, but there's no way I'm going to ask. The urge to do *something* is so strong, I channel it in a different direction. "One out of two."

Brayden quirks a grin at me when I turn to face him again. "You sure?"

"Let's go," I shoot back.

Our fists fly out, and on three, I put down one finger, and he puts down two.

Laughing in victory, I take a nice long sip of the coffee, burning my tongue a little bit, but not caring in the slightest, smiling at the group, who laughs with me, Brayden just rolling his eyes in mock annoyance at his loss.

"Everyone," Camille calls, and the music abruptly cuts off. "The competition is about to get started, if you could take your seats."

There are tables reserved for us near the front, mostly so the cameras can get our reactions as everything in Beijing is beamed back to our screen. I make sure to grab Maria and pull her into the chair next to mine, while Brayden slides in beside me.

"You ready for this?" he asks, his arm around the back of my chair.

"As I'll ever be," I say, suddenly nervous.

"It's gonna be okay."

Is it, though? There's a lot riding on Elisa's shoulders tonight. She's an underdog for sure, but a win, or really a medal of any color, would be massive. Not only would she be an Olympic medalist, but the sponsorships alone might keep Dad from having to mortgage the house. At least it should put a dent into the debt, right? That's the kind of thing Olympic victory brings.

But what if she loses?

Shit. What if she loses? I never even gave myself room to really consider that before. It was always a given. Elisa would go to the

Olympics and she'd win a medal and this constant pressure would ease, but what if she doesn't?

No, that's tempting fate. I'm not going to think about that.

Except now that it's in my head, I can't stop.

"I . . ." I trail off as the broadcast starts, the announcers introducing the competitors as they warm up on the ice, a cheer going up when Elisa skates across the screen, her blonde hair curled to perfection, ready to skate to her Taylor Swift medley the crowds always love.

"I'll be right back."

I can't even give voice to it, the sudden panic that I'm going to have to watch my sister succeed or fail at her lifelong dream in front of all of these people, on camera for the world to see.

I don't want to watch.

I *can't* watch.

I slide out of my chair. Maria doesn't even notice. I'm sure Camille does, but I don't look back. I just slowly move between the tables, smiling at everyone as I pass them until I'm at the door that leads downstairs. I slip through it and then stop in my tracks.

Freddie's there, silent as usual, but brow furrowed at my appearance. He looks over my shoulder as the door slams shut behind me and I cringe.

Everyone probably heard that and looked over and maybe now they're noticing that I'm gone.

"Are you—" he rasps, and then clears his throat. "Are you okay?"

I shake my head. "I don't think I can—"

He tilts his head down, his eyes finding mine, and the tension in his face softens. "Do you want me to get someone for you?"

It goes unspoken that he's not the person who can be there for me right now, even if he clearly kind of gets what I'm feeling. Of course he does. He always did. Like when my mom got sick and he stuck by me. A wave of memories hits me in a way I haven't let them in way too long. Like when he would sit next to me, holding my hand when everything hurt too much to skate. When he did the same thing at the wake and then the funeral and then the months after that when I couldn't bring myself to skate, not knowing if I'd ever be able to stomach getting on the ice again.

And how did I repay him for all that? When I grew faster than he did, I dropped him. I didn't wait for him, like he did for me, and he should hate me for it. Really hate me, and he doesn't. Maybe I hate myself enough for the both of us.

"No, I'm—" My voice cracks before I can force out the word *okay*.

"You're not—" he insists, and he's reaching out now, for my hand, and I pull back before he can take it because if he does, I don't think I'm going to be able to stop the tears that are already threatening to fall. His jaw twitches, his hand retreating to his side, clenched in a fist.

Great job. He's just trying to help and I made him feel like shit.

"I'm sorry," I start, and his expression softens. "I didn't mean—"

The door behind me swings open.

"There you are," Brayden says, clear relief in his voice. "She's about to go on and everyone's wondering where you went. Oh, hey, man."

Freddie quirks a grin at him over my shoulder and does that chin-nod thing boys do.

I close my eyes and take a deep breath before turning away from

Freddie and back toward the thing I was running away from just a few seconds ago. I don't really want to go back out, but I have to. What was I even thinking?

"Sorry," I say, sending Brayden a tight smile. "I needed some air."

"Inside?" he asks, raising his eyebrows and then glancing back to Freddie with an expression that clearly reads *girls, am I right?*

"Yeah, I needed some warm air. It's freezing out there," I correct. "Let's go before we miss it."

We slide back into our chairs as Elisa settles into the middle of the ice, moving into her starting pose and waiting for her music to begin.

As the harmonies of Taylor Swift's "Gold Rush" pour out of the speakers in the arena and onto the rooftop, Brayden's hand slides over mine, squeezing. I let out a breath and watch my older sister glide across the ice.

"Here's the triple loop she had trouble with during the team competition," the broadcaster says, and my stomach plummets before she even takes off. Because I've watched Elisa do that skill more times than I can count and I know what's about to happen. She put too much power into it, probably an overcorrection from when she fell the other night, and she can't control the landing and she's down before I can pull in a breath to hold.

The music keeps playing, but she stays down. Brayden's grip on my hand is like a vise and I lean forward, trying to get closer to the screen.

Then Elisa pushes up to her skates and relief slides through me, but it doesn't last long. She skates furiously, skipping through some of her choreography with perfunctory carelessness, something that will kill her performance component score. And then she goes into another jump, this one a combination, triple flip, triple toe, and she never makes it to the toe, just goes sprawling to the ice.

And she gets up again, her face red, her mouth set in a furious line, but it doesn't matter.

It's over.

Her dreams are dead.

Chapter 10

ELISA CAME IN tenth.

Top ten in the world; not bad, right? Especially with two falls. But somewhere along the line in the history of athletics, probably the original Olympics, now that I think about it, someone decided that only the top three count. Only first, second, and third get rewarded for their efforts and everyone else, fourth through last, goes home with nothing. And that's what's happening to Elisa today.

She'll be home, after more than a decade of training, with absolutely nothing to show for it. The February air is crisp this morning, but not the brutal frigidity of the last few weeks. The sun is shining brightly and it seems like it's capable of warming my face when I turn toward it. It hasn't snowed in days and for once the sidewalks seem pretty clear, so I'm taking a chance this morning and running outside. I . . . I need to get away. Everything about Kellynch right now feels suffocating, and it doesn't help that by tonight Elisa and Dad will be back home, adding two more complications to my already incredibly tangled emotions.

It's quiet, way too early for anyone else to be awake. It's too early for me to be awake too, but there's so much nervous energy racing through my bones that I need to burn some of it before the day really starts. I put in my earbuds as I leap off our front porch ready to sprint down past Kellynch House and the rink into the anonymity of Greater Boston. Once I'm over the river no one will even glance twice at me, just another girl from whatever college out for a run, they'll assume, no idea who I am, no idea what I'm going through.

No idea that thousands of people around the world have spent the last week blowing up my social media feeds, asking about Brayden, obsessing over every post, so much so that it's impossible to read all the comments and DMs or even scroll through the things I'm tagged in. As soon as we post anything, it's immediately dissected and analyzed and then thrown into a tribute set to a song or edited with a filter and reposted hundreds of times.

Brayden's so good at it. He keeps up with it, reposting and commenting, liking dozens of posts a day, creating even more chaos in our mentions. I'm not really sure how he does it. It's like he was made for this kind of life.

My feet slap against the pavement and I'm almost clear of our property, trying to find the right music for this morning's run when I hear the slam of Kellynch House's door and footsteps behind me answering my own. I glance over my shoulder and a flash of brown hair and a sharp jawline tell me all I need to know.

Freddie.

He sends me a tight smile, awkward and unsure, and I return it, hoping mine is a little brighter than I feel.

Last night sucked and he was there to witness it all, and is that why he's smiling at me today? Pity?

Ugh, the last thing I want is his pity.

"Hold up a sec," he calls, and part of me wants to take off at a full sprint, but that would be incredibly freaking rude, even ruder than I was last night.

"What's up?" I ask, turning as he catches up, trying not to relive the night before when I ran into him in a panic.

"You running into the city?" he asks, nodding over my shoulder in that general direction.

"Yeah," I answer, fiddling with my phone, pulling up my music.

"Mind if I join?" he asks, doing the same.

If this was two years ago, I'd roll my eyes and joke that he already had, but it's not, so I shrug and say, "Sure."

We used to do this all the time when we trained together— everything became a competition, who could run farther, faster, who could veer off the sidewalk and leap the bike racks lining the street like they were hurdles. Sometimes our arms would collide, and we'd shove at each other playfully and keep running, needing to make it back to Kellynch before we were late and Camille made us do laps.

I choose a random playlist that my thumb blindly finds on my screen, then tuck my phone into the pocket of my running jacket before taking off down the sidewalk at a good pace, knowing he'll be right beside me.

For a few blissful minutes, it's only me and the guitar riffs from The Band CAMINO pouring out of my earbuds, running through a mental checklist of the things I need to do today. First training and then later on I need to try on my costumes for the competition to make sure we don't need any last-minute alterations and then I need to pack. I'm nearly to the bridge when my earbuds lose connection, the song cutting off completely. Crap, I forgot to charge them last night.

The sounds of the city slowly waking up on a Sunday morning filter in instead—a few cars rumbling down the street, a couple of sirens in the distance, a plane overhead paired with the soft wind coming off the icy Charles River, and the slaps of our feet against the pavement.

It's not the worst thing to run to.

When I slow down to tuck my dead earbuds in my pocket, Freddie matches my stride and we run in silence, over the bridge into Boston itself, the river disappearing behind us. It's kind of nice, actually.

I could say something to him, though.

Should I say something?

I could . . . apologize, maybe? Apologize for what, though? For doing what was best for my career? That's not something to apologize for, is it? Maybe not, but why does it feel like it is? I never really got the chance to fully explain, though, that I was doing it as much for him as I was for me. It sounds like such an excuse, but it's the truth. We were a mismatch, physically; even if we were on the same page with everything else, it didn't matter. He hadn't grown yet, and I grew too fast. Neither of us would be here right now, ready to go to the Junior World Championships, if we'd had to sit out a year while we waited to see whether or not he'd be tall enough, strong enough to lift me up off the ice the way he can with Riley, the way Brayden can with me.

It turns out he is, but what if he wasn't? It's not like figure skating careers last forever and it's not like we could just push back the

Olympic Games because our growth spurts happened a year apart. That's the logic behind it, and it was logical, even if it still feels like I didn't do the right thing, like I should have waited, just like he did for me.

Still, there's something between us, a deep cut, not fully healed, and maybe it's scabbed over in the last couple of years, but for some reason this morning, I want to pick at it.

And it's perfect timing because I've hit the spot where I normally turn around, just as Fenway Park looms into view. I glance up at him and find he's already looking at me with his bright green eyes, but instead of the passive disinterest I've gotten for the last week, there's something there, some emotion I have no idea how to identify. Maybe two years ago I could have, but not now.

I slow my strides down to a halt and he does the same before coming to a complete stop just outside the ballpark. Wanting to say something, the only thing I can think of is, "I'm gonna head back."

"What?" he asks, pulling one of his earbuds out, and I almost snort when the exact song that was playing when mine died echoes out of the tiny speaker.

Actually, I did snort. Shit. "Your music."

"I thought you liked The Band CAMINO?" he asks, sounding genuinely confused.

"Yeah, I do," I say. "I'm gonna head back."

"Okay," he says, almost like he means "goodbye" or "see you later," but when I start up in the direction we came from, he follows, his stride matching mine again even though his legs are longer and can outpace me whenever he feels like it. I bet I can run for longer, though. He's not used to running in the cold anymore.

And if it was two years ago, I would have said that, I would have challenged him to a run until someone had to stop. But it's not, so we just run in silence and suddenly I'm annoyed. Annoyed at myself, annoyed at him. It's stupid, after all this time, to still be like this. Especially because my annoyance doesn't have anything to do with him, not really.

I open my mouth to say something, anything that might inch us away from this awful place of cold acquaintances with more history than most people could wish for in a lifetime when my foot catches on something. I don't even see what I tripped over before I'm falling, my body sprawling down toward the concrete. I don't reach out with my hands to break the fall; I roll, the way I was taught when I first started skating.

"Shit," I mutter, pushing up off the ground and examining my knee. It's barely a scrape, but it ripped open the fabric of my running tights and the skin is broken. I'm not hurt beyond that; I can put weight on both feet no problem, but it stings like a bitch.

"You okay?" he asks, his brow furrowed, leaning down to peer at my knee.

"Yeah, fine. You go ahead," I insist, waving him on. I'm going to have to walk home now. I'm pretty sure I'm okay, but running another three miles on it without really checking it out is probably a bad idea.

"That's okay, I'll walk with you," he says, even though he's still bouncing on his toes, like the energy in his body is colliding against itself inside of him, desperate to be let out. At least some things never change.

I'm not in the mood to argue with him, so I start walking and he follows. It's weird to walk together in silence, even though we had no problem while running. He seems to feel the same because he reaches up and pulls an earbud from his ear and offers it to me.

I take it and pop it into my ear. "Roses" is playing and we walk to the beat, nodding our heads along.

"Do you remember that concert we went to?" he asks, gesturing back behind us toward the rest of the city since the venue had been in that general direction. Of course I remember. "We thought we were so cool, at a concert by ourselves, meanwhile my mom was in the balcony the whole time."

"It was a great show, though, and it was cool, we were at a *club* and I remember feeling like we belonged there, you know? Like almost a grown-up."

We were down on the floor together, swaying to the music, tucked against each other to keep from losing one another in the crowd, his arm around my waist, holding me close, my head on his shoulder. The first time I'd danced with a boy, off the ice, at least.

It's a perfect memory.

Freddie laughs and grins down at me. "Yeah. I was so . . ." The smile slips from his face, clouding over with another thought. I don't have more than a few seconds to appreciate that this was how it used to be and how easily we slid back into it without even realizing it. But maybe that's how it is now, the happy stuff always overshadowed by the bad. Because that concert was only a few days before my dad and Camille sat me down to talk about the *realities* of my partnership with Freddie and how I had to make a choice and I had to make it soon.

A week later, he was gone.

It sucks and I want to make it not suck, so I ask, "What?" trying to bring back whatever the good memory was, and he glances at me, something shifting in his face while he swallows roughly.

"I guess it doesn't matter anymore," he says, rubbing at the back of his head, looking away.

I stutter-step, then just stop in the middle of the sidewalk and he stops with me. "It matters to me."

"Does it?" he almost snaps at me, the harshest I've ever heard his voice, and I'm too stunned to respond.

Looking up at him is still weird, that he has to duck his head to look fully into my eyes, but the way he's looking at me makes my breath catch in my chest. I'm not sure I've ever been looked at like that. A mixture of anger and hurt and something else that I *think* I recognize, but there's no way that's what it is.

It can't be.

But it looks like . . . like *want*.

I bite into my bottom lip, unsure, but when his eyes follow the motion, my heart flutters. His hand brushes against my wrist—and how did he get so close? So close I can see the darker green circles in his eyes and feel the warm exhale of his breath, and my stomach swoops sweetly when his eyes flicker down to my mouth, his tongue darting out and wetting his bottom lip, and I bite down on mine as his gaze meets mine again and I sway a little at the contact.

"Hey!" a voice calls from behind us. Freddie spins away and squints against the sun as a car pulls up. I fall back onto my heels, but I don't even remember pushing up onto my toes. When had that happened?

It's Georgia and Harry Croft. They're in the back seat of a cab.

"What are you all doing out this far?" Georgia asks.

"We wanted to get a nice long run in, but . . ." Freddie says to his sister, his voice flat, gesturing down to my knee, but refusing to really look at me.

"Oh!" Georgia says, catching a glimpse of my knee. "Adriana! Are you all right, sweetie?" Freddie leans over toward the car and mumbles something I can't hear. "Come on, we'll give you a ride home so you can get that cleaned up and Freddie can finish his run."

I start to protest. It's fine, I can ignore it, but Freddie's at my side, a hand at my elbow, leading me forward as his sister scooches over and makes room for me in the back seat. Then I'm in the car, the door is closed behind me, and through the window, I watch Freddie take off at a run before we leave him in the dust.

"Are you sure you're okay?" Georgia asks me again.

"She's fine, Georgia, don't fuss," Harry says. I haven't had much of a chance to get to know either of them. "We were coming back from a nice breakfast before the crowds hit. We have some leftover eggs Benedict, if you want one?" he offers, and when I shake my head no, he shrugs. "I don't know how you all do this. I don't know how *I* used to do this. Sunday morning runs instead of Sunday morning eggs Benedict, especially after staying up so late to watch the competition."

"It was fun," I say. It's not a lie. For a few minutes at that party, I was having fun. And if Harry didn't notice my disappearing act, that's fine.

"And did *it* finally happen?" he asks, a mischievous gleam in his eyes.

Panic, total and complete, rages through my veins and my heart clenches. They couldn't possibly know about . . . did they see us?

"It?" I ask, my voice cracking a little.

"Oh, you know, Riley and Freddie. I've got good money on them finally making it official before we fly to France."

Oh God. Riley and Freddie. I'd completely forgotten. How had I forgotten? I'm a complete idiot. Riley was going to tell him how she feels and I just almost—I don't even know what that was, but it was *something*. And clearly Freddie was freaked out too or he wouldn't have sent me along with his sister.

"You . . . you bet on them?"

Georgia rolls her eyes. "We bet the next show we're going to stream together. He thinks before we go. I think, not so much."

"Oh," I say, sending them a tight smile.

"Which do you think?" Harry asks. "Will my brother-in-law ever kiss that poor girl? Or will she get tired of waiting around for him and do it herself?"

"I—"

"Stop it, Harry," Georgia says, swatting at him playfully. "You're embarrassing her. Riley's her friend. She's not going to spill any secrets."

I play along and say dryly, "Yep, sorry. Even if I knew, I couldn't tell you. It violates section one, paragraph two of the girl code. Violators are punished with zero outfit consultations for a year and I can't afford to lose Riley's opinion. She's my tiebreaker if my sisters give me a split decision."

For a second there's silence, and then they both burst into hysterical laughter.

They're still laughing when the car pulls up to the house and we climb out.

"Thanks for the ride," I say as I lead them into the house.

There are suitcases strewn all over the foyer, clearly dropped after they were dragged inside. Elisa and Dad are sitting on the couch, facing us, their mouths twisted into the same expression.

My gaze catches the time on the grandfather clock in the corner. They're hours early. Their flight wasn't supposed to get in until later tonight. We'd planned a small welcome home dinner, nothing crazy, mostly because we weren't sure how much celebrating they were going to be in the mood for.

"You're home!" I say, moving toward them, but neither budges from their seats.

"Yeah, we are," Elisa says, frowning at me. Her eyes flicker from my face and then down to my scraped knee.

I try to push through the awkwardness. "You guys remember Georgia and Harry."

Dad, ever the crowd-pleaser, rises and shakes both their hands, wandering off with them and asking what they think of the house and the facilities. I can hear them assuring him that Kellynch is the finest rink they've ever worked out of, while I stand there with Elisa still sitting silently, arms folded over her chest.

Shit.

Chapter 11

"I, UM, I have to go clean up," I mumble, gesturing down to my knee, before Elisa can even open her mouth to respond. She's going to want to talk about the show and Brayden, and I do not have the energy for that right now.

I sprint back out of the house, ignoring the stinging cut on my knee, and head straight for the rink. Brayden and I don't have training for a while, but I always keep some of my things there just in case.

The trainer's room is empty since the first session of the day hasn't even started yet, and I mindlessly gather the peroxide and gauze and bandage I'll need, but when I push up onto the table and roll up the leg of my winter running tights, I stop and take a breath. And then another, sitting there letting time slip by.

The last half hour was too much.

First Freddie and our little trip down memory lane, and now Elisa, who is going to want to talk about the stupid love triangle plotline from the show. Brayden and I haven't actually figured out how this whole thing is going to work, but we definitely need to—and soon—because otherwise everyone is going to see right through it, especially Elisa.

Okay, one thing at a time. That's all I can do. So I go see the trainer to get my cut cleaned and wrapped before heading into the locker room to change for training. This I can do, this part is easy, and then when Brayden gets here, I can pull him aside and we can figure out how the hell we're going to pull this off.

With fake dating, like something out of a teen rom-com, there are always rules. That's what we need. Rules. Or guidelines. Something to keep us on the same page.

And that's a problem because I can already hear Brayden's voice in my head, telling me exactly how he's going to feel about that, and an hour later, when we've found an empty corner of the rink, stretching out while we wait for Freddie and Riley to be done with their training session, I nearly laugh out loud when he says, "Yeah, I've never been very good at rules."

"That's too bad," I say, keeping my voice down and glancing around to make sure no one else is near us. "The only way this is going to work, the only way I'm going to do this, is if we have rules."

"Rule number one, Adriana needs rules," he jokes, moving down into a standing lunge as I mirror his movement.

"Exactly."

"Fair enough, I guess. What's rule number two?"

"No one else can know it's fake."

"Duh," he says casually, "and three?"

Now that he's here and asking me, I know exactly what the rules need to be, and they come flowing out. "We only pretend in public. I can't . . . if we're going to do this, at least one part of my life needs to be real."

"Yeah," he says, nodding along, though his eyes sort of narrow at me, like he heard something in my voice he didn't like. "Listen, if you're having second thoughts . . ."

"I'm not," I insist, though that's not entirely true. I'm one giant second thought right now, but this feels like it's our only option. My only option.

"Okay, what else then?" he asks, still sounding skeptical.

"This might be the thing that kills it for you," I say, but he looks doubtful. "You can't cheat on me." He starts to respond, but I cut him off. "If this is going to work, there can't be some girl out there who can post that she hooked up with you. It'll defeat the entire purpose of this: good publicity that leads to sponsorships."

"You're right," he says, shrugging. "No one else. Which is what I was going to say if you'd let me speak."

"Really, it's that easy?"

"It's that easy," he agrees, shooting me a grin. "I do have *some* control over myself, you know?"

"Could have fooled me," I shoot back at him, but smiling. "Okay then, I think that's it."

"Not quite. I have some rules too."

"I thought you didn't like rules?"

"I'm evolving."

"Spit it out, Brayden."

"If we're in public, then we're in a relationship. Method acting. It's gotta be all or nothing. So if I do this," he says, leaning over to grab my hand and twine our fingers together, "no making a joke and pulling away."

"Fair enough," I say.

"And if I do this"—he tugs, pulling me closer, making me fall out of my low lunge, my hands landing on his shoulders, our faces millimeters apart—"you'll go with it?" he murmurs, his mouth hovering over mine.

"Yeah," I agree, my eyes flickering down to his lips and then back up again, half anticipation, half panic. Is he really going to do this here where anyone could see? But then again, isn't that the point?

He sends me a half grin and then leans back as my hands slide away from him. I exhale and swap legs into another lunge. "I take it back," I say. "I have one last rule."

"Okay?"

"If this becomes too much for either of us, we can call it off, no questions asked and no hard feelings. We tell everyone it didn't work out and we're still good friends and partners."

Brayden clears his throat and nods. "That sounds fair."

"So then there's just one more problem."

"What's that?"

"Telling Elisa."

"Fuck," he says, falling out of his lunge down to the ground.

"Yeah," I say, following him and stretching out into a split. "Exactly."

But then my attention gets pulled by something on the ice. It's Riley, up in the air, hands on Freddie's shoulders as he guides her through a complicated lift, her body twisting around before landing in a bridal position as they travel over the ice. It's a little slow, a little bit off the beat of the music, but it's clean. And from Georgia's shrieks of joy off the ice, she agrees. It's risky to be adding a move like that to a routine so late in the season, but I know Freddie and I know Riley; they're not afraid of a little risk, especially when it could launch them to the top of the podium.

"Wow," Brayden and I say together.

And suddenly telling Elisa is the least of our problems, but even as that registers, relief slides through me. This I know how to handle. It's time to get to work.

"YES! ADRIANA, THAT'S gorgeous; no, don't let it slip now. I can read your feelings on your face. Keep it up! Perfect, Brayden!" Camille yells as "Vienna" fades to silence and we finish up a run-through of our rhythm dance.

That was so good. There's nothing in the world like nailing a performance, and we've been on fire all session. Adrenaline is still sliding through me, and even though we've been out here for two hours, I feel like I could go ten more.

God, I love this so much. If only everything could be about skating.

We've been wrapping every training session with our full program, alternating the rhythm and free dances to make sure we're capable of doing both even when we're exhausted. We leave for Paris in a week and it's time to make sure we can hit our routines no matter what is happening around us, on or off the ice. Riley and Freddie can add whatever lift they want to their routine—if Brayden and I skate like this, no one can touch us.

Skating to the edge of the rink, I hear applause coming from the stands. Looking up, I squint and then blink and look again, completely convinced that it cannot possibly be my dad up there bringing his hands together over and over again for an ice dance routine.

He's standing and moving down the metal bleachers, and by the time we're off the ice, he and Camille are standing together waiting for us.

"Well done," he says, reaching out and clapping Brayden on the shoulder. "You can truly skate, young man"—and then he turns to me—"and Adriana, I have never seen you look so . . . captivating. There's something different about your performance—have you been doing those exercises I sent you about emoting?"

I shake my head. "No, sorry. I haven't had time."

"No?" he asks, but doesn't look upset, only pensive. "Ah, well, whatever works, right? Well done, you two, truly. Ah! There's Charles, I have to speak with him. Excuse me."

He says it like he's extricating himself from a conversation with acquaintances, which . . . I guess is kind of true. I can't remember the last time he said that many words to me unprompted.

"Well," Camille says, her eyes wide and twinkling. "Looks like you two have a new fan."

"Walter Russo, ice dance aficionado, who would have thought?" I ask, a small, slightly hysterical laugh escaping with the words. I've never heard my dad utter more than a passing half compliment to my skating before and maybe there'll be a day when that doesn't matter to me, but it's not today.

Camille wanders over to where Dad and Charles are talking, and when Brayden turns to me, I let out another excited noise.

"We are going to kick so much ass in Paris," he says as we walk through the doors leading out into the lobby.

Taking a deep breath, I slide an arm around his waist and lean in closer. "Yeah, we are."

For a split second, he tenses, but then he looks down at me with a smile and I feel his entire body relax. "So we're really doing this?" he whispers.

"Really *fake* doing this," I correct.

He barks out a laugh. "C'mere," he mumbles, and his arm comes around my shoulders. He's gross after a hard practice, but then again, I am too. I scrunch my nose while he brushes his lips against my temple, the contact sending a soft wave of warmth over my skin. Then he snaps a picture of us. It's casual and looks super candid and actually kind of adorable. "Post?" he asks.

"Post," I agree.

He types out a quick caption.

Training with @AdrianaRusso has never been better, even when we're both sweaty messes after practice. With #JrWorldChampsParis fast approaching our time as junior competitors is coming to an end. I've been thinking a lot about the last two years. We've grown so much together, and I can't imagine doing this with anyone else. She's my ride or die and I have her back #AllTheWay #RussoNElliot

God, I'm such a fraud, and for an instant I hate it, until he glances over at me after he finally posts it on our joint account and smiles. It's impossible not to smile back at Brayden when he's really smiling, when his eyes crinkle at the corners and that one dimple appears in his cheek.

"They all think . . ." I trail off when he reloads the app and hearts and comments start to appear on his screen.

"That we're together, yeah," he finishes for me. "I guess it's working."

I press my lips together and stare at the stream of notifications building on his screen. "Yeah, I guess it is."

"And not fake working."

"Definitely not," I say, laughing.

"What's so funny?" Elisa says from one of the tables lining the windows. It looks like she's been there for a while, a cup of coffee in front of her, her phone and a small notebook strewn around it. Some of the other coaches are standing around. Jimmy and Ben are stretching with Maria and Charlie in the corner. Out of the corner of my eye, I see Katya and Gillian are both at a table a few feet away. Great, we're doing this with an audience.

My laughter fades and I try to slide away from Brayden, but his arm tightens around my shoulders. I have no idea what to say to her. Still. Because there isn't anything to say. She knows what she's looking at, or at least what we want her to see. I look up at Brayden and he's already looking down at me.

"Really? My little sister and my ex-boyfriend get together behind my back and they have nothing to say? Fine," Elisa says, pulling our attention back to her. She's standing now, looking back and forth between us. "I cannot wait for this to blow up in front of the whole fucking world."

"Elisa," Dad's voice chides from behind us. "That's enough. I know you're still upset about what happened in Beijing, but that's no excuse for being cruel to your sister."

Elisa's eyes widen into saucers, her mouth dropping open, completely stunned. I wheel around, pulling away from Brayden, and blink at my dad too. I've never heard him use that tone of voice with her before.

Letting out a frustrated shriek from between clenched teeth, Elisa shoulders past, making sure to bump into me as she runs out the front doors.

I follow her, but by the time I make it through the doors, she's already nearly to the house. I could chase her, but I still don't know what I'd say. What is there to say? The only thing that would make it better is the truth, and I can't tell her that. We might not be super close, but we are sisters, and I hate that I hurt her, especially when, like my dad oh-so-sensitively pointed out, she's already hurting.

I can't make it right, though. There's nothing I can do right now, maybe nothing I can do ever. This is on me; it's what I decided to do and now I have to live with it.

THERE'S SOMETHING FAMILIAR about the two suitcases laid across my bed. A few weeks ago, I sat in Elisa's room helping her pack her bags for the Olympic Games. Now she's home and I'm in my room, staring at two empty suitcases, my closet door open, and not filling them.

It's not that I don't want to pack or don't know what to pack; that's easy enough. I've been packing for my competitions since I was eight. No, it's that packing for *this* competition feels different. We're headed to our last junior competition ever, the last time we'll skate out on the ice with that safety net. That's what it is, after all. Once you're *not* a junior, no one cares how old you are or if you've been there before or what your last name is. You go out onto the ice against the best in the world and you see whether or not you measure up, and if you don't, you don't. Simple as that. Elisa learned that the hard way.

Elisa, who, apparently, has decided she doesn't want to talk to me after all and has been pointedly ignoring me since her little outburst at the rink.

I square my shoulders against it, even though there isn't anyone here to see it.

With a deep breath, I dive in, pulling workout clothes from my dresser drawers and rolling them into neat rows inside the first suitcase. Shoes, boots, street clothes I might get at least some use out of if we have an off day to explore *after* the competition go in next. I glance at my costumes hanging on the knob of my closet door. We sent them to be cleaned and checked over after Nationals. I'm supposed to try them on before carefully putting them back into their garment bags, where they'll stay until I open them up again in France.

I should probably do that now. If there are any issues, we'll still have time to get them fixed before we leave.

The first costume is for "Vienna." We're supposed to be skating as a young couple caught up in the world's expectations, but letting our love slow everything down and keep us grounded against burning out too early, like the vibes in the song. Living life and not just existing. We brought that to our costume designer, and we decided we should look like a couple going out on a date. Simple, maybe, but I love the dress even more for its simplicity. It doesn't look like a typical ice dance costume. It almost looks like something you'd wear normally. A deep cream color, it has long lace sleeves and is designed to sit off my shoulders leading into a bodice of the same color in a very fine silky material. Sliding it on, I'm not sure I've ever felt prettier than when I'm wearing this costume. I check myself in the mirror, front and back, to make sure there are no stray threads or buttons. It all looks good, though. I look good.

"I love that costume."

"Me too," I say, catching Riley's eyes in the mirror as she peeks her head in through the bedroom door. I wave her in.

"Sorry, I texted you, but . . ." She trails off, stepping fully into the room and shutting the door behind her.

"I shut off my phone. After Brayden posted that last pic, it got a little bit insane."

"And speaking of Brayden . . ." she says, sitting down on my bed. "I want *details*."

I wave a hand in the air, turning to her. "You know, we sort of talked about it the other night and it felt like the right thing."

Riley's eyes sparkle playfully. "I don't want to hear about the *talking* part."

"Not much else to tell." And that's the truth, even though she shoots me a totally incredulous look. "Did you talk to Freddie?" I ask, feeling like I already know the answer.

"No, totally chickened out. I just . . . sometimes I think he really likes me, he's so sweet and fun to be around, but he's like that around everyone, so I don't know if I'm reading into it too much. What do you think?"

"You're asking the wrong person. I'm terrible with this stuff.

I'm . . . with a guy and now my sister is furious. And Brayden's not exactly known for long-term commitment, you know? I have no idea what I'm doing."

"So we're both completely screwed is what you're saying?" She falls back onto my bed with a sigh.

"Completely."

Chapter 12

I DIDN'T GET MUCH packing done, but both costumes are flawless and ready to go for Paris, and that'll have to be enough for now because Riley gets a text that everyone is downstairs and we're putting together a dinner order for tonight as a big group to celebrate Dad and Elisa's return home. It's probably not the home-coming my sister imagined at all: takeout with a bunch of junior skaters instead of appearances on morning shows and late-night TV and *Dancing with the Stars* announcements.

When we make it into the kitchen, Georgia and Harry are there, looking a little bit cornered by Dad. He's got out a photo album I know well, and from experience, I can tell he's only about a quarter of the way through it, which means there's at least an hour left of his career history.

Camille looks up from leaning on the kitchen island, studying a video, I assume from training today, just like always. "Sushi?" she asks, pocketing her phone.

Everyone agrees, and I swap the photo album out of Dad's hands with a menu for our favorite sushi place. There's nothing he loves more than being put in charge of things like that. He starts making a list of what we should order and over his shoulder Georgia mouths, *Thank you.*

Dad's wrapping up his list when Georgia says, "Oh, and add a spicy tuna roll for Freddie—and speak of the devil."

"Oh, I'm the devil now?" Freddie says, coming into the kitchen with Maria hot on his heels. She must have let him in the house. He heads straight for his sister and kisses her cheek. "Are you feeling any better?"

"So much," Georgia says, a hand on her stomach.

"Good enough for sushi?"

"Good enough for a California roll, anyway. No raw fish for at least a couple more months," she says, her eyes twinkling at her brother, the same way his do.

"They say it will be ready in a half hour," Dad says, ending a call. "Who wants to pick it up?"

"I'll go," I say. The restaurant is a few blocks away and I really don't need to be in the house when Elisa decides to come downstairs. And if I can avoid the way my skin tingles with Freddie this close—and yeah, across the room feels close—so much the better.

I'm halfway down the street when quick footsteps echo on the sidewalk behind me. For a split second my heart races in fear, and then I glance back to see Brayden jogging to catch up.

Clutching a hand to my chest, I grumble, "You scared the shit out of me."

"Sorry," he says, "I just got to the house and they said you went to pick up the food, so I figured you could use another set of hands."

"Or you're avoiding my sister as much as I am."

"Yeah, we never really talked about me and Elisa, did we?" he says as we fall into step together.

"We still don't have to," I say. "You don't owe me any explanations."

"I think I do, though," he says, his voice more serious than usual. "When I first got here, I didn't . . . I didn't think I was staying."

"What?"

"Yeah, I figured you'd call it after a couple of months at most, so I didn't really take it seriously, which is why I thought there wasn't any harm in hooking up with Elisa."

"Okay? I . . . but then?" I ask, pretty sure that's not all he was trying to say.

"But then we really started to click after a minute and I realized that we could be really great, which is why I called things off with her."

"You broke up with Elisa for me?" I ask, pushing my hands into my coat pockets, not quite sure I'm understanding him completely.

"For . . . well, for us, I guess. And I wouldn't call it a breakup— that's for people who are in an actual relationship, right? We were just . . ."

"I really don't need to know." I cut him off.

"It's not nearly as . . . scandalous as whatever you're thinking," he says with a shrug. "We made out a few times. That's all. It didn't mean anything."

"Kissing can matter. Especially if you haven't really done it before, and especially if you care about the person," I say, looking up sideways at him as we walk. And while I'm trying to defend my sister and her years-long crush on my partner, I'm pretty sure I'm not actually talking about her anymore.

"You're right," he says quietly. "It can matter, but what I'm saying is that it didn't matter with her and I wanted you to know that."

"You wanted me to know you were using my sister?" I snap. I know this is irrational and that I'm taking it out on him because this day has been a complete roller coaster of half joy and half disaster and I really don't have the mental energy for anything this important, but I can't stop myself. "I don't understand why you're even telling me after all this time. What do I care?"

He huffs, his breath turning into a soft white cloud of frustration in the freezing air. "No, you're right. It's stupid. I'm sorry I brought it up."

"Okay, then," I say, feeling the tension in my shoulders release. The restaurant is just up ahead. I tuck my chin into my chest to ward off the cold for the last few yards, but then Brayden's arm is up and around my shoulders, pulling me into his side, and it's like being pressed against a walking space heater. He's so warm I can't help leaning in closer. "Thanks."

"We're in public," he mumbles, nodding up ahead to the people coming down the street toward us. "Part of the rules, right?"

"Oh, right," I agree, and suddenly feel very stupid, like I'm in way over my head.

I probably am.

The sushi place is packed, just like it usually is on a Saturday night, and there's only a small corner to wait in while they find our takeout order. There's no real reason to, since it's warm inside, but Brayden puts his arm back up around my shoulders after a few minutes.

"What?" I ask, looking up at him.

"We've been spotted," he says, his eyes darting to his left for a second where a table of girls about my age are sitting, very casually—too casually—taking pictures of the girl with her back to us. "Should we?"

"I mean, this is what we wanted, right?"

"Right," he says, before turning to face them fully and sending them a megawatt smile. All of them practically melt on the spot. "Do you girls want a pic?"

"Oh my God," one of them mutters at being caught, but then she seems to think better of it and smiles back. "Yeah, do you guys mind? We're big fans of the show!"

We spend the next few minutes posing with them and then re-posting the ones they chose to put on social media. This is *exactly* what we wanted and it's working.

The rest of the restaurant watches in fascination as the girls take pictures with us in different combinations until our food arrives, and it's easy to watch the wave of recognition pass through them as they look us up on their phones or whisper to someone else at their table who we are.

It's wild.

"Thank you guys so much, this is awesome," the girl who first spoke says and we beat it out of the place before it occurs to them to leave too.

"That was so weird," I say when we're back on the street, carrying four massive bags of sushi between us. Apparently, they'd called in more orders after we left, and judging by the amount of food, everyone is going to be there when we get back.

"Yeah," Brayden says, looking back into the restaurant through the plate glass window where the girls are watching us go. "Hang on a second."

I stop and turn to him. "What's—?" I start, and then stop again. He's so close, close enough that his coat buttons catch against mine for a second.

"Do you think we could," he says, trailing off, his eyes flicking up toward the restaurant and then back to me and then down to my lips, "give them a show?"

"A show?" I ask, but I know what he means. Those girls won't be able to help themselves. If we do this, the pictures will be everywhere in a few minutes, with a sweet story about how we were nice enough to stop and take pictures with them before. It's perfect.

Brayden raises his eyebrows at me, and I nod once, but he shakes his head. "I need to hear you say it."

"Yes," I whisper, and that's all it takes.

He leans in close and, for a moment, presses his forehead against mine before one arm circles my waist and draws me closer, like he's done a million times on the ice, but then everything is different. My breath catches when he softly, but insistently, takes my lower lip between his. He guides me through the kiss. It's slow and sweet, like I'm being led in a dance, and just when I think I might dump the bags I'm still holding on the ground and wrap my arms around his shoulders to pull him close, to deepen the kiss and lose myself completely in this feeling, he pulls away a fraction, his nose brushing mine before he steps back and lets out a sharp exhale.

My experience with kissing is limited to a few quick pecks and one very sloppy attempt at French kissing with my seventh-grade boyfriend, Zac Brewer, who broke up with me two days later to go out with a girl who didn't spend every waking moment training and could actually go to his hockey games to cheer him on and go to parties to celebrate afterward, and I don't want to think about Zac Brewer right now, not after a kiss like that.

That is what kissing is supposed to feel like.

"Wow," I mumble, before I can catch myself.

Brayden clears his throat and nods. "Yeah, um, I think . . . I think that was good."

"Yeah?" I ask, biting my lip. He'd know better than I would.

He knows me really well, too well, probably, so he hears uncertainty in my voice. "Uh, yeah, Adriana, add kissing to your list of talents, okay?"

"Definitely something to put on my college apps."

"Come on," he says, "everyone's waiting for their food and I think those girls got their money's worth."

"Hmm?" I ask, a little distracted by how close he's still standing. "Oh, right . . . the girls."

He laughs a little and I want to be annoyed, but I can't muster up the energy. It was a good kiss, even if it was all for show, and I'd have to be dead not to appreciate that. "Shut up. C'mon."

We trudge back to the house, bracing against the wind as it picks up off the river. With our hands full, I can't bury myself against him, and by the time we make it to the front porch I'm starting to feel like a human icicle. We're barely inside the house when people start pouring out of the kitchen, almost all of them wearing shit-eating grins, led by Camille, whose eyes are dancing with mirth.

"So, what took you guys so long?" Riley singsongs as she skips up to me and grabs one of the bags out of my hand.

Oh God, that was fast. Had the pictures already . . . yeah, they definitely had. Elisa is nowhere to be seen in the crowd, but everyone else is there, laughing and pulling out their phones and showing us how many posts and reposts and edits there already are of the impromptu photo shoot and then us on the sidewalk after the fact. How are the fans so fast? It's barely been a half hour.

The sushi is divvied up and we all end up standing around the kitchen island eating, and for a few minutes it's nice, like I thought it would be when everyone first arrived. It's like a real team, with Charlie and Ben arguing over who gets the last piece of sashimi and Georgia complaining about her California rolls and Brayden, with his side pressed against mine as he steals a piece of my crunchy spicy tuna, teasing Jimmy, who lost a game of Odds to Ben and is flying around the kitchen looking for a carton of milk to cool the burn from the glob of wasabi he shoved into his mouth.

I'm still laughing when across the island, after managing to not even really clock his presence for the last hour or so, my eyes meet Freddie's, but just as quickly his gaze darts away. Like I caught him doing something he wasn't supposed to. He's focusing somewhere over my shoulder where I know there's nothing except bare wall. He must realize that, because then he shifts uncomfortably and tries to refocus on something Riley says to him. A couple of seconds later, though, his eyes flicker over to me again and this time when our eyes meet, they hold and my world sort of shifts on its axis.

I know that look. I remember it from our run the other day when for a split second I thought he was going to lean in and kiss me. And when the intensity feels like it's too much and I have to look away, he does first, but his eyes go to Brayden and his jaw clenches, the smallest twitch, and I know that look too because before everything went down, I knew Freddie O'Connell better than anyone else in this world. He's pissed off. Pissed off at Brayden, and there's only one reason he'd be pissed off at Brayden.

He's jealous.

My mind reels and I have to swallow back a groan building in my throat because something like guilt slides through me at the thought. Like I should feel bad that Freddie's unhappy. Like I should be the one to fix it. And that's insane because that's not my job. He's barely spoken to me in two years, we're not even really friends, and besides that, Riley likes him. But then he looks back at me again and this time I'm the one who's caught looking, a flush building in my cheeks as I stare down at the sushi in front of me and try to grab another piece with my chopsticks, failing miserably because my heart is beating like thunder in my chest and all from a few seconds of fleeting eye contact.

Oh no.

This is not good.

Not good at all.

Because a part of me, a way bigger part than I'll ever admit to, likes it.

"UGH," CAMILLE CALLS out as we botch another curve lift. Brayden has to let me go and push me away on the ice to avoid either of us getting impaled by our skates. "Okay, enough!"

It's our last skate before we leave tomorrow and it's been hours of massive struggle. My entire body feels like a gigantic bruise from the number of times I've eaten ice today and Brayden's not much better. We skate to her from opposite directions and stop, waiting for her critique. She stares at us for a second and then another, silently, her eyes flicking between us.

"Whatever is going on here, you two need to figure it out. You cannot go to Paris like this. At best you'll embarrass yourselves and me; at worst one or both of you is going to get hurt. Get out of my sight and don't come back until you're ready to work."

Retreating off the ice, neither of us head for our respective locker rooms, but instead to a small office we usually use for storage. Old clothing racks with long-forgotten skating costumes and hockey jerseys line the walls and boxes of equipment gather dust in the corners. Brayden closes the door behind us. He props himself against the desk, nudging a pile of boxes out of his way with his hip. I fall into a folding chair on the opposite side of the room, still not more than a few feet away from him in the tiny space.

"What is with you today?" he shoots at me when it's clear I'm not going to say anything.

"It's nothing," I lie, crossing my arms over my chest and shrugging.

Scoffing, he tries again. "Don't bullshit me. Was it the kiss? Did I cross some kind of line? I mean you said you wanted to, and it seemed like you were into it?"

"What, no? It was . . . it's fine, I just . . ."

He looks unconvinced and keeps pressing. "Then what is it?"

I can't say it, because I don't even know what *it* is. Or actually, I do know, but it'll sound insane. Sorry, Brayden, but this fake dating thing we're doing is confusing and kissing you is fantastic, but also,

I'm freaking out because a guy I thought was out of my life forever somehow makes me feel like I'm cheating on him with you even though you and I aren't even dating, he just thinks we are.

Yeah, that'd go over well.

"The last few days have just been a lot, okay? And I think I'm feeling the pressure more than I realized."

It's not *entirely* a lie, at least.

"Okay, so are we good?" he asks finally, standing up and holding out his hand to me.

I take it and let him pull me up. "We're good," I assure him.

Camille looks up from her phone when we reappear, her eyes darting back and forth, eyebrows raised in a silent question.

"Let's run through 'Vienna,'" Brayden says, and I nod. Camille gestures toward the ice and goes to the control room to cue up the music.

It echoes from the speakers seconds after we take our starting pose at the center of the ice. And then we're skating, hand in hand, spinning and twirling and stepping together. His hand feels like an extension of my own body as we shift with the music; the skills themselves are muscle memory at this point, which is why our issues earlier were so stupid. It's all a mental game now and with our entire focus on each other and the music and performing every note, every word, it's easy. On the ice, we're not Adriana and Brayden, not really. We're some kind of idealized version of ourselves, caught in a moment in time, pushing each other to be our best, but also taking the words to heart. We do this because we love it. That's the entire point. To love ice dance enough to train yourself and your partner into the belief that love will be enough to get you through. And maybe that's not an entirely foolish belief. Maybe it's real.

Brayden's mouthing the words as we glide smoothly down to the ice, falling briefly on our knees before we're both back on our skates and I'm pushing toward him. His arms come around me, one hand gripping my thigh, the other lifting under my arm until my entire body is held by his and he's spinning across the ice, carrying me through the uprise of the music, the moment the crowd usually buys in and shouts their approval of us and lifts us through the rest of the dance, and together we'll make them, and the judges, fall in love with us.

The music builds and builds before slowing to a close and Brayden and I drift down to the ice. My breathing is hard and fast, and I lift my hand to touch the back of his head, like I always do. It's the last bit of our choreography, but instead of resting on my shoulder, his face is hovering above my own, and as the last piano chords play out his mouth lowers to mine just as mine lifts toward his because right now, I don't want anything more than to be kissed.

It's brief, nothing like last night, barely a brush of the lips, but it feels so right, the intensity is the same, and it's enough to make my heart skip a beat and then pound out an uneven rhythm. This isn't real, but that doesn't mean I can't enjoy it. What's a kiss or two between fake dating friends?

We don't say anything as he lifts me to my feet. Our music is gone, replaced by the usual stuff that plays in between program run-throughs, but I can still feel my lips tingling and I press them together, trying to make it stop.

We skate to Camille, whose smile is wide. At the way we just skated? At the kiss? Both? Who knows?

"Oh my God, that was so good!"

It's Riley; she and Freddie are moving onto the ice.

Distantly, I hear Camille's comments and corrections, but mostly praise for the routine we put together.

I don't look away from Freddie. He's not looking at me, at least not at my eyes. His gaze is set firmly downward, where Brayden is still holding my hand in his. I pull it free as subtly as I can manage, but it gets Brayden's attention. He turns to me with a smile, and I meet it with one of my own, before he refocuses on Camille's words, but my eyes drift back to where Freddie stood a moment before. He's gone, though, skating across the ice with Riley.

Did he . . . did he see that last moment, the kiss?

Of course he saw.

But I have to . . . not care.

It doesn't matter if he's angry or jealous or annoyed that we're skating this well.

That's it. This is me, not caring.

What Freddie thinks about any of this shouldn't matter. The only thing that matters is that we keep skating like this once we get to Paris and bring home that gold medal.

Chapter 13

$\mathcal{U}$SUALLY WHEN I'M on an airplane my long legs are crammed up against the back of the seat ahead of me, but today there's plenty of room. We're flying first class, thanks to the NFSC, and the seats are huge. They're arranged in foursomes, with two chairs facing one another, but the cabin is mostly empty so there's plenty of places to spread out. Despite that, people seem to gravitate toward each other, and Brayden and I, almost instinctively, sit down together.

Dad and Elisa are a couple of rows away, also in first class, even though the NFSC is not paying their way. My whole body starts to overheat a little bit at the thought. I can't help it. It's force of habit. I calculate in my head how much it's costing us for them to sit in first class. Their extra checked luggage. Their hotel rooms. Food and souvenirs in Paris, which for both of them doesn't mean, like, a little Eiffel Tower figurine or a book from Shakespeare and Company. No, it'll be a bag from Louis Vuitton or a new suit from Versace. It will easily eat up everything I earned in the last few weeks doing product placements with Brayden since everything gets deposited into our family's joint account.

I twist around and look back toward Charles, sitting a few rows behind us. When we land, I'll ask him to set up more ads for during the competition, and if we win, then that might mean real sponsors, outfitting deals, the works. And maybe . . . maybe I'll ask him to set me up my own accounts, separate from Dad's. My heart rate goes back to normal. Yeah, that's a good idea. That'll make sure I'm in control of everything coming in, but more importantly, everything going out.

"You in there?" Brayden asks, and I shake my head, trying to bring myself back completely.

"Yeah, sorry, what?"

"I asked how long the flight is."

"Almost seven hours and remember, we're losing time, so try to sleep."

"Yes, ma'am," he says, sending me a mock salute, but then catching the eye of the flight attendant as she passes us. She's pretty, maybe in her early twenties, and when Brayden smiles at her, she stops. "Can we get two glasses of champagne? We're celebrating!"

She narrows her eyes at him, but they're twinkling with humor when she shakes her head no and continues down the row.

"We're not supposed to be drinking," I remind him when he starts to pout.

"There is no drinking age in international air."

"Last I checked we're still sitting on the tarmac at Logan, which is definitely still in the US."

"Nervous?" he asks, totally out of nowhere.

"What? No, I'm not nervous."

"I mean about Worlds."

"Oh . . ."

Is that what I'm feeling? Nerves? It might sound a little obnoxious, but I've never been nervous before, not about a competition. I know that's a normal thing for most people, but competitions have never made me freak out. Just, you know, literally everything else. Competitions are my happy place. I can control everything while we skate, even when the world is turning upside down off the ice.

"I don't know, maybe, a little bit?"

"About time there was something normal about you."

"Hey!" I protest, and gently smack his arm with the back of my hand. "I'm extremely normal."

The flight attendant comes back and hands us champagne flutes. She smirks at Brayden's wide smile. "Sparkling cider, enjoy."

"It's not a bad thing, not being normal," Brayden says, taking a sip of his drink. "You're not like most people, especially not most girls."

I shake my head, putting down my glass on the tray in front of him. "That's *so* untrue, and completely sexist, by the way. You just know me better than most girls. There are lots of fantastic girls out there. *Maybe* if you saw a girl more than one time, you'd know that."

Brayden shrugs. "Maybe." He seems unconvinced.

"Have you ever even been on a second date? No, wait, have you ever been on a date at all? Or has it just been hookups?"

"Wow, low blow."

"Sorry," I say, cringing. Maybe that was too far?

"No, you're right, though. I've never *actually* been on a date before. We should go on a date."

"A *date*? You and me?"

"Yeah, why not? Dinner or something."

"That doesn't count, though," I say. "We've had dinner together before, and besides, it wouldn't be . . ."

"What?"

"It wouldn't count if it was us." I keep my voice low, looking around to make sure no one was paying attention, but when I turn back to him, he's still looking at me, his face oddly earnest.

"What if I wanted it to count?" he whispers, his eyes darting away and then back again, unsure, and when was the last time I saw Brayden unsure of anything?

Oh God, what is he doing? This wasn't part of the deal.

"Brayden," I say, swallowing back the panic, and I have no idea what else to say, so the silence just grows between us.

The moment could get awkward—okay, it is awkward—but not for long, because Elisa is suddenly at our seats, rolling her eyes at us. "Could you guys detangle for like two seconds? Adriana, swap seats with me, Dad wants to talk to you."

She falls into my seat as soon as I'm up and moving a few rows ahead where Dad's riffling through a stack of papers, a tablet propped open on the tray table in front of him.

"Ah, Adriana, perfect," he says, gesturing to the seat beside him. "We never got a chance to sit down and chat after I got home from Beijing, so I thought this would be a good time to do so. What do you think?"

"Um, okay?" I ask more than answer, my mind still reeling from the last few minutes.

"It's the start of a new Olympic quad, so it's important to set up expectations and our goals for the next four years. Obviously, you're well on your way toward following in my footsteps, but I always like to discuss everything beforehand, make sure it's all laid out so there's no confusion as things become more high stakes."

"Sure, that makes sense," I say, furrowing my eyebrows, trying to read what's on the pages in front of him, trying to focus on this instead of the boy a few rows behind me. They look like a mix of financial statements and maybe some projections too. I see next year and the year after that at the top of some of the papers.

"I just want to make sure you understand the importance of upholding the family's legacy and how important it is for us to stick together. This past year's results were obviously disappointing, but I know I can count on you to do better. It's time we had another banner to hang from the rafters, and since ice dancing has come such a long way in the last few years, I would very much like to see your name enshrined up there with mine and your mother's."

"I want that more than anything." That, at least, is something we agree on.

"We can go over the details after this competition, obviously, but I just wanted you to be prepared. With my help, you can do great things and as you know, we'll need those sponsorships to keep flowing in if we want to restore Kellynch to its former glory."

"Exactly," I agree, but I feel like his definition of glory and mine don't quite line up. His probably involves construction on a second rink and who knows what else. Mine looks like a steady paying down of whatever debt we owe and making sure our house doesn't get mortgaged and then foreclosed on because we can't pay our bills. "But . . ."

"But?" he asks, raising his eyebrows. I know he and Elisa had chats like this all the time, especially once she became an Olympic contender, and I'm guessing she never even uttered that word.

"But remember, since I am an ice dancer," I say, pretending to not notice his flinch, "it's not just me involved. Brayden's a part of this partnership and he needs to have a say too."

I feel bad, using him as a buffer here, but he'll be cool with it. He knows how my dad can get. Except . . . maybe things are different now. I don't even know what just happened. How can I know how he'll react to this?

"Brayden is smart enough to know what's good for him."

"Yes, he is," I agree, but again, I'm pretty sure we don't mean the same things. "I, uh, promised Maria I'd sit with her for some of the flight, okay?"

"Oh, of course," Dad says, waving me away with a grin.

Elisa's still in my seat, so after shooting Brayden an apologetic look over her head, I keep my word and find Maria a few rows back, mostly relieved I won't have to sit next to him because I still have no idea what the hell I'm going to say.

"Yes, finally," she says as I land in the seat next to her. "I need your help." The captain makes an announcement that we're about to take off, so we buckle our seatbelts.

"Yeah?"

"Yeah, I want to get over Charlie and the best way to do that is to find someone else to like."

"Uh, I'm not sure if that's . . . I think the best way to do that is to recognize that Charlie's just going to be a good friend."

"Well, duh, I already did that part, are you not paying attention? But now I'm ready to find someone else and since you and Brayden are together, I figured you're the best person to go to about it. I think it should be Ben Woo. And before you say anything about his ex-boyfriend, I already confirmed that he's bi. I am *not* making the same mistake twice. He's kind of quiet, but maybe that's a good thing, you know? Since Charlie's the opposite of quiet. Or maybe Jimmy. He's really cool too and he *didn't* just get out of a relationship."

"Well, you could talk to them, I guess. That's the best way to get to know someone. Figure out if you like the same things, other than skating, obviously, or if he makes you laugh or . . ."

Maria wrinkles her nose. "I kind of want to figure out if either one of them wants to make out with me."

I laugh. "Yeah, that'd be a good sign too."

"Do you think I should ask Elisa what she thinks? She has so much more experience with this stuff. You know, moving on from a guy you like because he likes someone else."

I tilt my head and narrow my eyes at my little sister, who shrugs. "That's not . . ." But I can't even be mad because yeah, that's exactly what happened, or at least what everyone thinks happened, and Elisa has every right to be pissed about it. Guilt tickles at my conscience for a second, but I push it away. I'm doing what I have to do.

"It's true, right? I mean she's been throwing herself at Brayden for years and obviously she's *not* the Russo sister he wants."

"But . . ." I trail off. I was going to say that he doesn't want me, reflexively, but stop myself just in time because that's not exactly true, is it?

Maria shrugs, even though I don't finish my thought. She's

moved on and relief floods through me. "I think I want to sleep on the flight. After we take off, will you still sit with me anyway, like you used to?" When we were younger, after Mom died, whenever Maria was sick—or thought she was sick—I'd sit next to her bed and rub her back until she fell asleep. The seats in this cabin are big enough for her to fully recline.

"Sure," I say.

When did everyone get so opinionated about my relationships? I've never even had a boyfriend. Never even gone on a real date. And up until last week, I'd never been kissed. Not *really,* anyway. More and more I'm realizing that Zac Brewer shoving his tongue in my mouth does not count. Real kissing is something else entirely. Real relationships? Those I have no idea about.

Maria passes out less than an hour into the flight and I'm not far behind her.

When I wake up, it's hours later and we're somewhere over the Atlantic Ocean. Despite the first-class seats, every muscle in my body feels like it's coiled and pressed in a vise. I start to sit and stretch when I hear hushed voices across the aisle from me.

"I think she's too good for him, but whatever, they seem happy," Riley whispers. "Who knows, maybe it's one of those relationships where he's figured out what's really important, you know?"

"Or it's convenient," Freddie's low rumble answers. "He doesn't seem her type."

"People can change," Riley says, "and you can't help who you fall in love with."

"You definitely can," Freddie shoots back. "You can just decide.

If you don't want to love someone you don't have to and if you want to love someone, you can just decide."

"Have you been bingeing *Grey's Anatomy* again?"

"Riley," he sighs, exasperated, but I can hear the smile in his voice. "I'm just saying I don't get it. That's a pretty big risk to take, hooking up with your skating partner."

"Since when are you afraid to take risks?" Her voice is teasing, but I can hear the truth in her question.

"Never, but there are risks and then there's potentially throwing away everything you've worked for, for what? Infatuation?"

"So you think partners being in relationships is a bad idea? How can you say that? Your sister *married* her partner."

"I think it depends on the partners, and those two? Him, I get it. Her? I just . . ."

I shouldn't be listening to this, but there's no way to stop, and maybe Riley doesn't hear it in his voice, but I definitely do; there's . . . hurt there, in his voice. Hurt that I *wouldn't* take a risk with him two years ago for something he couldn't control and now I'm, at least from his perspective, *choosing* to make things riskier.

And maybe it's not just from his perspective. Maybe it is way riskier, what I'm doing, because it would be so easy for this to blow up in our faces.

Except he doesn't have all the facts. Doesn't know *why* I'm doing this, and the urge to sit up and explain, to tell him everything, is suddenly so strong, I literally have to bite my lip to keep the words inside.

But still, he's not entirely wrong.

The pair falls silent and it's not long before I hear their breathing even out. They're asleep again, like almost everyone else in the cabin. Even Brayden, his head propped against a neck pillow with Elisa out cold beside him, head thrown straight back against her seat.

What am I doing? When did my life become such a complicated mess, a tangled sort of flow chart of disaster? And suddenly I feel the urge to talk about it, all of it, but there's . . . no one knows the whole truth, and there's no one I can tell the whole truth to. What a freaking mess.

And then my eyes land on Georgia O'Connell-Croft.

She married her partner, like Riley said. She'd know better than anyone what I'm going through or at least sort of what I'm going through. I just need someone to listen, even if I can't spill everything. Or maybe if I ask her the right questions, maybe she'll hit on the solution I'm looking for. It's a shot in the dark, but it's my only option.

My feet are carrying me toward her before I can think about it for one more second. There's an empty seat across from her and Harry is snoring in the chair beside her.

"Can't sleep?" I ask.

"Exhausted during the day, can't sleep at night, one of the fun pregnancy symptoms they don't tell you about," she says, rolling her eyes.

"Can I ask you something?"

"Sure," she says, shifting around, trying to get more comfortable.

"If it's too private, you don't have to answer, but I was wondering, how did you know that it would be okay? Dating Harry, I mean."

Yeah, very subtle. She's definitely not going to know who I'm talking about. Yep, there it is. Her gaze turns to Brayden across the cabin and then she looks at me, her eyes softening at whatever she sees on my face.

"I'm not sure I'm the best person to ask, sweetie."

"You're really the only person I can ask," I whisper, and she sends me a sad smile.

"Well, for me, it was that despite everything, he was worth it."

"Worth everything falling apart and losing your skating partner?"

"Yeah, worth that. It's a big one, huh?"

"The biggest."

"So that's the question you have to ask yourself: Is what you're feeling, and presumably what he's feeling, worth risking all of that?"

"I don't know." I haven't even taken a second to really process what he asked me, let alone think about what I'm feeling. Do I like him like that? I didn't think I did, but . . . maybe it's like what Freddie said. Maybe you can choose? Can I choose to feel that way about Brayden? He's my friend, my partner, a really good kisser, stupidly good-looking, and he's been there for me through all of this. Isn't that enough? More than enough?

"That's okay, you know." Georgia cuts off my thought spiral. "You're allowed to not know things. Especially when you're sixteen."

"I . . . don't like not knowing things."

"I've noticed."

"Yeah, that's me, the control freak."

"From what I've seen, not so much a control freak as someone who takes too much on herself, which isn't necessarily a bad quality in someone who wants to win an Olympic gold medal."

"Not so great for romance, though."

"Maybe not. Okay, you got the easy part of the advice. Want the hard part?"

"Hit me with it."

"I've been watching you for a bit now, Adriana. You are incredibly talented and dedicated and the way you and your partner skate together, well, some couples never have that kind of chemistry, let alone as juniors."

"I sense a *but* coming," I say with a heavy sigh.

"All of those things I mentioned, they make for a great ice dance partnership, and those don't come along every day. I'm not going to tell you that you shouldn't explore that relationship beyond what happens on the ice, but I will tell you this. It's important to be sure because the decision you're thinking about making, it will impact the rest of your life. Here's the hard part: you have to talk to *him* about it. It's not a choice you should be making on your own."

"He seems to think it's a great idea."

"I bet he does, at least on the surface, but have you discussed the other things? The possible fallout?"

"We promised that if it didn't work out, we'd go back to how things were before."

"And you think that's possible?" she asks.

"I . . ." It had sounded so simple and easy when we made those rules. Except that was *before*, before he complicated everything by wanting to make it real. I don't know. There are feelings creeping in, feelings I didn't plan on, and now it feels like one false move could ruin everything. "I'm not sure."

She sends me a tight smile, but nothing else. There's nothing left to say, I guess.

"Could you not tell anyone we talked about this? There's enough crap with that stupid TV series and now the social media stuff."

Georgia pats my hand gently before raising hers to her mouth in a zipper motion. "My lips are sealed."

"Thanks."

She smiles and for a split second I wonder what it would be like to have someone like her as a big sister, supportive and kind and . . . there for you, and then I swallow that back along with a tiny lump in my throat, because all the wishing in the world isn't going to make that dream come true.

Chapter 14

"DON'T FALL ASLEEP," I warn Maria when she flops down onto the plush hotel room bed.

We're in Paris.

I mean, we're actually in a hotel room in Paris. The room is gorgeous, gilded and ornate fixtures with dark mahogany furnishing and glittering light fixtures. The walls are covered with intricately lined wallpaper, and a Van Gogh print hangs between the beds. That's pretty much all I've seen of Paris, beyond what I could catch outside my window from the airport to the hotel lobby, but we're actually, finally, here, after all this time. So many incredible things have happened in this city. Winning a Junior Figure Skating World Championship would probably rank pretty low on the list, but that it could be on the list at all is kind of amazing.

"But we left home yesterday and now tomorrow's already half over," she whines, covering her face with a pillow.

"That barely makes sense, and we have the Opening Ceremony soon, then the athletes' reception like right after. You know, we have to let the judges and sponsors see our brightest and shiniest faces."

"Sponsors?" she asks, pulling the pillow away.

"Yeah, Mr. Monroe has a couple of, he called them face-to-faces, set up for me and Brayden." Where we'll have to pretend to be a super-happy couple and I have no idea if I'm capable of that right now. I haven't had a chance to talk to him since the flight.

"I'm going to have to talk to Charlie. If his dad is already setting up sponsorships for you guys, then the least he can do is save some for his son and his son's partner."

I hum in response. Maria and Charlie are going to be junior competitors for at least another season, if not two, so there's definitely still plenty of time for things like sponsorships. "I'm going to steam my dress for the party. If you get yours out, I'll do yours too."

There's a sharp rap on the door and I go to answer it. Camille's on the other side, with a package in her hands.

"Hey," I say, waving her inside.

"The NFSC had these made for you guys. Team tracksuits."

"They're really into this now, aren't they?"

Camille shrugs. "They're pretty fed up with how we finished in Beijing. They want the generation coming up to succeed."

"And tracksuits equal success."

"A healthy team concept *before* you all make it to the senior ranks," Camille says, handing one to me and then tossing one to Maria, who sat up immediately at the mention of free clothes. "So yes, tracksuits."

"Happy to represent Team USA," I say, opening it up to reveal a dark blue set with red piping at the edges of the collar and wrists and matching bottoms. *USA* is emblazoned on the left lapel, in case anyone wasn't sure which country we were representing.

I had my first international assignment two years ago, the first year Brayden and I teamed up. It was an incredible jump from brand-new partners to skating for our country, and even though we finished dead last it was still exciting. Now? Just being here isn't enough. We're here to win.

"Get dressed. There's a bus picking us up in fifteen."

The bus is one of those high-end transports, with blacked-out windows and large leather seats. Brayden's already at the back of the bus, earbuds in, staring out the window, and maybe I should just rip the Band-Aid off, sit next to him and talk this through, but . . . I'm not that brave.

I slide into the seat next to Riley, who holds up her phone immediately for a picture.

"Maybe some of your internet fame will rub off on me? Maybe I can hit the hundred-K mark too," she says, laughing, tagging me in the post. I take the hint and immediately pull out my phone, like and comment on the post with a bunch of American flags and red and blue hearts to match our outfits.

"Two hundred and fifty thousand as of this morning."

"Do you know what we're going to have to do at this thing?"

"Literally nothing except go out on the ice and wave to the crowd when we're announced. Last year we did that part and left like right afterward. It's more a show for the fans. It should be pretty full, I think. Last year in China it was sold out and, like, figure skating is an even bigger deal in France than it is there."

"Especially ice dance," Riley says with a smile. "Papadakis and Cizeron are basically royalty here."

Thanks to nearly three Olympic quads where the ice dance competitors (including the French team, like Riley said) stole the show, our little corner of the sport is finally starting to pull in some real attention. Like, sometimes my dad's attitude about ice dance really gets to me, but it's easy enough to explain when you remember that no one paid attention to it when he was competing. Now, though, ice dancers are sometimes even more famous than the skaters in the other disciplines.

Fame isn't something I ever really thought I wanted. Growing up, we were already sort of semi-famous, and it seemed weird to want more than that, but every day my social media following seems to be growing and that's the true measure of fame now, right?

The bus comes to a halt outside the arena a few minutes later and it's starting to feel like the only way I'm going to see Paris is as scenery racing past a bus window. And not even that much of it because the arena isn't far from the hotel and we probably could have walked over.

We're hustled into a back entrance and through a tunnel that leads underneath the arena's seats toward the entrance to the rink. There are athletes in tracksuits from all the countries participating wandering around.

"It is very simple," says a tall woman with a headset, her English accented with the slightest hint of French. "You will skate out onto the ice, wave to the crowd, and when you hear the announcer call the next names, skate off the ice, still waving. Questions?"

We all look back and forth at each other and then at her, nodding.

"Bien. Attends ici," she says, slipping back into French, but we get the gist.

The teams are being announced in alphabetical order by country and then by discipline: girls, then boys, then pairs, then ice dance.

"Guys, we should line up how we're going to go out. Katya and Gillian first. Then Ben and Jimmy . . ." I trail off when Katya wheels around and glares at me with an eyebrow raised.

"We're *U*," Katya says, "it's gonna be forever."

"Actually, we're . . ."

"We're *E*," Freddie fills in. "We're in France, so États-Unis d'Amérique."

"Exactly," I say, and send him a small smile, which he returns. It's sort of soft and feels like the Freddie I knew before everything got so screwed up. A slight flush warms my cheeks and I have to look away.

Katya huffs, but the team gets into some semblance of order, Brayden and I falling to the back with Riley and Freddie.

"Hey, did you bring those pants?" Brayden asks out of nowhere, like the last thing he said to me didn't implode my brain.

"What pants?" I ask, staring at him like, *seriously*?

"The leather ones," he says, clarifying, eyes flicking down to my legs.

"Um, no, why?"

"Damn, those would have been good to wear tonight."

"You want to wear my leather pants?"

Jimmy and Ben lose it at that, laughing so hard they actually have to hold each other up to stay standing.

"Not for me," Brayden says, "though I could rock some leather pants. I mean for you."

I tilt my head. "Why would I wear leather pants to an athletes' reception? That'd be a little much, no?"

"Not for the reception. For after."

"After?"

"We're in Paris. Aren't we going out?"

He says it so casually, so sure that I'm going to agree. Are we just going to ignore what happened on the plane? Is that his plan? Pretend like it never happened. We've gotten pretty good at pretending in the last couple of weeks. What's one more thing?

"We have training tomorrow," I say, squinting at him. "We can't go out tonight."

"Sure, we can. Training's not until late and we're six hours ahead of where our internal clocks need to be."

"That is so not how jet lag works."

"C'mon, Russo, it's the city of lights! We have to see it."

"Well, I'm in," Riley says.

"Riley," Freddie and I say at the same time, to my total mortification.

"I know some people here," Brayden says, and I'm not even surprised. He knows people *everywhere*. "We'll keep it super low-key, no drinking, nothing crazy, just hanging out together. Think of it as team bonding."

"See!" Riley agrees immediately. "We go out, and see something that isn't the hotel for once at one of these? How much trouble could we get in?"

"The sheer possibilities running through my brain right now would be taller than you."

"I'm not that tall, so what are the odds," Riley sings at me, "that you're going out tonight?"

I groan and shoot a desperate look at Freddie, who shrugs. It's his stupid game, after all, but there's no helping it.

"One out of five," I say, and Riley smiles.

"Three, two, one, shoot!" she counts us down and I put down four fingers and, shit, so does she.

"Yes! Victory is mine!" she shouts, raising her arms in celebration. "We're going out."

"If you guys are going out tonight, we're coming too," Maria says from up ahead.

"We're going out?" Charlie asks, but then nudges Ben behind him. "We're going out tonight."

And by the time the news reaches Katya and Gillian at the front of the line, there's no more time to protest. I'm not sure this was the kind of team building the NFSC had in mind, but it's too late now.

"États-Unis d'Amérique!" the announcer calls, and our names begin to echo out immediately afterward.

Freddie and Riley go out before us, and then finally: "Adriana Russo et Brayden Elliot!"

I wasn't prepared for the shrieking.

The last time I heard a noise like that, it was when Elisa convinced Dad to take us to a Jonas Brothers concert. A spotlight follows us out onto the ice and the screams only seem to get louder. Brayden takes my hand and we skate at a measured pace, waving to the crowd as we go.

As we get to the edge of the rink, the cheers start to subside a smidgen. His grip tightens slightly, like it does whenever we're about to bow together at the end of our programs. I let him lead me into a spin underneath his arm, but he doesn't let go entirely and instead pulls me into a low dip, which sets the crowd off again. It feels like magic is swirling around us, sending every nerve ending a jolt of pure joy, flaring out from where his fingertips are pressing into the small of my back, even through my jacket and the shirt underneath. A shiver slides through me and he sends me a wink.

Okay, then, pretending he never said anything on the plane it is.

I can do that.

I can do this.

I throw my head back and laugh, playing it up a little before he spins me back to my feet and we skate off the ice as the next country is announced.

"THE POWER OF social media," Charles says, shaking his head back and forth. "I'm not sure I'll ever fully understand it, but it seems as if it's working."

"I'd say so," Dad responds, before taking a sip from his glass.

The reception is back at the hotel, in one of its massive ballrooms. I've been to parties like this before, usually at Nationals, but those are held at, like, a Hilton or a Marriott. This hotel is wildly different. It looks like something out of my history textbook, all columns and intricately carved sculptures and actual candelabras lining the walls, with a gigantic chandelier at the center of the room. I'm extra glad I packed a decent party dress for this. Walking in here in a Team USA tracksuit was not going to cut it. Instead, I'm in my favorite black dress and the one pair of heels I own, a set of strappy black sandals that I used when Brayden and I took a salsa class about a year ago. I basically tower over everyone in the room, except for a couple of the men, Brayden and Freddie included. Everyone else seems to be appropriately sized for figure skating.

"We should take advantage of this now," Charles says, and I refocus on the conversation as best I can. "I've already had some calls with a few of the companies you've been doing ads for, but I've also decided to set a threshold for the two of you, financially speaking. We don't want too many demands on your time, so we'll make sure anything you do is something that's worth your while."

"Sounds like a plan to me," Brayden says, squeezing my hand.

"And I've had calls from Nike."

I choke on a sip of seltzer. "Nike?" I ask through a cough.

"Nike," Charlies confirms. "It's early days and we have a bit of a negotiation ahead of us, but they see the wisdom in signing you two up this far out from the Games. You give them a bit of a discount for the length of the deal, but we'll have it set to renegotiate in four years, so you can profit on your fame now, but have a chance to really cash in if you do well at the Olympics."

Shaking my head, I take another sip of my drink. Slower this time, in case he has any more surprises to throw at us. "Let's not jinx us, okay?" I manage to say, still in total disbelief.

"And while I have you here," he says, mostly to my dad, though, "the film crew that worked on Kellynch, they're interested in filming again, maybe as these two get prepped for Senior Worlds next month?"

Figure skating isn't a sport that takes a break for an Olympic year. They still hold their Senior World Championships as scheduled, regardless, even though most of the competition is watered down after the Games.

Dad nods. "Of course, it'll be even bigger as we'll have three athletes."

"We don't even know if we'll be sent to Senior Worlds," I say, cutting in quickly, the panic rising at the idea. "We're still only juniors."

"Two weeks from now you won't be," Charles reminds me, "and the senior teams basically fell on their asses in Beijing. The NFSC is going to want you there. Count on it, a month from now you'll be flying out to Senior Worlds."

I shake my head. Senior Worlds had always been a good possibility this year, but it was just supposed to be for the experience, no pressure. "But we're not ready, not to, like, actually compete. We'd need to add an extra . . ."

"Camille's well aware of what you'll need to do to get prepared for a senior competition," Charles insists, and he's not wrong. "I have full confidence that you'll do well. Not win, of course, but a good starting point for next season. It will show Nike you're ready for the big time as we negotiate."

Charles turns back to Dad to say something, but I don't hear it. There's buzzing in my ears until Brayden nudges me a bit with his elbow. "You okay?" he mumbles.

I look up at him and he takes a deep breath and squares his shoulders, like he's about to say something, something important, something like what he said back on the plane, and you know what, I was perfectly happy ignoring it, so I cut in before he can utter another word.

"Do you still want to go out tonight?"

"Yeah," he says, furrowing his brow, studying me carefully, like he's trying to figure out where I'm going with this. Good luck to him, because I'm barely sure where I'm going with this.

"Well, then, let's go out."

"Okay, then," he says, a wide smile playing over his face as we excuse ourselves from the conversation.

"Let me grab the other girls," I say, pulling up our group chat on my phone. "You get the guys. We'll meet in the lobby in fifteen minutes?"

He doesn't respond, a funny look playing across his face.

"Brayden?" I ask, tilting my head.

"Right, yeah, I'll round up the boys and we'll get going."

Fifteen minutes later we're in the lobby and five minutes after that we're in cabs setting out to a place the hotel's concierge recommended.

"Are we famous?" Ben jokes as we make our way into the club, past a line of waiting people, by a bouncer who holds a velvet rope open for us.

It's not completely dark inside, like what I've always pictured a club looks like. It's got a chiller vibe than that. The walls are made of old stone, so it looks like the entire place was built out of an ancient tunnel or something, but there are neon lights lining the ceilings, changing colors and blinking with the pulsing beat of the music being spun by a DJ at the back of the room.

"How did we get in so easy?" I ask Brayden, who's standing beside me.

"I . . ."

"Charles called and mentioned that I might be stopping by with some friends tonight," Elisa says, answering for him and smiling.

"He said we'd *all* be stopping by," Brayden says, quirking a smile at Elisa, who actually flutters her eyelashes at him in response. I don't think I've ever seen anyone in real life do that before and I try to stifle a laugh, but it's tough. Brayden doesn't manage it quite as well as I do, and he tries to mask it in a cough.

"I need a drink," Elisa says, looking around for the bar.

"I think we all do," I mutter, and Brayden laughs again, "but part of the deal was not drinking, right?"

"Right," he says, nodding.

"C'mon, we got a place to sit," Jimmy says, and we follow him to a corner of the club, a little set away from the sea of people out on the dance floor, drinks in hand.

There are large leather couches roped off with a small sign on it that reads RÉSERVÉ.

"Charles got us, like . . . what is this, a VIP section?"

"This is wild," Riley says, her eyes wide as she takes in the rest of the room. "I've never been clubbing before and the first time I go I get to do it in *Paris*! Dance with me!" She grabs my hand, and as she does, I grab Maria, who grabs Elisa, who grabs Katya, who grabs Gillian, and we're able to wind our way through as a group to a relatively open space on the floor.

"We should have brought the guys!" Elisa shouts over the music, but I'm content to ignore her. The bass is pulsing through my chest and this is why I wanted to go out tonight. I wanted to let the music completely surround me, so loud and obnoxious that there's nothing else I can do but dance and ignore every other thought swirling in my head. Thoughts about sponsorships and medals and winning and pressure and nerves.

Because that's the only thing that conversation with Charles and Dad and Brayden did for me earlier. It wasn't exciting or thrilling or a dream come true. It was terrifying. I should have expected this. It's what I set myself up for, isn't it? Attention that leads to sponsorships, which leads to financial security. That was the plan, but now that I'm here and it's possible, I just . . . it's a lot.

Because it was never supposed to be me. I wasn't the Russo people talked about when we were growing up. That was always Elisa. She was Mom brought back to life on ice. She was supposed to be the legacy. And, yeah, maybe I resented that a little bit, but there was also some freedom in that. Freedom to be too tall and to skate for the sheer joy and love of it. The only time I made a decision that was driven by anything other than those things was when I split with Freddie, and I'm still dealing with the fallout from that choice.

Now, though? Now it's different. People *expect* results from us. They expect us to win. They're even betting money on it. A lot of money. Nike doesn't play around. They wouldn't even talk to Charles about Elisa late last year, even when it was clear she was going to make the Olympic team.

It's all way too much.

So instead I dance.

Chapter 15

THE PULSING BEAT of some kind of EDM I don't recognize is pounding in my chest, but it sets the perfect beat for Riley, Gillian, Katya, and I to bounce around, arms in the air, completely unknown in this sea of people. Maria and Elisa drifted away at some point, and the boys are somewhere in the crowd too. Every once in a while, I've spotted them rocking out to the music.

This was such a good idea. We needed this. I needed this.

The song fades for a second and Riley leans in. "I have to pee!" she yells.

"I have to pee too," Gillian says, wheeling around.

"Me too," Katya agrees, and they look at me expectantly.

"I don't. You guys go. Meet me back here."

They give me a funny look, but then they're disappearing into the crowd.

Someone behind me stumbles and I have to spin out of the way to avoid flying into a sea of gyrating bodies. As I catch my balance, I look up and Freddie's right there, blinking at me like maybe he thinks I'm not really there. The crowd surges a little and forces me closer to him. I reach out and brace myself against his chest.

There's no air on the dance floor, but that's okay. He's so close, his hands at my hips, fingertips pressing into the silk of my dress.

I look up into his eyes, the green blown out almost entirely black, meeting my gaze and holding it. One of his hands slides around to the small of my back, drawing me closer, so close he can lean down and press his mouth to my temple. His cheek brushes against the damp strands of my hair pasted against my forehead.

"Is this okay?" he rasps, his voice somehow carrying over the thump of the bass.

"Yeah." I don't know if he can hear me, so I nod.

We shouldn't be doing this. I shouldn't be doing this. Freddie doesn't belong to me and I don't belong to him.

But it's easy to dance with him. We'd skated together since we were little kids and when his body moves, mine follows reflexively, as my arms come up and rest on his shoulders, his hand twitches against my hip and then pulls me in, our bodies totally pressed together. And it's that cinnamon scent and his lips brushing against my temple and his strong arms around me, being totally surrounded by him. It's everything.

We lose ourselves in it and the crowd closes in around us, insulating us, making us just another couple in an anonymous mob, and there's a freedom in that lets us stay like this. All I want to do is stay like this, with him, for as long as I can.

But then he's gone, and my eyes fly open—when had I closed them?—and Riley and Katya are there in front of me. When I look around, the rest of the group has found us, and Freddie's retreated to the edges of the tight circle they've made in the midst of the crowd. Riley shoves a water bottle in my hand, and I take a sip before handing it off to Gillian and it's almost like it never happened, but it did. I know it did because he won't meet my eyes, instead shouting something down at Ben before sliding away from us, and then when Brayden finds me and smiles widely, before pulling out his phone to take a picture of us to post, I lose track of him and don't see him again for the rest of the night.

"UGH, TURN IT off!" Maria demands as the alarm on my phone blares out its usual morning sirens.

I answer with a groan, rolling over and swatting at it on the nightstand that separates our beds.

I slide my feet out from underneath the covers immediately. If I roll over or do anything other than get up right away, I'll fall back to sleep, and it'll be twice as hard to get up. "We should not have stayed out that late."

Standing, I stretch my arms above my head and twist at the waist, trying to get my blood flowing. We have practice and there will be judges milling around. I don't want them to be able to see any weaknesses when Brayden and I take the ice, even in training.

"It wasn't that late," Maria says, before she buries her head under her pillow, but it's too late to block out the sun as I tear the curtains open. It's not even that early. Our training is during the afternoon session.

I'm not really awake either, though, but I have to at least put on a show to get Maria going. "It was late enough. Come on, let's go! I get first shower."

There's a small café attached to the hotel and most of the team is there when we make it down, mostly because I literally had to pull the covers off Maria's bed and threaten to dump a pitcher of water over her head to get her out of bed.

Brayden waves me over to the bench beside him and nudges a bowl of fruit and a croissant in my direction, along with a steaming cup of coffee.

"You're my favorite," I say as I lift the mug to my lips.

"Damn right I am," he agrees, and sits back as Charlie leans over to tell him something.

I don't really hear anything, though. I allow the caffeine to do its thing. I'm sleepy, sure, and like I told Maria, we shouldn't have stayed out as late as we did, but I'm actually feeling okay. I take a bite of some melon and chase it with a flaky piece of the croissant and another sip of coffee.

"Hey, everyone," Freddie says, looking around the table and finding the only open seat next to me.

I shift over as much as possible on the bench and he slides in beside me, and I try not to think about the last time he was this close to me, just last night, bodies moving together in the dark . . . and yeah, I'm definitely thinking about it.

"Adriana, what do you think?" Riley asks from across the table.

"Sorry, what?" I blink at her and she laughs at me.

"Did the caffeine kick in yet?"

"Almost, what am I supposed to be thinking about?" I assume it's not how Freddie felt pressed up against me at the club last night.

"Is winning the most important part of the sport?"

I furrow my brow and take another sip before answering. "I mean, that's sort of the point of sports, isn't it?"

"See, I don't agree. Most people showing up at this competition are pros or want to be pros soon and they know they don't have any chance to win and they're still here. Are they all just delusional?"

"Ooh, philosophy in the morning after a late night, sign me up," Jimmy jokes, and my partner laughs and leans back, putting his arm over the back of the bench, which basically puts his arm around me while the boy on my other side stiffens and I can't help but let my eyes drift to him. He's looking back at me for once and I shift forward on the bench away from Brayden's arm.

"What do you think?" I ask, turning toward Freddie.

Freddie's eyebrows lift in surprise at the question, but he considers it. "I . . . I think that the love of something is the most important part. Does winning even matter if you don't love it?"

And that makes me think, really think. It's never occured to me before, that some people skate without loving it. "I don't know. I don't know if I'd want to win without loving it. But I also really want to win."

"Yeah, I know."

And suddenly we're not talking about ice dance or hockey or anything other than each other.

Then Freddie tilts his head, thoughtfully. "But don't you think that there's something admirable about people who do this just because they love it, knowing they won't win?"

"That makes sense. For some people, skating is necessary, like breathing."

"And we're back to it depends on the person because what's necessary to me might not be necessary to you. You need, what, three cups of coffee to function in the morning? I don't need any. It's not *necessary* for me, but it is for you."

"Right," I say, "but as long as we're up and doing what we need to in the morning, does it matter?"

"Depends on what you mean by 'need.' Do I need to get up and train every morning? No, but I do it because I love skating. So maybe I'm more like that than I thought."

"And because by training every morning, it gives you a chance to win." I smirk, thinking I've won.

"If winning was the only reason I got up to train every morning then I'd have a hard time getting up. Haven't won anything outright in a while."

My smirk disappears.

The last time he won anything outright was with me. The Intermediate National Championships. We were so good that night, skating to "(I've Had) The Time of My Life" from *Dirty Dancing* because I was obsessed with it. It was our first and last gold medal together. One year later, Brayden and I won Junior Nationals, proof positive that I'd made the "right" decision. Had I, though?

"I said a chance to win, not actually winning, which you agreed with a couple of seconds ago," I say, managing to correct him slightly, but it doesn't matter. "If everyone who didn't win quit, the sport wouldn't exist."

"There *are* more important things than winning."

"I'm not disagreeing with you."

"It sounds like you are."

"No, it sounds like *you* are."

"Okay, you two," Brayden says, interrupting us with what sounds like forced laughter. "Save it for the ice."

The rest of the table seems to agree, and more than one of our teammates are shooting us a confused look. I sit back against the bench, not realizing how much I'd shifted forward in my seat.

"Sorry," I mutter, mostly to myself, but Freddie clearly hears me. "Me too."

He has nothing to be sorry for, I want to say, but somehow it feels like he's not apologizing for whatever that stupid argument we were having was, but something else. Was he saying sorry for last night? It feels like it didn't even happen, like maybe I dreamed it, but he must be. My eyes fly open wide at the thought, but then he's gone, just like last night, pushing off the bench and heading toward the café's counter, probably to order something. For a half a second, I think I'm going to follow him, though what the hell I'm going to say, I have no idea.

"Ah, good, you're all here," Camille says, wandering into the café. "Bus is pulling up. Finish up and be outside in five."

It takes more like ten minutes, actually, but eventually we get our bill paid and venture outside to board the bus for our first training session. The sun is barely peeking out between low cloud cover and the morning air is crisp but comfortable. It's warmer in Paris than it was in Boston, no biting cold that makes your nose go numb and your eyes water. But I still rub my hands together against it as I wait for the rest of the team to get onto the bus.

"Here," a voice says from behind me, and I turn. Freddie has a small cup of coffee with a lid firmly in place and he's holding it out to me. "You only got through one at the table."

"Thanks," I say, taking it and grinning. "That was sweet."

"Nothing sweet about that. It's black, like you like it."

"Yeah, bitter," I say, trying to make it sound like I'm talking about the coffee.

"Adriana, I . . ." he says, and stops, like he doesn't quite know how to put it into words, but I bail him out.

"I know," I say, before looking up into his eyes. *"I know."*

Do I, though? No, I don't. I'm completely full of shit. Everything feels like a riddle between us right now, one that I'm not even close to figuring out. Has he forgiven me? Like, really forgiven me? Does he . . . does he want to be friends? My mind flickers back to the night before at the club and the way dancing with him felt, like I was finally back where I belonged. Is that what he wants? Is it even what I want? And even if it is, is it possible?

No. No, it's not. Not if I'm "with" Brayden. Not as long as Riley likes Freddie.

I just have to put it out of my mind. It's not going to happen. Too much has happened.

He nods and takes a deep breath before letting it out in a heavy sigh. "Okay, then," he says, gesturing ahead of me. "Let's go."

We're a well-oiled machine at training. We've gotten so used to sharing the ice over the last few weeks that it's easy to let those routines take over. We're spaced out on the ice, working with our coaches to break down different skills, and then we rotate easily to run through our short programs. When our time is almost up, it feels like we should all be able to leave together and walk back to the Kellynch House and maybe have lunch, watch some TV, or even sit together in the living room and scroll through our phones in a comfortable silence, interrupted only when someone has something hilarious to show us.

The team is so efficient that we have a few minutes left after Brayden and I finish up "Vienna" and everyone glides back out onto the ice to work on whatever little problem spots they encountered during the session.

Brayden swings me up into our lift easily and holds me steady as we finish up.

There, it's perfect. We're ready to go out there and kick ass tomorrow.

"One more time," Riley calls out from the corner of the ice she and Freddie are using to work on their lift too. We skate past them and for a split second my eyes meet Freddie's. I send him a tight smile, one he returns.

"Fine, one more time," Freddie agrees, and grabs her hand. "Gotta show these two they've got some competition."

They take off down the ice, building some momentum before Riley slides into his arms and Freddie lifts her up against his chest, her legs flying out and holding as he takes her weight against him, and when they go to change positions, something goes wrong. I think her hand slips and it throws off his momentum.

"Shit!" Freddie yells, when his skate goes out from under him and sends him sliding in the other direction. Riley's not so lucky, trying to turn herself in the split second she has in the air, but it's clear she's not going to make it. There's not enough room. Before she lands, Brayden and I are already sprinting across the ice in that direction.

Then she goes down, her knee cracking against the ice before her head whips back and does the same.

"Riley!" Charlie shrieks, leaping over the boards and skating out to his sister.

A small ice shower coats Freddie's pants when Brayden and I stop in front of them. He's still standing there, staring down at Riley's horrifically still form, one leg twisted at an odd angle, her eyes shut. No movement.

"We need the trainer," I say, snapping out of my horrified fascination and dropping to my knees beside her. "Don't move her."

Brayden skates away at top speed and I can hear people skating to us. Somewhere behind me, Maria is screaming bloody murder.

I check the ice around Riley. There's no blood. I don't know if that's good or bad. I grab her hand and squeeze it. "Riley, can you hear me?" I say, leaning in close, hoping that she can, even if she can't respond. "Riley?"

For the briefest moment, she opens her eyes, but there's no comprehension there. She doesn't see me, just stares at me, and for a panicked second, I think she's about to have a seizure. I know that can happen when people hit their heads hard. Her eyes close again, though, and at least that's something.

A strangled sound escapes from Freddie, who still hasn't moved away. The trainers arrive on the ice and I pull back to give them room to work. In a blink, they're examining her, shifting her carefully onto a stretcher, and getting her up and off the ice. Sirens are wailing in the distance and I jerk at the sound. It sounds so much like my alarm on my phone that for a second I instinctively want to check it, but it's not my phone. An ambulance is on its way here.

That was fast, unless it was already close by. Sometimes it's even in the arena in case someone gets hurt, like the event organizers don't want to tempt fate by not having one here.

So much for that.

As a group, the trainers move an unresponsive Riley off the ice toward the sounds growing louder by the moment. Freddie whispers, "My fault."

"No," I whisper back, but he shakes his head and follows them.

Then Brayden's there, beside me. "Come on, we can go with them to the hospital."

I let him lead me off the ice.

There are dozens of people in the rink and everyone has their phones out, videoing the stretcher being wheeled away from the ice and out toward the ambulance.

"Fucking vultures," Brayden says, nodding at them. That's what finally snaps Freddie out of his daze. For a moment, I think he's about to dive into that crowd and smash every single phone on the concrete floor, but Ben and Jimmy fall into step with him and practically perp walk him out of the arena with the rest of us.

Vaguely, my brain registers that we're in a car following the ambulance as it winds through Parisian traffic. The city I wanted to see so badly a few hours ago is a five-minute blur, then we're in an emergency room, where everyone speaks French, so there's a lot of confusion at first until Mr. Monroe arrives, his phone pressed to his ear, and he's able to shout loud enough to find someone who can speak English and then take him and Charlie to where they brought Riley.

The waiting room is small and cramped and there are barely enough chairs for us to sit down.

Who knows how long we've been sitting here? I check the clock on the wall. It's the early evening now. It was barely three in the afternoon when we were finishing up our practice session.

Two hours and no word.

That can't be good.

"Maybe we should go back to the hotel and wait for news there," Camille says.

"I'm not leaving," Freddie says, his eyes never leaving the doors they took Riley through.

"I'll stay with you," Georgia answers, putting an arm around her little brother's shoulders even though he's a good foot taller than her.

Camille nods. "We should go then."

"Can we wait for—" I start, and stop.

I can't quite get the words out, but Camille nods. "We'll stay until we get some news."

"We'll go get everyone coffee," Jimmy says, and he enlists Ben to go with him.

Brayden stands up. "I need to stretch my legs anyway. I'll come too."

They disappear in the general direction of where a sign with a coffee cup illustration is pointing.

"I'm going to hit the ladies' room. Do you want to come?" Camille asks after a few silent minutes, but I shake my head. Georgia stands to join her.

Sighing after they leave, I sit back in the hard plastic chair and run my fingers over my hair. The bun I put it in this morning is falling down, but I can't be bothered to redo it. I lean forward and put my head in my hands, pressing the heels of my palms into my eyes.

Maybe this is a terrible dream. Maybe the sound of ambulances around me is my alarm trying to wake me up. Maybe none of this actually happened.

"It's my fault," Freddie says, and I turn my head enough to see him. He's a full seat away from me, staring out ahead into the middle distance now. "If only I'd—"

"It's not your fault."

"I wasn't thinking about anything except winning and beating—" His eyes fly to me as he cuts off his thought. "Training was over. I should have called it."

"It's not your fault," I repeat firmly. "Falls happen."

He shakes his head. "*This* fall didn't have to and now she's—"

"Hey," I say, shifting over a seat and grabbing his hand. He's got it clenched so tightly that once I pry it open, I can see little half-moons in his palms from his blunt fingernails. I hold one hand in both of mine and squeeze. "She's going to be okay. She has to be."

"You can't know that," he protests, but his hand flexes and then relaxes in mine.

"No," I say softly. "You're right. I don't know, but I have to believe it. I can't do anything else. I'll believe it for you, if you need me to."

He nods and he squeezes my hand again. "Adriana," he rasps, and I look up at him. He doesn't say anything else, just looks at me and something thunks in my chest, hard and fast, and then it blossoms into a soft hum through my blood.

Bam!

The door that leads from the waiting area to the emergency room swings open and slams against the wall. Charlie's rushing through it at full speed. Together, Freddie and I fly to our feet and meet him halfway, as he skids to a halt in front of us. His eyes are red and puffy. Oh God, he's been crying. What happened back there?

I try to speak, but the words get caught in my throat, then Freddie squeezes my hand and I'm able to force them out.

"Is Riley okay?"

"She's awake and she's going to be okay."

A Mack truck of relief plows through me, but no, that's Freddie pulling me into a crushing embrace, his arms wrapped around my body. For half a second, I stiffen against it. We were this close last night, but this is different. There's no doubt that this means something because he's not pulling away and neither am I. And when he turns his face into my neck, his lips brushing my pulse point, I sink into him, my forehead tucking into his shoulder. I tighten my arms around him, my hand burying itself at the back of his head, sifting through the soft hair that's grown a little too long at the nape of his neck.

Then a throat is clearing behind us. Shit. Charlie's still standing there, probably with more news about Riley. Freddie pulls away like he touched a live wire and I fall back on my heels as we blink at each other in utter shock.

With a shake of his head, Freddie turns to Charlie. "Can I see her?"

"Uh." Charlie hesitates, looking back and forth between us before he says, "Yeah, sure, c'mon."

Then without a backward glance, Freddie follows him through

the doors that lead into the emergency room. I want to follow, but I don't; it's not my place, and when I turn back to my seat, there's Brayden with a steaming cup of coffee and a tight grin.

"Thanks," I say, reaching out for the cup and letting out a heavy sigh as I sit back in my chair.

"She's going to be okay?" he asks, still staring at the door Freddie and Charlie disappeared through.

"Yeah, she's going to be okay."

Chapter 16

"THE HOSPITAL KEPT her overnight. It's a concussion and a partially torn ACL," I say, and Dad frowns beside me from our seats at the arena as the pairs program gets underway.

"That's a year, maybe more," Elisa chimes in from his other side.

"But it could have been so much worse. She's lucky," Brayden says. He's all the way over on the end of the row, as far away from me as he can get. I don't think he did it on purpose. Elisa sort of maneuvered her way beside him as we were sitting down.

"When are they going to release her from the hospital?" Camille asks from my other side.

"Not for a couple of days, and she can't fly right away, so she'll be sticking around Paris with us."

"Well, why wouldn't she want to stay in Paris, regardless? It's Paris," Elisa cuts in.

I stifle a retort about how that's exactly what she did after she lost in Beijing, not staying and waiting through the closing ceremony, but returning home and hiding from the spotlight. She doesn't wait for me to answer, though, just turns to Brayden. "Did you see the boots I snagged yesterday at Dior?"

She extends her leg as far as she can without kicking the man sitting in front of her in the head.

He takes his time perusing the length of her leg before he says, "They look good, Lis, like always."

She lets out a soft giggle and he grins at her, but then her eyes flick to me. She's trying to make me jealous, and if any of this were real, maybe I would be.

"Représentant les États-Unis d'Amérique, Maria Russo et Charlie Monroe!" the arena announcer calls out, cutting into my thoughts. The crowd applauds. It's as full as the Opening Ceremony, easily one of the biggest audiences I've ever seen for a junior figure skating competition. It was the same for the singles' short programs yesterday, and this morning it's pairs and then ice dance tonight. I hope the International Skating Coalition takes notice and has competitions in bigger cities from now on. There's nothing better than a packed arena to skate to.

Charlie and Maria skate onto the ice and get set in their starting positions, but Elisa is still giggling at Brayden. She swats at his chest and he lets her, but when he looks up and meets my eyes over her head, I look away.

It's annoying how she flirts with him like this and even more annoying that he's letting her. Like there's anything between them beyond a one-sided crush and maybe a physical attraction.

I could probably put a stop to it, if I wanted. I could go all in, move to the empty seat on his other side, grab his hand, interlock our fingers, and rest my head on his shoulder. I could pull him away from the group and give him a long, lingering hug in full view of everyone and their phones, setting off another social media deluge. It would be so easy. Everyone in this arena knows who we are and fans in Europe have zero chill.

Charlie and Maria's music filters through the speakers, a remix of songs from *Aladdin*, Maria's favorite Disney movie. I hold my breath as Maria and Charlie perform side-by-side double axels and land them with no problem.

So what's stopping me from doing that, from marking my territory?

Elisa wouldn't hesitate.

I sigh and then answer my own question. We're not exactly close and if we weren't sisters, I'm pretty sure we wouldn't even be friends, but . . . that doesn't negate the fact that she *is* my sister and that it probably hurts her to see me with Brayden. It might be a fake relationship, but she doesn't know that. Her feelings for him are genuine. I can tell the difference easily enough. She's unsure around him; the confidence she normally carries herself with is a shadow of itself when he's around. Her laughs are a little too loud. Her tone is a little too insistent when he doesn't respond as enthusiastically as she'd like. So much physical contact is initiated by her and never by him.

And I'm the one standing in her way. At least, that's what she thinks.

Charlie lifts Maria up into the air and spins beneath her as he holds her over his head, her legs extended out and an arm up to show how much control they have over the skill. Not one wobble. They're strong out there, a solid partnership, like me and Brayden.

The audience applauds and I do too as realization washes over me.

That's what I want. That's what matters.

Riley went down on the ice yesterday and her dreams are put on hold, at least for a year, maybe more.

Life is too short and figure skating careers are even shorter.

Maria and Charlie pick up momentum on the ice as they move into the throw jump, the same thing that Riley fell on, though they handle it with no problem and the fans cheer.

This is what I want. A crowd cheering as I skate and afterward, a gold medal.

I want to win Junior Worlds, and now that I've had time to let the idea settle for more than a split second, I want to go to Senior World Championships. I want to see where we rank among the best of the best, regardless of age. I want to know how far we need to climb from now through four years from now when we'll be in Milan for the Olympic Games.

For now, I'm going to try to focus on that.

And because I've decided to do that, green eyes and chestnut hair and strong arms and a warm embrace slide through my memory.

Freddie.

The program is almost over, my little sister and her partner spinning side by side, and then they grab hold of each other, twirling at the center of the ice as the song finally crashes to an end, and finish with their arms raised over their heads, breathing hard, but sheer joy plastered on their faces.

That's it. That's the ending I want for Brayden and me tonight. That feeling, knowing you went out and hit the way you've been training, doing your best at the exact right moment. That's everything.

"C'mon," Brayden says, past Elisa and Dad, looking directly at me and standing up as Charlie and Maria skate off the ice. "We should get going."

He's right. We should. We have to warm up. I have to get my hair and makeup right and then get into costume. They'll clean the ice after pairs and open up the ice dance competition.

We warm up in silence, both of us with earbuds firmly in place as we pace around the dressing room we've been assigned to prep before the competition begins. I try to clear my head and replace everything swirling there with nothing beyond each and every moment of our rhythm dance. "Vienna" is on repeat and every stroke of the piano keys pulls me further and further into the character I'll be playing out on the ice. Brayden is doing the same, I think.

Camille comes in the room and nods. That means we should get our costumes on.

I unzip my garment bag and stare at my dress. It's as gorgeous as I remember. The cream color will set off my hair and eyes, especially since I really nailed the smoky eye I've been trying to perfect for a long time for this routine. I take out my earbuds and change quickly, not even concerning myself with Brayden in the far corner of the room. Checking myself in the mirror hung on the wall, I make sure the dress is sitting correctly, no tears, no undone buttons, and then nod before moving to get my skates on.

Stretching my feet and ankles as I do it, I wrap the back of my heels for support and then lace up my skates tight, like I do every day, before standing and testing how they feel.

Perfect.

"You good?" Brayden asks.

"I'm good," I say with a nod.

"Good," he replies, and then steps forward.

He's handsome in his gray trousers that look almost like casual dress pants and a burgundy shirt that's a little more open at the neck than most people would wear normally but looks a bit disheveled and flat-out hot on him.

I turn and see us in the mirror, our eyes making contact and holding. We look older somehow, too old to be juniors. It really is time to move on, like we planned. His arms skirt around my waist and he tugs me back toward him and slowly we breathe together. Then he leans down and whispers, "We've got this."

Nodding, I bring my hands up to rest on his and we stand there for another moment before Camille comes in.

"Five-minute warning," she says, eyeing us carefully, and then nods at whatever it is she sees, like she approves.

Walking toward the mouth of the tunnel underneath the area that leads to the rink, Brayden grabs my hand and squeezes. Whatever happens, we're in this together.

The area announcer is introducing the ice dance competition and the rest of the athletes in this subgroup are milling around, waiting for the signal that we're allowed on the ice to warm up.

Camille holds out her hands and we give her our skate guards.

Warm-ups are a blur except for the shrieking that echoes the reaction we got the other night when our names are introduced as part of the group and our images are splashed on the huge screen hanging from the arena's ceiling. It's something we'll have to get used to. I've never been a fan favorite before. Hell, I've never had *fans* before.

It's so surreal.

A chime rings out and the rest of the skaters finish up their last bit of practice and then retreat off the ice, but we simply skate to the gate to where Camille is waiting.

"Go out there and do what you do in training and you'll walk away today in the lead." She holds out two fists and I bump them. Then Brayden follows before holding his fists to me too. I knock mine against his and then grab his hand.

"Représentant les États-Unis d'Amérique, Adriana Russo et Brayden Elliot."

The shrieking is back, somehow even louder now than before.

This is it. Everything we've been working for and now we finally get to take the first steps. My body knows what it has to do. Hours upon hours of training have ensured that. Now I just need my expression to match that, like Camille has been begging me for years to do. I'm going to do my best.

At the center of ice, we start a few feet away from each other and when "Vienna" begins to play through the speakers, I push off down the ice slowly, knowing he'll be following close behind. He catches up and takes my hand to spin me around into his arms and ready to dance across the ice for the next two minutes and thirty seconds.

His free hand finds my waist and mine, his shoulder, and for a split second, barely half a note of the music, we stop and stare. His eyes twinkle at me and the choreographed smile I'm supposed to be wearing is very real and then we're off.

The program flies and it is showstopping. We're perfection the whole way through, not a hand slip, not a misstep. Even our twizzles are flawless. It feels unconscious, no thought, nothing to stop us, the music in time with every scrape of our skates, and when Brayden lifts me against him and we spin out across the ice, the screams from the crowd overpower everything and we have to rely on our instincts to pull us through the last few seconds of the dance, and then the music fades and it's over and we find each other again at the center of the ice, me bent back over his arm, his forehead pressed to my shoulder. His lips graze against the pulse at my throat and it sends my heart rate soaring beyond what I've ever felt before on the ice, and the fans' reaction echoes it, somehow growing even louder.

"Adriana Russo et Brayden Elliot!" the announcer calls as we stand together and bow to each part of the crowd, our hands still held firmly together.

There are stuffed animals being chucked onto the ice and little girls in sparkling skating costumes are rushing around to gather them for us as we retreat to the gate where Camille is waiting for us, the biggest smile I've ever seen her wear plastered across her face.

"Brilliant!" she shouts, as Brayden lets me leave the ice first and then follows behind me. Camille pulls me into a hug and then grabs Brayden too. For a second, I'm crushed between them as we all laugh together. We grab our skate guards and click them in place before we move to the Kiss and Cry, the booth where we'll wait for our scores. We're the first competitors on the ice, so no matter what we'll be in first place, but we're setting the standard for everyone else, I'm sure of it.

A man slides onto the bench, holding a camera at his side to get our reactions. I hold up my hands in a heart to everyone watching and Brayden's arm slides around me. His eyes are trained up at the scoreboard flashing on the arena's screen.

"That was beautiful, Adriana," Camille says, leaning over to whisper it in my ear. "I felt every moment of it."

I squeeze her hand tightly.

My breath is finally starting to even out as the scores come up.

"Les scores, s'il vous plaît," the arena announcer calls, and then there's a pause. I take a deep breath. "Le score d'Adriana Russo et Brayden Elliot dans la danse rythmique est de 75.49!"

I don't hear it at first, but then my eyes catch our names on the scoreboard and the numbers beside it.

> 1. RUSSO, A./ELLIOT, B. (USA)
>
> TECHNICAL ELEMENTS: 40.02   PRESENTATION: 35.74
>
> TOTAL SCORE: 75.49

I've never seen scores that high. Not for us. Not for juniors.

And then the announcer confirms it.

"Il s'agit d'un nouveau record du monde junior pour la danse rythmique!"

Record du monde. That I understand. A world record. The crowd loses its mind and so do I, nearly launching myself across the few inches that separate me from Brayden, pulling him into the tightest hug I can manage with my hands nearly full of stuffed toys.

For the first time in my life, Camille is speechless when I turn to hug her and then Brayden comes in from behind me and I laugh wildly.

One down. One to go.

A few minutes later we're back in our changing room and it's the way we left it despite the world being totally different after that skate.

"Ah! I can't believe how awesome that was!" I say, collapsing into the same chair I sat in less than a half hour ago to lace my skates.

"It was great," Brayden says, but his tone is flat, so far from the joy that spilled over in the Kiss and Cry that I feel like I have to be misinterpreting it.

"You were amazing. We've never skated like that."

"No one has," he says, shrugging lightly. "New world record."

The tone is familiar, that half-joking, half-serious voice he uses to tease about important things, but his eyes won't meet mine.

"Are you okay?" I ask, tilting my head at him. "Did you hurt yourself or something?"

He barks out a laugh, harsh and quick. "No, I didn't hurt myself."

"Then what?"

"Don't worry about it, Adriana," he snaps.

Is he . . . is he mad at me?

"I don't understand, we skated the greatest rhythm dance in the history of Junior Worlds and you're mad at me?"

"Yes! No! I'm not . . . just go, okay? I'm sure you want to celebrate with O'Connell."

"What does Freddie have to do with anything?"

"You tell me."

I still don't really understand. And I'm starting to feel stupid. He's looking at me like I should know the answer to this ridiculous whiplash he's given me while my head is still spinning with the high of competition. And then a thought flies to the front of my mind and stays there, like a big red siren flashing, and I remember that moment on the plane and . . . had he seen us in the hospital? Now that I'm thinking about it, he must have. Shit.

"Are you jealous?"

"Jealous? What are you talking about? I'm not jealous, Adriana. We had an agreement. We made rules."

"I definitely haven't broken any of the rules."

He raises an eyebrow. "No cheating. I saw you two yesterday and it looked . . . it looked like something."

"That wasn't . . . Brayden, you're being ridiculous."

"So you're saying you don't have feelings for him?"

"I'm saying even if I did, it wouldn't matter. It was just a hug." The protest sounds weak, even to my own ears. "I don't know if you've noticed, but we didn't exactly stay besties after we stopped training together. It's nice that we can be friends again, sort of. Okay?"

Brayden stares at me for a long moment, so long and so intently I start to fidget under his gaze. "Maybe this was a bad idea," he says finally.

A sharp spike of panic flies through me. "What?"

"This, us, the fake dating thing. Maybe we should just call it."

"But . . ." my mind spirals, images of money flying up into the air out of my grasp, a For Sale sign going up outside of Kellynch, my dad's eyes flashing in disappointment. "Is that what you want?"

He's quiet for a second, a hand coming up to sift through his blond hair, tugging on the ends in frustration. "No, but, if it's what *you* want . . ."

"It's not."

"You're sure?"

And the For Sale sign is gone and the money is back in our accounts and my dad's disappointment shifts to pride and relief.

"I'm sure."

Chapter 17

$\mathcal{T}$HE LIGHTS IN the arena are down low and music plays softly in the background as we wait for the presentation of medals. There's a red carpet laid out over the ice and a podium at the end of it. A few officials from the ISF are standing beside event volunteers holding trays with the gold, silver, and bronze medals and the bouquet of flowers that will accompany the prizes. Dad is down on the ice with them too. When the event organizers realized he'd be here for the duration of the competition, they asked him to be the one to give out the medals to the winners. Dad, never one to refuse a spotlight, obviously agreed.

We spent the last two hours watching the best junior men's skaters in the world battle it out.

"Médaillé de bronze, de la Fédération de Russie, Vladimir Fedorov!"

The Russian skater sprints out onto the ice and presents himself to the crowd with a flourish before skating to the podium and carefully stepping up onto the lowest platform.

"Médaillé d'argent, du Canada, Bastien Roy!"

The crowd goes wild for the French-Canadian skater and he shows appreciation for their support when he moves out onto the ice, turning to each section of the arena and placing a hand over his heart with every bow.

"Le médaillé d'or et le champion du monde junior, des États-Unis d'Amérique, Ben Woo!"

"WOOOOOOOOO!" Brayden and I stand up and scream as Ben appears on the ice, waving up at the fans with both hands and a huge smile on his face. He skated brilliantly in the last couple of days, something I would have noticed if I hadn't been caught up in my own drama. I'm so proud of him, though, from not being able to skate less than a year ago to the Junior World Champion is obviously impressive.

Maybe he'll be coming with us to Senior Worlds in a month too. The medal ceremony doesn't take long and then we're all standing while "The Star-Spangled Banner" plays through the stadium speakers. In the far corner of the arena, the Russian, Canadian, and American flags rise, and Ben's face is up on the screen as he sings along with the song.

Our free dance is in three days.

Will we be up there at the top of the podium?

Or will we be like Jimmy, standing on the sidelines after finishing a disappointing fourth?

Yesterday after our rhythm dance, when that score came in, I thought nothing could touch us. I thought there was zero chance that we don't win this whole damn thing and skate off to the senior career we've been working toward for four years. Training today was okay. Not bad, but not great, at least I thought so. Camille didn't say anything about it, so maybe it was better than I thought. I still feel kind of off-balance though, after what Brayden said about Freddie. I think I was able to reassure him, but . . . now it feels like maybe I wasn't being entirely honest, not with him and not with myself.

"I've gotta go," I say, once the anthem is over and the lights come up.

"Where are you going?" Elisa asks. "Dad made reservations for us tonight for dinner after this. Apparently, it's the hottest restaurant in Paris."

"I promised Riley I'd visit her in the hospital," I say, shouldering my bag and shrugging.

"Isn't she getting out tomorrow?"

"Yeah, but I told her I'm coming. I'm not going to blow her off."

Elisa shrugs. "Brayden, are you coming?"

He looks to me and raises an eyebrow.

"You should go. We'll hang out later, okay?"

For a second he looks back and forth between us and then nods, leaning down to brush a kiss on my cheek. Gotta keep up appearances, after all.

"Have fun," I say, turning away, and scroll through my phone, pretending I'm way more confident about ordering an Uber in Paris than I am.

Instead of exiting the arena with everyone else, I use my athlete's credential to get down into the locker room area underneath the stands and by the time I make it down there, Ben is finishing up his last interview.

"You won!" I yell, and reach out to pull him into a hug.

"I did! You should try it. It's amazing."

Giggling, I reach out and hold the gold medal that's still around his neck. It's *awesome*.

"Where are you headed?"

"I was going to visit Riley in the hospital. You know, try to cheer her up a bit."

"Give me a few minutes to say hi to my family and I'll go with you."

"Don't you want to go out and celebrate?"

Ben shrugs. "We're going to do dinner later tonight, but I've been where she is. Some things are more important."

True to his word, ten minutes later, Ben is showered, dressed, and meeting me outside the changing room, skating bag over one shoulder where I assume his gold medal is safely tucked away.

"You must be freaking out," I say when the car pulls away from the arena.

"I am. I didn't think this was possible."

"You worked hard."

"Sometimes hard work isn't enough," he says with a shrug. "I'm really proud of myself for not giving up."

"That's what matters, in the end."

His phone buzzes, so I focus on the view out the window. It's raining today. It's been raining since before we woke up this morning. I don't read a lot of poetry or anything, but it feels poetic, like Paris can't be sunny and happy when Riley is stuck in a hospital bed.

I glance over to Ben. He swipes out of whatever conversation he was having and turns to me. "It's not only figure skating where that matters, you know."

"What?"

"Not giving up. It's a universal thing."

"Yeah, I know."

"Do you?"

"Ben, what are you—"

"Just," he says, cutting me off, "sometimes you think something is over or that it can't be fixed, no matter what you do, but I'm living proof that's not true."

I blink at him. Is he talking about his injury? It sounds like he could be, but it doesn't feel like he is.

There's no time to ask him, though—not that I'd even know what to ask exactly—because the car pulls up to the hospital. He gets out on one side, I on the other, and by the time we're walking inside, it feels like it would be too awkward.

We sign in and get visitor badges from the nurse at the front desk using a translating app and pulling out Ben's gold medal as proof that we are who we say we are. I'm pretty sure she's violating their policy by letting us through, but whatever works.

"Hey, guys," Riley says quietly when we knock on the open door. There's an empty bed next to her and she's hooked up to a bunch of machines, which is super scary, like the beeps and toots are proof that she's really not okay. She looks so small in that bed wearing a hospital gown that's definitely at least three sizes too big. "You just missed Freddie. He's been here for hours and won't stop hovering, so I made him leave and go get snacks. I'm so glad you're here."

"Of course we came," I say, trying to ignore that any minute now Freddie is going to be back here. I perch on the end of the bed since

Riley's feet don't come anywhere near the footboard while Ben sits in the chair beside it. "How are you feeling?"

She shrugs. "Still kind of woozy, but the doctor says that's probably more the meds for my knee than the concussion. They scheduled the surgery for when we go back at the end of the week."

"You're staying till the end of the competition?"

Smiling, she nods. "Yeah, I want to cheer you guys on and see you kick everyone else's asses instead of mine, but right now talk to me about literally anything other than skating. What's up with you and Brayden?"

"Why would anything be up?" I ask quickly. Too quickly.

"Do you guys need, like, girl talk time?" Ben asks. "I can go."

I roll my eyes. "It's fine. We're fine. I think—"

"What?" Riley asks, leaning forward, clear interest in her face. This is what she needs right now, a distraction.

"I think he got jealous over something really dumb and now things feel weird."

Riley laughs. "Brayden Elliot gets jealous?"

"I thought that dude had two modes: confident and more confident," Ben says.

"Yeah," I say, kind of wishing I could just tell them. Or, well, at least Riley. It would be so nice to be able to talk about this weird tangle I've gotten myself into, but I can't. I promised Brayden. "We figured it out, though, and we're good to go for tomorrow. Hazard of mixing skating with other stuff. Things get weird off the ice and it's a domino effect."

"Yeah," Riley says softly. "That's what you were worried about before, right? You never really said anything, but I feel like that's what it was."

"I mean . . . it's fine, though, as long as you talk, which, you know, Brayden and I did so it's fine now. Everything's fine."

She doesn't look convinced.

"I don't think it's the worst thing in the world," Ben says carefully, "but then again, I don't skate with a partner."

"The frustrating thing is that he got so worked up over something so small," I say. "I really need him to, you know . . . not."

"That's so immature," Riley says. "Aren't you worried that if he can't handle this now, what would it be like if you broke up?" Some kind of panic must show on my face, though, because she grimaces. "Sorry, the meds have, like, removed any filters I had."

She's right, though. *Really* right. It's not about whether or not Brayden and I could handle dating and being skating partners, because we're not actually dating. It's about what it would be like if it all blows up in our faces somehow. What if he meets someone or what if . . . what if I do? Then what? From what I can tell, it would be like the last couple of days, but you know, way bigger. It would totally destroy us and our dreams along with it.

"I don't know," Ben says. "There are no guarantees in figure skating. Sometimes you gotta take a risk and hope it works out."

I tilt my head at him. "Says the boy who already has a gold medal."

"Touché."

"Anyway," Riley says. "Look at it this way, you've already made one huge, life-altering decision to try to go to the Olympics, and you still have a really good shot to do it."

It's super clear she's not talking about me with that last part.

"Hey, so do you! It's four years until the Games. You're going to come back stronger than ever."

"Maybe," she says, picking at the worn cotton of the hospital blanket. "But I can't ask Freddie to sit out a year and wait for me. It's not fair."

"Did you talk to him about it?" I ask softly.

"No," she says, and there are tears welling in her eyes.

Reaching out, I grab her hand and squeeze it as the first tears start to fall. "Talk to him about it. Trust me. He might surprise you. In fact, I'm pretty sure he will." I know he will, he did for me. He'll do it for her too.

"But it's not fair to him." One tear falls and then another.

"Let him be the judge of that," I say, and she nods, squeezing back and then letting go to wipe at her face.

"Here," Ben says, reaching over and handing her a box of tissues.

"I'm such a mess," she says, laughing through the tears.

"You have a pretty decent excuse," I joke.

"I guess so," she agrees, laughing harder, but then the tears win out. "I don't know how I'm going to do this." She tries to muffle the sobs with the edge of her blanket, but it doesn't do much good.

I move toward the head of the bed to hug her, but Ben's ahead of me, an arm around her shoulder, pulling her into him and making soft hushing noises. He gets it. Just over a year ago he was in a hospital bed like this one. He'll know what to say to Riley when she's all cried out.

A throat clears from the doorway. "Uh, everything okay?" Freddie asks, walking into the room with a cardboard tray of fruit and a couple bottles of water. Smoothly, he drops it all on the table at the center of the room before stepping gingerly toward the bed.

Riley makes some kind of noise in the back of her throat, but Ben shakes his head and eyes Freddie with clear meaning, a silent conversation between bros. And its meaning becomes clear as soon as Ben speaks. "Could you two give us the room? I need to talk to Riley in private, ACL patient to ACL patient."

"Uh, yeah, I was going to head back to the hotel anyway," I say, biting my lip. "I have some stuff I need to take care of." I don't, but it's an easy excuse.

"It's pouring outside," Freddie says, moving over to the table. He grabs an umbrella and holds it out to me. "Take this. I walked over here earlier."

"But then you'll get soaked on the way back," I say, shaking my head, trying to clear it. We haven't talked since he released me from that hug, and it shouldn't be weird, but it is. It's so polite and awkward and weird and I hate it.

"Please," he says, practically pushing it into my hands. "I don't mind the rain."

"Or here's an idea, you two could just walk together, umbrella looks big enough for two."

"Shut up, Ben," Freddie snaps at his best friend, but then bites his lip when his eyes land on Riley again.

Ben snorts, sending him a rude gesture with his fingers. "Shutting up. Now get out."

And then we're out in the fluorescent glow of the hospital hallway, staring at the closed door.

"I guess we should," Freddie says, gesturing down the hall to the elevators.

"Yeah."

We head outside and he was right. It's pouring, way harder than it was when we left the arena, but the hotel is only a few blocks away and there's something that feels new and extremely grown-up about walking down a Paris street, cafés and shops on one side, the Seine on the other, blending in with the city. To the people we pass, we probably look like a couple, huddled under the same umbrella, walking with purpose in, well, at least not completely awkward silence. The walk is a short one and we jog up the steps to the hotel, where a doorman holds the door open.

"Bienvenue," he says, nodding to us as we pass by. Freddie closes the umbrella and holds it out dripping on the spotless marble floor and I smile apologetically at the doorman, but he waves us away and we head for the elevators.

We're on the same floor and the tinkling music in the elevator is the only sound as we rise up.

His room is a couple of doors into the hallway and I'm farther down.

"Thanks for not letting me get soaked," I say when he stops at his door.

"Anytime," he says, shooting me a grin before I turn and head to my own room.

I pass the key over the scanner and the door clicks open. It's pitch-black inside, curtains drawn, lights out. There's a Maria-shaped lump in the center of her bed; she and Charlie probably just got finished with training for the day. She always naps after practice.

In fact, a nap seems like a really good idea. I pass a mirror on the way to the bed and grimace. My hair might be a lost cause. The rain barely touched it, but the moisture in the air was enough to make my curls a puffy mess.

I pull the bulk of it into my hands and twist it around into a ballet bun, keeping it loose enough that it doesn't look like a poop emoji on the top of my head, which has definitely happened more than once. A few pieces fall out the back of it and my bangs aren't quite long enough to pull back, so they frame my face nicely. Not that it matters. I'm going to curl up with some French TV show I don't understand and let myself drift away.

There's a knock at the door. I bet Maria ordered room service, forgot, and then fell asleep. I don't even check the peephole before opening the door.

"Freddie?"

"Yeah," he says, rubbing a hand over the back of his neck. "I know you said you had some stuff to do, but I thought maybe—"

"Maybe?" I prompt when he stops talking to just look at me.

"Right. I thought maybe that instead"—he hesitates before saying in a rush—"what are the odds you want to get out of here, go somewhere?"

"Me and you?"

"Yeah," he says finally, holding out his hand, ready to shoot for it.

I shake my head instead, smile, and grab my bag. "Even odds. Let's go."

Chapter 18

WE PASS THE same doorman as earlier and I send him a smile as he holds the door open for us and we step out into the early evening. The rain has almost completely stopped and the air smells clean, like the downpour washed away the grime of the city, at least until tomorrow when everyone will dirty it up again.

"So, where are we going?" I ask, falling in step with him.

"We could just wander?" he suggests. "I've heard that's the best way to see Paris."

Seeing Paris. That sounds nice and it's something I've been dying to do since we arrived. The Seine is right across the street, and I know enough from our car rides back and forth to the arena that if we follow it, we'll probably see a lot of the city.

"Let's walk along the river," I say, nodding toward the Seine.

"Let's," he agrees.

The city is older than Boston by almost two thousand years, but it's been rebuilt enough over the centuries that the stone and the buildings and the bustle of people going about their daily lives almost feels like I could be at home.

"It almost feels like home," Freddie says, echoing my thoughts.

"Like Atlanta?" I ask, not turning to him, but looking out over the river.

"Atlanta's not home. It's just where I train."

"Oh."

He means Boston, then. Boston is his home. Just like it's mine.

It's still winter, technically, but despite the clouds and the earlier rain, it's actually not that cold outside, which is a relief since I didn't think to put on a jacket before we left. I didn't really think about anything at all, except how much I wanted to go.

The silence stretches out in front of us and I eventually give in to it.

"Ben's still with Riley?"

"Yeah," he says, "I hope he can get through to her. I told her that she'll come back better than before, but I don't think she believed me. It might resonate more coming from him. He's been there, you know, with the injury."

"She's afraid you're going to drop her as a partner."

"What?" he asks, his eyes flying wide open with panic. "There's no way I'd do that. I would never."

"I know," I say softly. "That's what I told her."

"Good."

"You should tell her, though."

"I will."

"Good."

I could kick myself for bringing this up. There's too much baggage here, but when am I ever going to get another chance to do this?

"I never thanked you, you know, for staying with me, back then. I should have."

"Adriana, you don't have to—"

"Yeah, I do, especially after I didn't—"

He shakes his head, stopping dead in the middle of the sidewalk. "You did what you had to do. It took me a little while to realize that, but it was the right call, for the both of us. I wouldn't have been able to make a call like that."

And just like that, two years of awkwardness are erased, and my shoulders feel light and I pull in a breath of crisp air.

"We should get food," I suggest randomly.

"Food?"

"We're in Paris and all we've done is eat at the hotel restaurant. We should have food."

"French food?" He sounds unsure.

"I mean, it's Paris, there's probably all kinds of food. We could probably find a McDonald's if you want. We could be *those* kinds of tourists. The ones that come to Boston and eat at Red Lobster."

He sighs. "French food. Let's do it." And then he hesitates for a second. "What are the odds you'll try snails?"

"Ha! One in five. Same for you, though."

He wrinkles his nose. "Forget it, no snails."

We find a bistro with a menu outside where we recognize at least some of the words and order a few things the waiter insisted are *light* because if I'm going to win a World Championship in three days, gorging myself on French food isn't a great idea.

I take a few bites from each plate, one with veal, another with crepes, another with gratin potatoes, and yet another dish called coq au vin that I'd definitely order for my last meal if I ever found myself on death row. Freddie finishes them off. I drink water, and he drinks wine the waiter recommended, which feels like a very grown-up thing to do. This entire day has been a lot of grown-up stuff, to be honest, but there's something about the way he sips the wine from the glass instead of chugging it like people down beer at parties that feels right. Like the way walking down the street earlier felt.

"Is . . . is everything okay with you?" he asks, sopping up the last bit of sauce from the coq au vin with a piece of flaky bread that I kind of want to snag out of his hand for myself.

"Uh, yeah? Why?" I blink at him.

"I don't know, maybe I'm way off base here and you can tell me to shut the fuck up if you want, but it feels like something's wrong, like something's been wrong for a while."

I sigh, falling back against my chair. "But we were having such a good time."

"You don't have to tell me," he says with a casual shrug that I know is anything but casual. He's worried, I think.

I don't have to tell him anything. And that makes me want to spill my guts even more, because sitting across from me isn't the guy who could barely look at me when he first got to Kellynch, or even the guy who looked at me with cold detachment outside of Fenway Park on a cold Boston morning, and not even the guy who I pressed against in the club while for a second I let myself forget everything else in the world. He's just Freddie O'Connell, the boy I grew up with, the boy who knew me better than anyone. Him? I can tell him anything.

Except I can't. I promised Brayden.

Shit.

"It's just, you know my dad. Money's tight and there's a lot of pressure and now this thing with Brayden is a lot and confusing," I say, trailing off, hoping that's enough for him to get it.

"Is he pressuring you or something? I'll kill him." And he looks serious as he shifts forward in his seat, like that's not an idle threat.

"No," I say, in a rush. "Nothing like that. It's all just a lot. Have you ever gotten in over your head with something, thinking you wanted one thing and it was the right call and you sort of wish that it wasn't?"

Freddie sits back, clearing his throat roughly, his eyes avoiding mine. "Yeah, yeah, I have."

"So now I'm sort of stuck and it's not a bad stuck, necessarily, but it's still *stuck,* and I don't really know what to do about it or if I even should do anything about it, especially since I definitely thought I was doing the right thing at the time. Is any of this making any sense at all?"

For a moment we sit in silence and then Freddie leans in his chair.

"I honestly have no idea," he says, "but at least we can distract you from it a little. C'mon, we've barely seen any of Paris and it's getting dark. We should watch the Eiffel Tower lights and then get . . . is it gelato in France or just ice cream?"

"Glacé," the waiter says helpfully as he lays the check down on the table.

Freddie smiles at him. "Glacé," he repeats.

I pay, which makes Freddie grin.

"Charles has really come through with sponsorships," I say with a shrug, and it's true. Every other day or so we post another random thing about a headband or a type of makeup or socks that we wear after training, and while the money isn't huge amounts, like the contract he's working on with Nike, for now, I feel more than able to pay for this meal and maybe the ice cream too.

"Big-time," Freddie says with a laugh.

"I guess."

"I'm sorry, mademoiselle," the waiter says, coming over with our check and my card. "It was declined."

My brow furrows and I take the card back from him. "Declined? That's impossible." And then realization washes over me.

Elisa's new boots.

Dior boots.

Those things can run into the thousands. She must have used the same credit account to buy them and I'd been too distracted by this thing with Brayden to notice.

Well, so much for big-time. I'd be mortified if I didn't feel like such a fucking idiot. Where did I think the money came from? Thin air? Ugh.

"It's okay," Freddie says, pulling out his wallet and handing his card over. "I've got this."

The waiter takes it and makes himself scarce, but that doesn't stop the fiery heat building from my chest, up my neck, my blood boiling. I can practically feel the steam coming out of my ears.

"I'm *so* sorry," I mumble, fumbling with my phone to check the card's balance. Sure enough, there's Elisa's boot purchase from this morning for more than two thousand euros, maxing out the card.

"Family," Freddie says carefully. "Family is hard."

"Easy for you to say. Your family is wonderful."

"They are pretty awesome. I'm lucky," he says, and when I don't respond, he drops it entirely. "C'mon, let's get out of here and see more of this city."

Stepping outside into the early evening, the sun is setting in the distance and the sky has lightened, with streaks of orange and pink. It's warm for March, but still cooler than earlier and I shiver, shifting the collar of my sweater a bit so it covers both shoulders a little better.

"Can you believe we made it here?" I say as we fall into step again on the stone walkway along the river. If he's willing to ignore what just happened, I want to do that too, at least for a little while. "We always talked about Worlds when we were kids, getting here, and we did it."

"Well, second time for you," he says, laughing, though when I glance up, I can see some tension in his eyes, "and while I'm here technically, not so much with the competing."

I wave it off. "Temporary setback. Riley will recover and you two will be on the ice again in no time at all."

"Yeah, though whether she'll ever trust me again after what happened . . ."

"You know that it's not your fault, right? There's nothing you could have done. But the good news is, when Riley wants something, there's no stopping her. Like I said, you guys will be back."

He shrugs and I'm pretty sure there's nothing I can do to convince him.

We walk silently until a breeze kicks up and I catch the spicy cinnamon scent he wears and I'm suddenly hyperaware of him. When our arms swing as we step, our hands are *so close* to brushing and it wouldn't take much to reach out and take his hand, linking our fingers together as we walk.

But . . . no, I can't do that. He thinks I'm with Brayden.

Although maybe I could. We're friends now. Friends hold hands, right?

Plus, he's the one who hugged me after we found out Riley was going to be okay, and neither of us have said a damn thing about it or about the dance at the club that I've tried my best to just chalk up to a moment of insanity, but maybe if I grab his hand, he'll know that it was okay and it would be very okay for him to do it again, now or maybe in a little while when we've reached the Eiffel Tower and the sky is fully dark and we're standing under the glittering lights.

It's not okay, though, I remind myself. Because we're out here walking around and seeing Paris for the first time even though we've been here for almost a week and Riley is in a hospital bed, concussed with a torn-up knee and she likes Freddie and I'm fake dating Brayden and what a shit show this is.

"Ah!" Freddie says, grabbing my hand and making my entire internal monologue completely pointless. "Glacé!"

There's an ice cream shop ahead and I let him pull me along to it, holding on tight for as long as it lasts.

"Glacé in front of la tour Eiffel?" he asks, in a terrible French accent when we emerge a few minutes later. He has what looks like a Leaning Tower of Pisa cup of ice cream that's pink and green and purple, though I have no idea what the flavors are, which makes my little cup of vanilla look pathetic. It's still delicious, though.

Our hands are full now, cups in one hand, spoons in the other, and part of me wants to throw them away so he can take my hand again.

This is hard. Harder than I thought it would be. It feels like we're friends or maybe at least on the way to being that again. But I don't know if I can be friends with Freddie. Not really. Can I? The way I'm friends with Brayden? Affection and a smattering of attraction and trust. Friendship.

I glance up at Freddie, not bothering to brush away the curl that's dangling in my eyes. More than a smattering of attraction, way more, and I care about him, a lot, yeah, but . . . it's different. Just as deep, just as important, but way different.

We're getting closer to the Eiffel Tower. I can tell because when we emerge out of a side street, the crowds are thicker, and everyone seems to be headed in the same direction. We finish up our ice cream, but even with our hands free now, I don't dare to reach out for him.

As we walk, the streets open up to a beautifully manicured garden with green grass and fountains in a row perfectly in line with the tower on the opposite side of the Seine, rising up from the streets already lit up against the night sky, but every hour it glitters like the stars that are blotted out by the city lights.

"Five minutes till the hour," Freddie says, checking his phone. "Let's take a picture."

He holds his phone out with his long arm, and we crouch down enough to get the full view of the garden and the tower behind us.

"Should we post it?" he asks as we both smile down at it.

I shake my head. "It should be just for us."

"Like a secret?"

"No, not secret, *private*. Not everything is for everyone."

His brow furrows for a second, looking at me the same way he did back in the restaurant, like something about me doesn't quite add up, but he hums in agreement and pockets his phone. It must be eight o'clock because the crowd gasps together as the tower starts to shine brighter, flickering strobes traveling up and down the spindly tower all the way to the top where a light rotates, sending a signal off into the distance like a lighthouse greeting boats off the shore.

Everyone else has their phones raised, capturing the moment, but we stand there watching, our shoulders nearly touching.

"Beautiful," I say, taking in maybe the most famous light show in the world.

"Yeah." Freddie exhales and his breath ruffles a loose curl at my forehead, sending a shiver through me that I'm sure he must notice.

We watch for a few more minutes, waiting for the show to end, and then finally the lights steady out back to the simple golden outline of the metal structure.

Turning together, we head back the way we came.

I check my phone, and there are enough missed texts and calls, not only from Brayden, but from Camille too, that I send an *I'm fine, be back soon* message to my coach before pocketing it again.

"Hey, look," Freddie says as he nods and points down a side street.

There's an outdoor skating rink. There's a sign beside it promoting the Junior World Championships, which makes sense. Paris seems to be doing a great job marketing the event, since there hasn't been a session with more than a few empty seats.

"Oh no," I say, laughing. "You're not serious?"

"Why not?" he asks, smiling, and that's what does it. I can't refuse him.

There's a skate rental off to the side and I lace up the cheapest and smelliest pair of skates I've worn in my entire life. Freddie's not even wearing figure skates; they only had hockey skates left. After tying the worn strings as tight as I can manage—a sprained ankle now would be a ridiculous way to lose the World Championships— Freddie and I slip into the crowd together, skating along smoothly while music plays in the background.

"I wonder if they do requests," he muses, and right on cue, a song I haven't heard in years starts to play and I send him a quick side-eye.

"I guess they do," I say as he laughs.

"(I've Had) The Time of My Life" was the song we skated our free dance to when we won the Intermediate National Championships, the year before my growth spurt ended our partnership.

"Do you remember this?" he asks, wiggling his fingers at me, palm up and hand open, waiting for me to take it.

I smile and shake my head. "Of course I do." As soon as he takes my hand, he spins me toward him and we find some space at the center of the ice, away from the circling crowd. "Do you remember the steps, though?"

With a soft laugh, he pulls me closer and leans down to whisper against my temple. "I remember everything."

He doesn't just mean the dance, and the weight of it, wonderful and torturous, settles over me.

The steps come back easily. We worked on that routine for two years and it's easy to fall back into the rhythm of it with the music playing in the background. We've even drawn a bit of an audience as we skate, not going full-out because there isn't a ton of space, but clearly performing rather than skating.

His hand is firm in mine, just like it used to be, but our height difference is way bigger now. He's improved, though, obviously. His footwork is stronger, his posture is better, and everything about being this close to him feels more like a dream than anything else. There is nothing about this routine that would make my pulse pound, except that it's Freddie's broad shoulder under my hand and it's his forehead that rests against mine when he pulls me closer as we dance.

His breath is warm against my already flushed cheek as he leans down into me, his hands sliding from my waist to my thighs, and reflexively my body responds the way it's supposed to, moving into his momentum and letting him lift me up against his chest and carry me across the ice, my back foot popping up into the air as my hands circle his neck. I don't need to, though; his hold is strong and if I want, I could throw my head back and lift my arms in the air, no fear of falling. So I do, feeling safe and protected and wild and free all at once. The rest of the ice rink, the rest of the world, melts away so easily.

Just like back at the club, this is everything.

Being with him is everything.

I look down into his eyes. His face is serious, but then he wrinkles his nose at me sweetly and I laugh and it's just so wonderful, the lightness and the intensity.

Then it's over.

The music ends, the DJ barely letting it finish before he starts playing another song, and there's a scattering of applause as we finish skating, but it brings the world back into focus around us.

"I think that's enough," I whisper, still in his arms after he's lowered me to the ice, the finishing pose we stood in all those years ago.

"Yeah," he agrees, and releases me gently.

"It's getting late."

"We should go back."

Somehow the walk feels so much shorter now. Before, it felt like we wandered and time passed by slowly, if at all; now, though, I spot the hotel in the distance almost right away.

The same doorman is still on duty and he tips his cap to us, holding the door open as we make our way inside.

"Bonsoir," he says. We nod to him before heading for the elevators.

One opens almost immediately, and we step inside. The doors close and a faintly buzzing song plays as the car rises. We ride in silence and get off at the same floor again, but this time Freddie doesn't stop at his room. He follows me all the way down to my door, like he's walking me home from a date, and I have to take a deep, steadying breath because in this moment I want that to be true so much my chest actually aches.

"This was nice," I say, knowing it's maybe the most massive understatement I've ever uttered.

"Yeah, it was," he agrees.

Unlocking the door, I look back at him and pause, because he's rocking back on his heels, like he wants to say something or do something and he's hesitating. Then he settles and lets out a frustrated breath.

"Good luck in the free skate. You . . . you deserve to win."

"Thanks," I start to say, but then he's leaning down and his lips brush against my cheek. My breath catches and I freeze because his mouth is right there, all I have to do is turn my head a fraction of an inch. My nose bumps gently against his and his bottom lip slides against mine. And it's like a bolt of lightning explodes from my heart.

I reach out and clutch at the knit of his sweater, pulling him closer as he surges forward, my mouth opening beneath his as I fall back against the hotel room door.

It's pure relief, reckless and heady, but the most natural thing in the world. This isn't just what kissing is supposed to feel like. This is what they write those songs we skate to about, this feeling of knowing it's right, knowing this is the person you're supposed to be with. And when his arms wrap around me, I want to stay like this forever and that's the thing that sends me plummeting back down to Earth because we can't.

We can't do this.

"Freddie," I manage to gasp out when his lips move from mine to the line of my jaw, "we . . . can't."

He groans, his forehead falling to my shoulder. "Shit," he rasps. "I'm sorry. I shouldn't have—shit."

"No, I—I'm sorry," I stutter, and gesture vaguely behind me at the door while he pulls away, stepping away, his sweater sliding through my fingers, and all I want to do is pull him back to me.

"I'll just go," he manages, and he straightens his shoulders before nearly tripping over his own feet when he turns to head down the hallway.

I watch him go because maybe his resolve will break, maybe he'll change his mind and turn back around and stride to me and kiss me senseless . . . again . . . and we'll figure out the rest after, figure out a way to tell Riley and figure out how to end this ridiculous sham I'm currently living. Because that kiss? That was everything I've ever wanted and so much more. I'm dizzy in the best possible way. I want to do that again and then tell him everything, how I feel, how I've felt for so long, even after he left.

But he gets to his door and sends me one last glance, before pushing it open and disappearing behind it. I wait a second and then another. Maybe he'll change his mind, maybe if I wait another second or ten or a hundred, he'll come back out.

Or maybe not.

Chapter 19

"*D*AMN IT, ADRIANA!" Brayden shouts after another aborted lift halfway through our run-through of the program. The training rink is nearly empty and his voice echoes through the entire space. "I'm *not* going to drop you."

I push away from him and drift out toward the open ice. "Your arms were shaking."

"Because you didn't lock your body. It's like trying to lift a squirming snake."

We only have to train one program now. *Thrones* was always tough, but now it feels impossible. Every time Brayden goes to lift me today, it feels unsteady, like I'm about to fall face-first into the ice and he won't break my fall. And it's probably my fault. After yesterday everything about this feels wrong. I need to tell him what happened with Freddie. Keeping it a secret, even just overnight, is weighing on my chest.

"Enough!" Camille commands, skating out toward us. "You sound like children."

"We are children," I mutter petulantly, but the glare Camille pins me with is enough to shut me up.

"You," she says, and points at Brayden and then hikes her thumb back behind her, "hit the showers and call it a day." Brayden throws his hands up in frustration, but then leaves without protest. "And you." She turns to me. "We need to talk."

We glide off the ice and onto the bleachers that adjoin it. Camille waits until Brayden disappears into the locker room and then she raises her eyebrows. She doesn't ask; she waits.

I finally give in, if only to get this conversation over and done with. "What do you want me to say?"

"I want you to tell me what the hell is going on. I can't fathom that a team who broke the world record a few days ago looks like *that*. I don't even have a word for it. I've never seen either of you skate this badly."

"Thanks, Coach, so inspiring."

"Adriana, be serious."

"That's all I ever am," I mumble.

"What?"

I shake my head, not wanting to go down that road. It's a little too real. "Nothing, I'm fine."

"You're not fine and Brayden's right, you're the one not trusting him. Did something happen between you two?"

"No, it's not like that, I just . . . I can't tell you."

"If you don't tell me, I can't help you."

I sigh and say, "I know."

"Then you need to figure it out." I glare at her and she raises her hands in defeat. "Because skating like that is unacceptable and, frankly, dangerous."

"What if I can't?"

She's the one who sighs this time. "Then you better start looking for another partner."

My stomach drops and twists as bile rises in my throat at the idea. Another partner. I don't want another partner. Brayden and I are great together . . . were great together. Now? Who the hell knows what we are? And that's on me. I broke our rule.

Camille pats me on the knee and stands. "You coming to the ladies' competition this afternoon?" she asks.

"Yeah, of course I'll be there."

"Good. We're going to do a family dinner in between, before Maria and Charlie's final. I invited Brayden earlier, before I knew, well, before we spoke. I hope that's okay?"

I nod. "It's fine," I say, though I have no idea if it is, really, and then she leaves me to my thoughts.

It's a decent day outside, so I don't bother getting a car back to the hotel. I want a hot shower and to get ready for the ladies' competition this afternoon. Katya and Gillian are down in eighth and tenth places after the short program, but I still want to be there to support them while they skate.

We've been a team all the way through this and we're still a team.

Maria isn't in the room when I get back. She's at the rink with Charlie and their coach, getting ready for the pairs' final tonight. I shower quickly and pull my wet hair back into a bun. There's no time to dry it, but if I leave it up for a few hours, it'll give me decent curls when I let it down.

I'm checking my bag, making sure my phone and my hotel room key are in it, when there's a knock at my door. When I look through the peephole, I nearly shriek when all I see is the top of a head with braids dangling over a pair of shoulders.

Flinging the door open, I squeal when Riley, with a huge smile across her face, swings forward on her crutches and hugs me.

"I thought you were getting out tomorrow morning!"

"These two busted me out," she says, nodding back at Ben and Jimmy.

"Come in, guys, I'm almost ready."

"You're gonna sit with us, right?" Riley says, moving past me, while the boys seem more hesitant, but then follow her.

"Yeah," I say, "I have to do family dinner after, but, like, obviously."

"Uh, yeah, my dad was invited and he's making me go too. No offense."

"None taken. I'm glad you'll be there with me."

"Same," she says. Then she asks, innocently enough, "Is Brayden sitting with us now?"

"Uh, no, probably not."

Riley shoots me a questioning look that I ignore, twisting the bracelets at my wrists as a distraction.

Jimmy checks his phone. "We're waiting for Freddie too. He said he's coming and will meet us in the lobby," he says, but he's looking at me when he does.

"Oh, okay," I say, trying to keep my voice even, but failing spectacularly.

The hotel's lobby is always bustling, but with the competition today and then another one tonight, it feels like Fenway before the Sox play the Yankees.

We spread out over two chairs and a couch, watching the people come and go, while I ask Riley about when her surgery is scheduled and how long the doctors think she'll be out, when finally, the elevator dings and Freddie steps out with Georgia and Harry right behind him.

We stand up, and his eyes find us almost immediately, but then he stares in shock, mouth open at Riley. In a few long strides he's across the lobby and pulling her up into his arms. His relief is palpable and my chest pangs at the sight. They look right together, and I suddenly feel so guilty I want to sob an apology to Riley right here in the middle of the hotel lobby.

Riley can't walk to the arena, obviously, so we grab two cabs. Ben holds Riley's crutches for her; she slides into the car and then he follows.

"We'll get the next one," Jimmy says when he notices there's no more room.

The three of us squeeze into the next car with me in the middle, even though Jimmy is shorter than me, and I find nearly one side of my entire body pressed up against Freddie.

"Sorry," I mumble.

"Don't mention it," he says, sending me a shy smile, and I tilt my head in confusion.

Is he flirting? Even after what happened last night?

Why is all of this so confusing?

The ride is short, and we make it in through the entrance used by the athletes, coaches, and media easily enough while the lines of fans wrap around the arena.

"There you are," Elisa says when we're inside, and I blink at her. It doesn't sound like she's happy, either, though what the hell she could be angry about is totally beyond me.

"Guys, give me a second. I'll meet you at the seats."

"You're sitting with them?" she says, and even though it sounds like a question, it's not. It's a judgment.

"My friends. Yes. What do you want?"

"Charles wanted to talk to you about an interview he needs you and Brayden to record."

"And you thought you'd remind me?" I ask, like that's some sort of smart comeback.

Elisa rolls her eyes. "Whatever, Adriana."

"Fine, I'm going to sit with my friends. Tell him that we'll record it tonight after pairs."

"Will do," she says with a shrug, before turning on the heel of her brand-new Dior boots and walking away.

KATYA AND GILLIAN don't even come close to medaling, but that doesn't mean we don't cheer our heads off for them as they skate through their programs. What I'm most interested in, though, is one of the Russian skaters. There's a girl skating with a quad axel, one of the first women—actually, she's barely thirteen—to attempt the skill. That's four and a half rotations and she doesn't quite get it around, but it's a close thing and she stays on her feet. And she's not the only junior with a quad jump. I almost wish I was sitting with Elisa, to get her reaction. She didn't win a medal in Beijing and now she's got this crop of juniors coming up behind her who can jump like that. It's wild.

"I bet I could do a quad," Riley mutters, and all of us turn to her in horror. "Bad joke, sorry! Too soon?"

Shaking my head, I laugh, and so does the rest of the group.

"Come on," I say as the crowd starts to thin out. "We've got, I don't know, is this even dinner, or lunch? It's like three o'clock?"

"Whatever it is, it won't be hospital food, so I am *in*," Riley says, and we say goodbye to the boys.

It turns out it's the same restaurant Freddie and I stumbled into the other day, and the maître d' even recognizes me. I flush, wondering if he remembers how dinner ended, but he says, "Ah, mademoiselle," as Dad gives his name for the reservation. "Bienvenue."

The group looks at me, but I shrug and smile blithely. Camille's eyes narrow, though, and as we're led to a table, she ends up next to me.

"You've eaten here before?" she asks. "Would that be the other day when you disappeared for hours and nearly made me call the metro police to find you?"

"Don't be dramatic," I whisper, making sure Riley can't hear me. "Freddie and I walked around a bit and we ate here. Nothing crazy."

She slides into the seat beside me and with Riley on my other side it's one of the nicest family dinners I've had in a long time.

I haven't eaten much all day, so I don't hesitate to order the coq au vin and savor every bite. I even take a picture of my meal and tag the restaurant in it when I post. The least I can do, with my nearly five hundred thousand followers now, is give a shout-out to an awesome restaurant.

Dessert is on its way when Dad turns to Charles and asks, "And how are the negotiations with Nike proceeding?"

Charles nods and smiles. "Stalled a bit. Brayden and Adriana, could be a little bit more active on social media, that'll help the cause for sure. They were impressed with your performance the other night, certainly, but they'll want that gold medal to get things going again."

It's nothing we haven't heard him say before, but suddenly the full implications of me not being able to get through a full hit routine with Brayden seems to mean a lot more. I need to talk to him. Tonight, after the pairs' competition. We'll talk and we''ll figure this out and get back on track.

"MÉDAILLÉS DE BRONZE, des États-Unis d'Amérique, Maria Russo et Charles Monroe!"

Our section erupts in excitement. I hadn't given a ton of thought to my little sister and her partner's chances at these Worlds, but they totally rocked their free skate and edged out a couple from Canada for the bronze medal. And that's a gold and a bronze for Team USA so far with me and Brayden left to compete tomorrow night.

My stomach twists at the medal missing from that haul. A silver.

Would a silver medal be that bad?

No. A silver isn't bad, but when you step back and look at the whole picture, the lead we have on the field, the expectations from our coaches and from our potential sponsors and from ourselves, a silver wouldn't be what we came here to do. It would mean we didn't hit our free dance the way we're capable of, or at least the way we used to be capable of before everything went to shit.

It's my fault. I'm the one up in my head. I really do need to talk to Brayden.

By the time we get back to the hotel, the café attached to the lobby has fully converted into a bar, and it seems the entire junior figure skating world has converged on that small space.

Our group has managed to carve out a corner of seats. Ben's regaling them with what looks like a full reenactment of when he hurt his knee two years ago, a story we've all heard dozens of times, but it's Ben, so it's fine.

There's someone missing, though, and my eyes dart around the room looking for him and finally I find him, across the room sitting with his sister and brother-in-law and chatting with someone I vaguely recognize as a Canadian coach. He must feel my gaze, because it's not long before he looks up and makes eye contact and my breath catches in my chest.

Why does he have to be Riley's partner? And it'd be great if he could stop looking at me like that. Or, you know, look at me that way forever. Either is fine.

I manage to tear myself away and search for Brayden. He's standing with Charles in the far corner, near where the lobby opens up into the café-turned-bar, and I head in that direction. I don't even pretend to be subtle.

"Sorry to interrupt, guys, but Brayden, can I steal you for a few minutes?"

He raises his eyebrows and shrugs. "Sure," he says.

Charles smirks a little bit at us, like I'm pulling him away for an entirely different reason.

There's almost nowhere quiet inside, so I walk through the bustling space, weaving us through the groups of people laughing and drinking and generally totally oblivious and having a great time.

When we make it outside the air is crisp, colder than it's been the entire time we've been here. I shiver against it, but turn to Brayden with purpose.

"We need to talk."

"We do," he agrees.

"I'm sorry for how I've been in training. It won't happen again." He nods and then heaves a heavy breath. "Good."

"Good," I agree, and maybe it's as easy as that. We just agree and move on. "We should go back into the party before anyone misses us." I turn away, but his voice stops me.

"You know, if you'd just told me the truth, we wouldn't be in this mess."

I spin back to face him, but I can't deny it. He's right. I have been lying to him. I broke our rules and didn't come clean and yeah, it's time to face the music.

"How long have you been in love with him?"

And that's *not* what I expected him to say.

"What . . . I'm not . . ." but I can't bring myself to finish that sentence. "How . . ."

"I know this whole fame thing is new, Adriana, but skating across a public rink in the arms of another guy in the middle of a major skating championship? Someone was going to see you."

"It's not—"

"It's not online," he says, cutting me off, "one of the guys on

Team Canada saw you and sent me a pic. He's too nice to post it. Even made me watch him delete it from his phone."

"Thank God."

"So were you ever going to tell me?"

"I was—I just . . ." I stop and take a deep breath. "I *was* going to tell you about it. I just sort of chickened out. It . . . it doesn't matter."

"So you're not with him?"

"No."

"But you want to be with him?"

"I . . . like I said, it doesn't matter."

"Yeah, Adriana, it does matter. Do you really not get it, after all this time?"

"Get what?"

"How I feel about you?"

Oh.

Oh God.

"How . . ." I swallow down the panic. I thought, I hoped, when he asked me to dinner on the plane it was just a stupid mistake, a one-off something we could ignore, but, apparently not? And God, I'm such an idiot for pretending otherwise. "How long have you—"

"Long enough."

"Brayden, that's—"

"Ridiculous? Yeah, I know."

"You're *always* talking about your hookups and how you have plans and the parties you go to."

"That I *always* invite you to. Always. What did you think that meant?"

"I—I don't—I didn't—"

"It's fine, Adriana. Really."

"It's not," I argue. "Brayden, I'm so—"

"Don't," he bites out. "Don't apologize, it's fine. C'mon, we have an interview that Charles set up for us right after this to thank everyone at home for watching."

Yeah, it's definitely not fine.

Chapter 20

"**I**'M A WORLD medalist," Maria says for maybe the hundredth time since we turned out the lights in our hotel room to go to sleep. It's past two in the morning and I'm happy for her, but I have to get up early tomorrow.

Brayden and I made it through that interview, barely. Thankfully, it was over the phone so the reporter on the other end couldn't see us sitting on opposite ends of his hotel room, barely looking at each other as we muttered answers to the standard pre-competition questions, and since it was a figure skating magazine, most of it was centered around actual skating and nothing about our lives off the ice. There's no way we're going to be able to avoid that forever, though. Eventually, someone is going to ask us and I have no idea what I'm going to say. Not to mention, we have to actually go out and compete tomorrow, somehow, after everything. Does a relationship ever recover from unrequited feelings or is it just doomed forever?

Because they are unrequited. I know that for sure. Maybe if Freddie had never come back into my life, maybe then, but he did come back and I know what that feels like and it doesn't compare. Not even close.

Maybe we'll be okay, though. Maria was in love with Charlie for

248

years and they're fine now. They went out today and killed it on the ice. So maybe Brayden just needs time? Time to heal? Time for him to get over whatever it is he feels for me?

We don't have time, though.

We have like—I check the clock—eighteen hours, most of which I'm supposed to spend sleeping.

"You're a world medalist," I repeat back to my little sister, shifting against the mattress, trying to get comfortable. "You did so well today."

"Is it weird that it's under my pillow?"

"No," I whisper, pulling the blankets closer to my chin and feeling my eyelids start to droop. "That's normal."

"I mean, we came in third and we still have another year or two as juniors. Maybe we'll even be ready for Milan instead of waiting for another Olympic cycle. I mean, like, you and Brayden didn't even medal last year and look at you guys now. You're like huge stars. We are going to be so *famous*. I talked to Charlie's dad about sponsorships at the party tonight and he said he's going to look into it. Can you believe it?"

"I can," I say. "You've worked hard. You deserve it."

"Maybe he'll be able to talk to Nike about us too. I mean, if they're signing up one Russo sister why wouldn't they want another? Everyone knows that people care about pairs more than ice dance. No offense, but that's the truth. It would be *wild* if we were able to bring in that kind of money. I wonder what else Charles could get us. Those big money sponsors love Olympic athletes. We'd never have to worry about money ever again."

She's still talking as I drift off to sleep, but it's the last thing I hear and the first thing I remember when my alarm goes off eight hours later. I might not be able to do anything about the complete shit show that has become my personal life, but the business stuff? That I can handle. Or at least I have to try. If the last few weeks have taught me anything, it's that there's only one person responsible for my happiness and that's me. And I refuse to let what happened to Elisa happen to me too. I love my dad, but my money isn't his and I need to make sure that's clear.

I don't mind helping out, but after what happened at the restaurant, I need those accounts to be in my name only. No more handing my card off to be swiped and rejected because Elisa decided she needed a new dress or Dad felt like splurging at Brooks Brothers. And once that is out of the way, I'll be able to focus on the only thing that should matter today: Brayden and I going out there tonight and bringing home a gold medal.

One problem at a time, though.

Maria is already up and about, her bronze medal around her neck while she digs through her suitcase.

"I need to figure out what to wear to the party tonight."

"The party?"

"After you and Brayden win, obviously."

"You say that like it's guaranteed."

"False modesty isn't cute."

What she doesn't know is that it's not false modesty. Not at all. We set a world record the other day, but this is still ice dance and without a great free dance there's no way we'll win gold. There are no guarantees in this sport.

I roll out of bed, moving right to the floor to start stretching out.

In the corner my skating bag is already packed, my costume is in its garment bag. Everything is ready to go. We'll leave in a few hours for the arena, but first, I need to find Charles. I send him a quick text and ask him to meet me at the café in an hour and he responds with a thumbs-up emoji.

He's already down there, waiting at a table when I arrive.

"Good morning," I say, sitting down, ordering a grapefruit and coffee. "Congrats on Charlie's bronze, by the way. They were really amazing, weren't they?"

"They were," Charles says, and smiles. "He's a good kid and he and Maria seem to suit each other."

"It's not the weirdest partnership I've ever seen."

He laughs. "Fair point. Anyway, before we get started, I wanted to tell you how thankful I am for how kind you've been to Riley, not just in Paris, but during training. I know how difficult and competitive this world is . . ."

"Riley's my friend," I say, cutting him off and trying to tamp down the guilt I've kept at bay for the last few weeks. Some friend I am, kissing the guy she likes.

"I know, but still, it's not unheard of for friendship to take a back seat in figure skating," he says, raising his hands a bit. "Anyway, what can I do for you this morning?"

"I want my money moved to separate accounts with only my name on it."

"I think that's a prudent path for you, though I'm not sure it's possible. Your father has a right to control your funds until you're eighteen, though we could set up a legal trust. He wouldn't have access to the monies, but then it's likely neither would you until you turn eighteen." He pauses and then purses his lips. "Of course, there's always emancipation."

He says it so casually, like that wouldn't be a huge deal, separating myself from my family. Probably having to leave Kellynch, because I can't *imagine* Dad being okay with me skating there after something like that. And they're my family. But Charles has known my family for years and maybe understands my situation better than anyone. Plus, he's a dad. A good one. If that's the solution he's suggesting, then maybe I should consider it?

Sure, there's some stuff I'd change about them and maybe they're not the cuddliest group, but they are my family. If there's a way to avoid a complete break, I want to try that first.

"I . . . don't want to do that . . . at least, not yet. Can you look into the trust first?"

"Of course."

"Thanks."

"If that's all, I have a meeting with the Nike reps on your behalf this morning?"

"That's all," I say.

"Good luck tonight, though I don't think you'll need it."

"I'll take it, though."

Maria still isn't dressed when I get back to the room.

"Where were you?"

"I had a meeting with Charles about making sure my money is put where it needs to go. You should talk to him about it too, actually, once he gets you those sponsorships you talked about. I don't mind helping out with bills and stuff, but Elisa's shopping sprees are not what it's for."

Maria snorts and nods. "I'll make sure Charlie talks to him about it for us."

"Good."

"What do you think?" She spins around in a bronze sequined shirt and winter-white jeans that match the white of the medal's thick ribbon.

"You brought a bronze shirt?"

"I brought a gold, a silver, and a bronze shirt, you know, just in case."

"Smart."

Maria beams at me, a little too brightly for such a small compliment, and I resolve to give her more in the future. I know how overlooked she feels sometimes.

There's a knock on the door and I know that knock, which is ridiculous, but if you know someone long enough you know weird things about them like that. Brayden knocks firmly, almost impatiently, like he's going to pound on the door next if you don't open up in a few seconds.

"You ready?" he asks when I open the door.

"As I'll ever be."

"What's that supposed to mean?" he snaps.

I shake my head. "Nothing. Let's go."

Yeah, this is going to go great.

THE TRAINING RINK is bustling when we arrive. There's only one competition left to go, ice dancing, but tomorrow the winners from every discipline will skate in a gala to celebrate the ending of the World Championships. So a lot of the athletes are around working on their exhibition routines. It's one of the things sort of unique to figure skating, having a fun routine set aside to celebrate the sport and not for competition. Brayden and I skate to the finale song from *Grease* and it's so campy and over the top that it's a blast to skate.

That's for tomorrow, though.

Today is all *Thrones* and making sure every detail is perfect for the judges. There's only one thought in my head as we warm up, skating simple patterns to get ready to train. I'm not even worried about my expression today. After everything that's happened, channeling emotion is not going to be a problem. I'm more concerned with keeping it under control, making sure none of this stuff spills out onto the ice. We need to stay in control. Our first order of business is to get that lift right, the one that caused so much stress the last couple of days. If we can nail that right at the start of training, hopefully everything else will fall into place.

And that's exactly what Camille asks for when we get started. "Show it to me safely and we'll go from there."

We skate together, building up some momentum like we'd have if we were in the middle of the program, and when I start to let him take my weight, he bails completely, doesn't even try.

"What the hell?" I say, skating back to him.

He's got his hands down on his knees and he's breathing hard, even though we've barely done anything yet. He lifts his head a fraction, and I can see there's some kind of panic in his eyes.

"Brayden, are you hurt? What's wrong?"

He shakes his head and takes a steadying breath, circling away from me. "Let's go again."

We do and this time he manages to lift me a little bit more, but not much, and he sets me down on the ice, before skating away from me, hands on his hips.

"Fuck!" he yells out, and it bounces off the ice to every other competitor and coach in the rink.

"Can do you this?" I mutter to him. If he can't, I need to know.

"I'm fine. I can do it. Let's go again."

"We need to nail this lift if we want to win. If you can't do it, you need to tell me."

He glares at me, eyes flashing. "I said I'm fine."

"Again," Camille calls out, "but don't kill each other, okay?"

"C'mon," I say between gritted teeth. "Get it together."

I don't even know if I'm talking to him or to myself. Maybe it's both of us, but if he can't lift me, then it's over. The last two years will have been for nothing. Giving up skating with Freddie would have been for nothing.

"Brayden," I say as my hand falls into his, our starting grip for the lift. "We can do this."

"Yeah," he bites back.

"I mean it," I say, looking up at him, squeezing his hand tightly. "We can do this. You and me, remember? All the way."

He stares at me for a second and then another, his eyes holding mine and I don't look away. I need him to know I still believe in us, even if it's not in the way he wants.

Brayden exhales and then closes his eyes. "Yeah, all the way," he agrees, and when he opens his eyes again his gaze is softer, but focused. "Let's nail this."

We move across the ice, finding the edges of our skates together, and then his hands slide around my waist and with a pull I'm up in his arms, in the air, his grip firm, his hold sure, and I let out a breath as he sets me down again.

There it is.

That was perfect.

"Perfect!" Camille shouts at us. "Now do it again!"

And we do, three times before it feels good to me and, maybe more important, before Camille's satisfied that our inability to do it was a total fluke. And maybe it was, maybe we'll be fine out there, even with all this bullshit between us.

No, that's not fair. It's not bullshit. It's just . . . a lot. Maybe I was oblivious to how Brayden felt and yeah, maybe I've been avoiding thinking about it too much because it's scary as hell. If he feels this way and I don't . . . how do we get past it long term? Is that even possible?

The training rink is directly across the street from the arena and once our session is over and we've had a light lunch, in complete silence, we simply walk over with the other skaters and their coaches. The competition is going to start in a few minutes, but with twenty teams competing, we won't be out there for a while. In the free dance, the teams compete in reverse standings and since we're in first place, we'll compete last.

When we get into the arena and walk through the tunnels toward the locker rooms, the announcer is introducing the judges to the crowd to polite applause.

It doesn't sound like all the fans are in their seats yet, which I don't get. Who buys tickets to something and then doesn't show up on time?

And that's the extent that I'm able to distract myself. Because who cares if people are here on time when there are way more important things to focus on. Like the program I'm supposed to go out and skate.

Love and betrayal, that's what our routine is about, and I've had more than my fill of those things in the last few weeks. Part of me would rather go back to a time before I understood exactly what my character was supposed to be feeling, but there's some sense that at least, even though it all sucked so much, I'll be able to use it for good, that my performance will be that much better for it. Maybe, hopefully, it'll leave the judges in awe and maybe make the audience shed a tear or two?

Part of being a figure skater is knowing how to kill time and I've become a pro at it over the years. My routine is simple. Stretch, meditate, listen to a classical music playlist that keeps me calm, and repeat. Then as we get closer, I add in our music and do some choreography run-throughs, but keep alternating the stretching and meditating. Somewhere in the middle of all that, I lose track of time and it all melds together until Camille knocks on the door for our time check.

Brayden and I change into our costumes and then I get my hair and makeup ready. My entire career up until now I always competed with my hair up, but playing this character, a dragon queen, my hair has to be down. I pull the sides away from my face, but then let the rest flow down my back in loose curls.

The music for the last of the session's competitors comes to an end and a few minutes later they have their scores and the announcer is calling for the warm-ups to begin for the final group.

When I turn to Brayden, he's dressed in all black with a silver wolf embroidered on the shoulder.

We look as badass as we're about to be on the ice.

"Let's do this," I say, holding out my fists for him to bump, which he does, and that soft look from training is back and I know what it is now. He's in love with me and if that's what's getting him through today, then maybe for right now, that's okay.

We march out of the changing room and fall into line with the four other couples that will be battling it out for the medals. They're all that stands between us and that gold medal we've been working toward our entire lives.

After the ice is cleaned, we're let out onto it to warm up and be introduced to the crowd. When the announcer gets to our names, the wall of sound that flows down from the seats is incredible and makes me glance at Brayden, who shoots me a half smile. We run through some of our dance patterns and twizzles, making sure to avoid colliding with anyone else out on the ice.

Then we leave as the fifth-place team gets ready to start their program. As we move through the gate, I catch the section our team is sitting in out of the corner of my eye. Charles, Dad, and Elisa are at the edge of the row, with Gillian and Katya beside Elisa, but my gaze travels down the line and there they all are, Riley and Ben and Jimmy and Maria and Charlie, but there's one face missing. I scan the section, thinking maybe he's sitting with Georgia and Harry, but they're in the row behind the others and no Freddie, not even an empty seat.

He's not here and . . . yeah, that's okay. I get it.

"You okay?" Camille asks when she catches the direction of my gaze.

I tear my eyes away. No amount of staring is going to make him suddenly appear. Nodding my head, I follow Camille as she leads me back through the curtain to wait out the next four routines before I skate out on the ice with my partner and win this whole damn thing.

Chapter 21

"CELA LEUR DONNE un score combiné de 177.78 et ils sont maintenant à la première place!"

My eyes fix on the score up on the screen, listed under the Canadian team who just finished their program, smiling and hugging their coaches in the Kiss and Cry and generally seeming happy with their performance. And why shouldn't they? They're sitting in first place with one team to go.

Unfortunately for them, we're up next.

"Représentant les États-Unis d'Amérique, Adriana Russo et Brayden Elliot!"

As one, we skate out onto the ice and raise our hands to the crowd. The noise they make now is still astoundingly loud and sends a chill down my spine the way the actual ice hasn't in a long time.

At the center of the ice, we stand back-to-back and lace our fingers together and wait for the music to begin. The harp strings are being plucked softly and then two cellos join it as "Rains of Castamere" starts off the medley, slowly and tragically.

Brayden and I move around each other, hands twining and then releasing, back and forth, our actions mirroring each other until a drum rolls in the distance and the deep bellowing of the main theme builds and builds. He grabs my hand, twists and pulls me into his arms and then we're off across the ice as I pull away into our twizzle sequence, spinning in perfect unison, our footwork as aggressive and forceful as the music. As we reach the other side of the rink, our hands find each other again and we're waltzing, cutting a perfect pattern across the ice before our first lift, a simple one, me in his arms as he spins.

The music reaches another crescendo and then pulls back as my skates hit the ice, and the song slows a fraction before building again. Then it's full-out all the way through the end, every part of our bodies working together to tell the story of Daenerys and Jon, and maybe, somehow, of Adriana and Brayden too. As the music finds its peak, I move into his grasp and he lifts me, my knees pressing into his chest as he circles the ice, holding me up toward the rafters as I lean back, arms extended, and the crowd gasps at the right moment.

But my legs give a little, a fluke, nothing to do with betrayal or trust, just a weird shift of my weight and I'm destined for the ice, where I'll crash headfirst and knock myself senseless, probably worse than Riley did, but instead, Brayden's grip is solid at my thighs.

He has me.

He's not letting go.

And then I'm down again, my skates on the ice, finding my edges, secure and firm as always, and the music is coming to an end; we go into a spin, the same pose as the lift, except this time, it's part of the choreography as we fall together and Brayden mimes a sword stabbing me and together we're down and breathing as the music ends. There's silence for a split second and then the crowd is back, louder than I've ever heard them, somehow, but I'm still able to hear Brayden say, "That's what I'm talking about!"

I laugh, wrapping my arms around his neck as he stands and pulls me with him.

"Yes!" he yells again as we raise our joined hands together to take our bows to the judges and the crowd. They're on their feet applauding—the fans, not the judges, they'd *never*—and we make sure to turn to each corner to send them the same amount of love they've shown us this entire time.

After our final bow, Brayden pulls me to him again.

"Thank you," he mumbles in my ear.

"We did it," I mumble back, hugging him tight.

We skate off the ice as the crowd is still cheering, throwing stuffed animals for us, and I head straight for Camille, who is hysterically crying, like a full-on ugly cry of joy. She hugs me tightly and then grabs Brayden and we rock back and forth together for a moment.

"You two, that was *incredible!*" she shrieks.

I try to catch my breath once we get to the Kiss and Cry, but it's almost impossible. It's not the routine. It's the moment. The scores will come up in a second and I don't know exactly what they'll be, but I know we've done what we set out to do.

"I almost went down there for a second," I say as we settle onto the couch.

"Yeah, I felt it, but I had you," he says.

"You did." I grab his hand and hold on tight as the announcer interrupts the music playing to entertain the fans while we wait for the score.

"The score, please," she says, almost sounding like a robot.

"Le score d'Adriana Russo et Brayden Elliot est de 104.32, ce qui les place à la première place de la danse libre, avec un score total de 179.81, un autre nouveau record du monde junior!"

My brain still can't translate the French, not completely, but that last part sounds familiar and I look up to the scoreboard and see:

RUSSO, A./ELLIOT, B. (USA)

TECHNICAL ELEMENTS: 53.11   PRESENTATION: 51.21

TOTAL SCORE: 104.32

TOTAL: 179.81 (1)

We won.

Holy shit.

We were always supposed to win. We were the favorites coming into the competition, but after everything we've been through, after the impossible highs and lows of the last few weeks, we actually did it.

I can't breathe because I'm squashed between my partner and my coach and I think maybe I'm crying? Which is insane and impossible because I never cry. Ever. But there are hot tears running down my cheeks and my throat is thick and I can barely breathe and my eyeliner is probably streaking over my face and I don't care at all.

"Your mom would be so proud of you," Camille says, and I know it's true, which just makes me cry harder.

When we finally pull back, the lights in the arena are going down. Event workers are rolling out the red carpets over the ice and the podium is in one corner, waiting for us to stand atop it.

"Here." Camille shoves a box of makeup wipes into my hand. God, I probably look like a total mess. We race back to the locker room, with everyone we pass shouting congratulations at us along the way and right before we get there, through my blurry vision, I think I see a tall, dark-haired figure disappearing down the long tunnel toward the exit, but then we're at the locker room door and Brayden is leading me inside so we can get camera-ready for the medal ceremony.

Was that Freddie? Did he watch? Why didn't he sit in the stands with everyone else?

I don't have time to think about it because I have to get my face looking like I didn't spend the last few minutes snotty and gross. I smooth back my hair when I look in the mirror and take a makeup wipe to the edges of my eye makeup, which mostly fixes the major issues, and then I reapply my lipstick. I have to be done, though, because a man with a headset is knocking on the door and speaking rapidly in French, waving us out of the room.

Brayden grabs my hand and we walk together back to the black curtain that blocks off the rink, and there's some kind of orchestral music playing that sounds like it should be backing an epic battle in a fantasy movie.

The announcer is introducing everyone and it's mostly a lot of French blending together, but then I hear "Walter Russo" and it occurs to me, though why I didn't realize it before is kind of ridiculous, that Dad is out there and he's going to be the one to put the medals around our necks.

My grip on Brayden's hand tightens and he squeezes back.

"It'll be okay," he says, and I believe him. Besides, this is *my* moment. Not Dad's.

"Médaillés de bronze Vera Petrova et Alexi Volkov de Russie!"

"Médaillés d'argent Rosalie Martin et Thomas Nelson du Canada!"

"Médaillées d'or et nouveaux champions du monde juniors de patinage artistique Adriana Russo et Brayden Elliot!"

We skate out onto the ice hand in hand, pulling up before the podium, where we stop and wave to the roaring crowd. Then it's easy. A kiss to each cheek for the bronze medalists and then to the silver medalists before Brayden holds out his hand and helps me up onto the podium and then follows.

We stand tall as the event workers walk out with the medals on their trays, holding them for Dad to put around the necks of the Russians and then the Canadians. The movie trailer music is still playing as he approaches us, but all the air and sound and people seem to be sucked out of the building and it's just us. Brayden leans down first and Dad puts the medal around his neck with a smile and a firm handshake.

Then he turns to me and meets my eyes firmly, but it doesn't feel like he sees me, not really.

Not that that's any different from normal.

I thought maybe, though, in this moment, things wouldn't be normal.

"Well done, Adriana," he says as I lean down for my medal. "Very well done."

He kisses each cheek and then he's stepping back. The world

returns to normal, the music still playing, the crowd still cheering.

"Mesdames et messieurs, veuillez-vous lever pour l'hymne national des États-Unis!"

"The Star-Spangled Banner" begins to play, like it did for Ben earlier this week, and I have a pretty good view of where our friends are sitting. They're all standing, singing along, and so I do too, focusing on the flag rising above the others toward the rafters, slowly but surely as the music swells.

I mouth the words to myself, but Brayden sings, mostly off-key, and we laugh as the music ends and the crowd cheers again.

Then we're being led down from the podium, a worker ushering us toward a row of photographers all bunched together off the ice. We pose with our medals held up, with our medals down, with our arms around each other, and with flags they have for us to put around our shoulders. Then they send off the Canadians and Russians and the pictures are of only us, the clicks and flashes and their instructions, mostly in languages I don't understand, blurring together.

The worker doesn't let us pose for long and eventually, he calls off the small on-ice photo shoot and motions for us to leave the ice.

That's it.

It's over.

All that work and it's over.

And the work begins again.

A month until the Senior World Championships, if Charles is right about what the NFSC is going to want. And then two more Worlds after that until Milan.

No. No, it's not over yet.

We have a party tonight. We're going to celebrate and enjoy the moment.

Enjoy our win.

But first, the media.

It might only be the Junior World Championships, but the crowd of reporters waiting for us once we leave the ice is the largest I've ever had asking me questions at any competition, even the US Nationals, where people are usually curious about Walter Russo's daughter and Elisa Russo's sister, and I'm pretty sure I have our newfound fame to thank for it.

Now, though, the questions are rapid-fire, most in English, but those that aren't are translated by someone from the NFSC and my head is spinning, but Brayden has a charming smile and a quick quip for everyone.

Then, finally, though I'm surprised it didn't happen earlier, one of them asks, "There is a lot of speculation that the two of you are a couple off the ice. What's the status of your relationship? Are you dating? Are you just friends?"

I open my mouth, but no words come out. We've been pretending for a while now, but we've never *officially* confirmed anything and in the mess of the last few days, I never came up with an answer, but then Brayden leans forward and says, "I love this girl, so much. She's my best friend, maybe my only *true* friend, and someone I'd trust with my life. She's my skating partner and there's no one else in the world I'd rather skate with, no matter what. Maybe people don't understand that, hell, sometimes *we* barely understand it, but I wish everyone could have a partnership with someone like Adriana so they could know that being *just* her friend is worth more than anything."

And I'm crying again and manage to choke out a laugh. "Am I supposed to follow that answer? What he said, every bit of it. I'm so proud to skate with him and I'm so proud of what we did here in Paris and I can't wait to see what's next!"

"Okay, that's enough," the NFSC official says, and we're led away from the media pen and back toward the locker room. It's the last time we'll be in it and I'm going to miss this bare-bones room with its sad paste-on mirror against the wall and little, completely empty water jug in the corner.

"Did you really mean that?" I ask as I reach for the zipper of my dress.

"I did," he says, and looks me dead in the eye. "I . . . I haven't been fair to you. This whole time, I was just, I was hoping . . ."

"It's okay."

"No, it's not, but I think . . . maybe it will be. If you meant what you said, I mean. We won gold and that should be enough. I'm invoking our last rule. I'm calling it. I don't think I can pretend anymore."

"Yeah," I say, nodding, and his shoulders deflate because I think maybe he was hoping I'd disagree and maybe that was his last bit of hope and God, this sucks. I want to give him something, anything to make it better and I don't have much, except, "I meant what I said too, you know. Every word."

Brayden nods and then heaves a sigh.

Silence reigns for a minute and it's awkward and awful and I need to fill it. "So what do we tell everyone?"

"Who cares? Let them wonder. It's more mysterious that way.

Social media will go crazy. Sponsors aren't going to care *why* we're famous, just that we are." He sends me a mischievous grin, and it doesn't quite reach his eyes, but that's a Brayden I recognize, at least. "Charles said they're going to want us to go to Worlds. I kind of like winning golds, and we set another world record tonight. Why don't we go for another? What do you say to youngest *Senior* World Champions ever?"

"I say you're completely cracked, but it'll be a hell of a lot of fun to try."

His grin widens and his eyes crinkle at the corners and yeah, okay, there he is, finally. Maybe we're going to be okay. "Yeah, I think so too."

"C'mon, there's a party waiting for us back at the hotel and we should celebrate tonight because it's back to work tomorrow."

AS SOON AS we step through the doors the doorman holds open, the lobby bursts into cheers, like what I imagine the sound the most epic surprise party would make, except it's not a surprise, it's our just desserts.

Drinks are flowing, not only in honor of our victory, but because with the close of the ice dance competition, the competitive part of World Championships is over. Charles and the reps from Nike are tucked away in a corner. Apparently they're about to make us an offer, a big one, and they never even mentioned our supposed romance. They think we're gonna crush it in Milan.

"You won!" Maria says, stumbling into me with Charlie in tow and I'm pretty sure someone gave them alcohol because they're both giggling like idiots. "You're in trouble, though."

"I'm in trouble?" I ask, grinning at Brayden, who rolls his eyes.

Maria looks around, like she's worried about being overheard and then she stage-whispers, "Dad *knows* and it's not my fault, I told Elisa and she told him like right away because she's Elisa."

"Wait," I say, holding her by her shoulders and trying to get her to focus. "What does Dad know?"

"He knows about your . . . emancepanda."

"Emancipation," I say, groaning. "Damn it. That's *not* what's happening."

"S'what he thinks, and he's *pissed*."

I leave Maria and Charlie near the door and step into the mass of people, my height letting me see over them easily enough, and I spot Dad, sitting in a corner with Elisa and Camille. My coach is talking, but it doesn't look like either of them are listening. Elisa is staring across the room at Charles and the reps from Nike, but Dad? He's looking at me.

Shit.

"I need to go handle this," I say to Brayden, who followed me closely.

"You want me to come with you?"

"No, I need to do this myself."

Steeling my shoulders, I head straight for them and don't mince words.

"We need to talk."

Dad raises his eyes to me and nods. He stands and Elisa follows. Camille furrows her brow at me, in confusion. No, he wouldn't have said anything to her. That would be embarrassing. They're pissed, but not enough to air their dirty laundry. Never that.

"What's this I hear about you emancipating yourself from this family?" Dad asks as soon as the door of a small room off the lobby is closed behind us.

"You heard wrong," I say. "I asked Charles to look into setting up a trust for me to keep my money safe until I turn eighteen."

"Safe from me," Dad says, his tone clipped.

And there it is. There are two paths ahead of me. I can do what I've always done and smooth this over. Reassure him and Elisa that it's not true. Or instead I could . . .

"Safe," I repeat, but I continue before he can respond, using the voice I've developed over the years answering calls from bill collectors and angry parents. It makes me sound way more grown-up than I feel, but that's the point. "I plan on contributing a portion of my earnings to Kellynch and giving myself a monthly stipend, but mostly the money should be in an account, gaining interest. I might want to go to school someday or, I don't know, something, but that's what I plan on doing. I don't want to be emancipated, but it was suggested that would be a solution, if you have objections to these ideas."

Dad raises an eyebrow. The implication is clear, let me do this or let the entire world know he wants my money.

That's an easy choice for him.

He waves a hand dismissively. "Well, it sounds like you've thought it through. Your mother was always good with finances too. I'll tell Charles that he should set it up as you've outlined."

"Thank you," I say, and when he leaves, I let out a shaky breath of relief.

"I hope you're happy," Elisa says as the door clicks shut. I'd almost forgotten she was there.

"I am, actually, for the first time in a really long time."

"You say that now, but you don't understand what comes next. The pressure, it's . . . it's impossible."

"I think I'll be okay."

I know I will. I have Brayden and Camille and my friends and Charles . . . maybe even Dad now.

Elisa's shaking her head. "You don't understand what it's like. No one expected you to be great. No one ever has, especially not Dad. You've been able to skate in the shadows your entire career and get away with it. I was the one who had to live with the pressure of our family's fucking legacy. I was supposed to medal in Beijing and I didn't. I choked and now I have to live with it, but you think you'll be okay? Great. Just one more thing you can take away from me."

She's angry. She's lashing out. It doesn't have anything to do with me.

I know that, deep down.

But it doesn't make it hurt less.

It also doesn't mean I'm going to let her get away with it.

"You know what, I'm done. I won a gold medal tonight. I'm not going to let you ruin it. I deserve to enjoy this. I wanted to enjoy it with you, but apparently that's asking too much."

I don't let her respond, but as I stomp from the room and head back into the party, I hear her let out a choked sob as the door clicks shut behind me.

Chapter 22

HE CRUSH IN the lobby is immediately too much. There are too many people. Too much noise. Too much light. This party is basically for me and I can't stand to be there for one more second. I duck my head and make for the elevators, smiling and nodding at everyone who greets me along the way, but not stopping.

I fold my arms around my middle while the elevator's floor number runs down from four to three to two to one and then finally the doors open.

There are people gathering behind me. So much for a private elevator ride where I can sob to my heart's content. When the doors open, I step in and immediately move to the back, pressing myself into the corner, hoping they don't notice me. They're wearing bemused expressions, like they weren't a part of the massive crush of a party, so my shoulders relax a little bit. They won't recognize me. They'll have no idea that I'm Adriana Russo of the Kellynch Russos and that I shouldn't be upset or angry right now. That I should only be feeling joy and accomplishment and all the other things that go along with winning a gold medal.

"Quatre, s'il vous plaît," I say in my best attempt at a French accent and one of the men in the group presses the fourth-floor button for me and I'm relieved to see they'll be getting off at two.

We ride in silence and they leave without a word, and as soon as the doors close behind them, I feel the tears burst forth like a tsunami. There's no way to stop it or choke them down.

I shouldn't have to threaten my father with public embarrassment in order to keep him from stealing from me. Because that's what it would be, even though he would never see it that way. It's entirely fucked up and it's my family and there's nothing I can do about it except cry.

Twice in one day.

Probably some kind of record.

Those were happy tears, but these?

It's not only sadness. It's frustration and disbelief and anger at my own disbelief because how could I be so naive to not see any of this coming?

Blindly, I tread down the hallway and unlock my hotel room door before shutting it behind me and bolting it. Maria's at the party. She won't be back for a while, but I definitely don't need her to see me like this. She wouldn't be able to handle it.

And that's fucked up too, because even after all of this, I'm *still* thinking about what my family needs and wants before me. It might actually be good for Maria to see what Dad and Elisa think is important, more important than me and very likely her as well. Money and prestige. That's it.

I'm not really sure why I assumed anything else mattered, but I won't make that mistake again.

Lesson learned.

I step into the room and kick off my shoes and my foot lands on something, a small packet of paper I can't really make out as I lean forward in the dark. Patting the wall beside me for the light switch, the small hallway that leads into the main part of the room is suddenly lit in a warm golden glow from the ornate sconces that sit on each wall.

It's an envelope, a pretty thick one, with my first name scrawled across the back.

"What the hell," I mutter to myself, like I'm Alice wandering around Wonderland. I roll my eyes, again at myself, and then laugh.

Well, at least I'm not crying anymore.

Picking up the envelope, I move into the room and sit down on the edge of my bed. My name is printed across the back in handwriting I haven't seen in years but recognize immediately.

It's Freddie's.

He left me a letter . . . about what?

I'll never know unless I read it.

Taking a deep breath, I slide a finger beneath the seal, and it pops open. There's a small card tucked inside with a recipe written on it. It's for coq au vin and the card is embossed with the logo for the restaurant we went to the other day. *Thought you could try this when you get back home* is scrawled in the corner of the card in Freddie's precise handwriting.

A teardrop rolls off my cheek onto the corner, smudging the ink a little. He noticed I liked it, and what? Went back to ask the chef for the recipe, even back when he thought Brayden and I were together? I struggle to pull in a breath as a tsunami of affection crashes over my heart. I . . . I love him so much. What the hell am I going to do?

I glance down at the envelope and there's a thick sheet of paper still folded inside of it. Pulling it free, I see it's a piece of hotel stationery with the same handwriting neatly covering every inch of space.

Dear Adriana,

I'm writing this letter before you go out on the ice and skate, completely confident that by the time you read it, you'll be a World Champion. You were always meant to be standing at the top of the podium because you're the hardest-working person I've ever met, not to mention the best skater I've ever seen.

You'll probably deny that. You're already listing all the skaters who have superior skill and technique in your head. Stop it. None of them are you, so to me, all of them fall short.

You're probably wondering what this letter is even about, why I'm writing and if you should keep reading. I hope you will, but I understand if you don't. This is my third draft and I hope I'm able to finally put down exactly what I'm feeling, but I've given up on making it much more than just a ramble.

So here it is, the truth. My truth.

When Georgia told me that we'd be training at Kellynch before Worlds, I was furious. In fact, I'm not sure that fully covers it. But I was terrified too. I was so scared that going back to the place where my world crumbled out from underneath me would destroy everything I built in the last two years. That it would destroy the person I've become. I learned to live without you in my life and it pissed me off that you were being forced back into it. I tried to pretend, pretend that being around you didn't eat away at me, pretend that not only was I over you, that I was stronger and happier and better, even, than the decimated sixteen-year-old who left Boston heartbroken and never looked back.

I wasn't wrong. I was right to be afraid. The layers I buried my old self under were peeled away, every day, every hour until I couldn't hide from it anymore just by being near you.

I know I made you feel like maybe I still resented you. That I blamed you for making the choice you did. And then you confirmed it the other night and it's been driving me nuts ever since.

Maybe I did blame you, at first. I've been stewing in that anger and resentment for years. It's what fueled me. It's what got me out onto the ice every day. It's even what made me first ask Riley to be my partner. She was as different from you as I could find, in every way. She looked nothing like you, she skated nothing like you. And it worked, for a while. It let me see who I could be without you and it turns out that's a pretty damn good skater and, when I'm not being blinded by jealousy, a decent partner. I failed Riley, in more than one way, and I'm determined not to fail her again. I'm going to be better. For her.

Which is why I have to tell you how I feel, how I really feel, because I need to be honest with myself. I've been in love with you since I was ten years old. I might not have known what to call it back then and up until a few days ago I would have denied it with my dying breath, but that's the truth.

I love you.

I always have and I always will.

I tried to stay away from you. Tried to just ignore you and avoid you and I failed. I've never been happier to fail in my life because I think that maybe I'm not alone in this. That maybe everything I'm feeling, you're feeling too.

Maybe this is the coward's way out, leaving you a letter like this, not facing you and telling you, but I know I'm probably crossing a line here and you've probably moved on, but if there's the slightest chance, I can't leave it unsaid.

A look or a word will be enough to let me know if I've read this all wrong or if, somehow, I've read it right, but no matter what you decide, I'll respect it.

Love always,

Freddie O'Connell

I release a long breath because I held it the entire time I was reading.

He loves me.

He's always loved me, even when he tried to convince himself to hate me.

Just like I loved him, even when I tried to convince myself I was over him, when I tried to convince myself it was okay that he was over me.

We're such idiots.

And yet, even though this letter is everything, even though all I want to do is run out of this room and find him and kiss him, I can't do that. He must not know how Riley feels. Though, how can he not?

And suddenly, I know what I have to do. I need to talk to Riley, right now. I'm going to tell her, be totally honest and whatever she says, that's what I'm going to do, because I owe her that much at least. Both Freddie and I do.

Pulling out my phone, I go to text her, only to see that there's already a message from Riley waiting for me.

Where are you? Everyone wants to celebrate with you!!

I tuck the letter inside my suitcase, burying it under my clothes, splash some water on my face, fix what's left of my makeup, and then head back down to face the crowd. This day has been wild, but I've had way worse, and right now it feels like anything is possible because I'm a World Champion and Freddie O'Connell loves me.

When the elevator doors open again on the ground floor, the crowd has thinned a little bit, but not much. It's getting late, nearly midnight, but most people are still going strong. Including Brayden, who is leaning against the bar chatting with one of the girls from the French team. He catches my eye and I raise my eyebrows and he shrugs helplessly before refocusing on the brunette.

Scanning the crowd, I catch a glimpse of Riley's crutches leaning up against the far wall, near the café, and there she is, sitting at a table with Ben and Freddie, because of course.

I take a deep, steadying breath and then release it before heading right for them.

"Hey, guys," I say, hoping my voice doesn't sound as squeaky as I think it does.

"Hi." Freddie's voice cracks a little and he's standing up out of his chair so fast it rocks back and nearly crashes to the floor, but Ben catches it.

"Hi," I say back, and smile.

"Hi," he says again, and a small smile starts to form on his face too.

I have to close my eyes to keep from getting lost in his and I'm about to ask them if I can talk to Riley in private, when Riley beats me to it.

"Boys, go away, it's girl talk time," she says, shooing them away.

Ben stands, clapping Freddie on the shoulder. "Let's go see if they have any more of those croquettes."

Freddie hums an agreement, but he stumbles a little when he tries to follow Ben without turning away from me.

"Ah, they're gone, okay, sit down, I have to tell you something," Riley says, grabbing my hand and pulling me toward the chair that Freddie vacated, and I brace myself because she's giggling, and I know that giggle. It's the same one she used when she talked about Freddie back in Boston or when she thought Brayden and I were together.

My stomach sinks.

"Ben kissed me!" I blink at her and wait because there's no way I heard her right. "Adriana, did you hear me?"

"Yeah, I think so. Did you say *Ben* kissed you? Ben Woo?"

"Yes!" she squeaks.

"Um, did you want him to?"

Riley grins widely. "I never even thought about it before, but then he was kissing me and I was kissing him back."

"So, you and Ben?"

"I know, right? Could you think of two more different people? He's so serious and I'm . . . well, not, but they do say that opposites attract, and I don't know, it could work. He came to the hospital every day, even after he won his gold, you know, to make me feel better, like I won't always be hurt and that I could come back. Part of me, like a really, really tiny part is glad I got hurt because I don't think we'd ever have figured this out and I'm so glad we did. I really like him. What do you think?"

"I . . ." I trail off, trying to process all of this. "That's awesome, Riles."

"Really? You don't think it's too weird?"

"Why would it be weird?"

"Because I thought that maybe Freddie and I would be a thing and then—"

"You're entitled to feel however you feel and if you like Ben and he likes you, then I don't see a problem."

"No, let me finish, though," she says, cutting me off. "I thought that it made sense, you know? Freddie and me? And then I realized that he just didn't feel that way about me. I mean, Freddie isn't the kind of guy to not ask a girl out if he likes her."

"You're right," I say. "He's not and . . . well, he might have . . . I think I might . . . I like him, Riley." Her eyes go wide. "I'm sorry, I should have told you so long ago, but then Brayden and I decided to pretend that we were . . ."

"You were *pretending*?"

"Yeah, it was such a stupid idea because—"

"Because Brayden is super for real in love with you."

"It was that obvious? Ugh, I'm such an idiot."

Snorting, Riley nods. "Yeah, kind of, but you guys are okay?"

"Yeah, we will be, but I had to tell you about Freddie because I think he might . . . no, I know he feels the same way, but if you aren't okay with it . . ."

"Are you kidding me? I'm so relieved. It was like he became someone else completely when we got to Kellynch and I couldn't figure out why, but it was because he was going to be around you, and God, it makes so much sense now."

"Yeah, we were all being ridiculous, weren't we?"

"Speaking of ridiculous," Riley says, glancing over my shoulder. "The puppy eyes he's shooting across the room at you right now are pretty intense. You should probably go put him out of his misery."

I turn, my eyes darting around the room, looking for Freddie. I scan the crowd in the direction Riley's staring and there's a head of brown hair over the crowd across the room, like when I caught a glimpse of him at the arena. That had to be him. He came and he watched me, but first he left me that letter. That's why he wasn't in the stands.

I stand from the chair so quickly I knock it to the ground, but I leave it there. I can't lose sight of him again. Not now that I finally have hope.

I battle through the crowd, which is getting rowdier by the moment, with fewer people but more alcohol. Charles shoots me a thumbs-up from across the room where he's standing with the Nike reps, but I pretend I don't see him and instead focus on Freddie's back. He's talking to Georgia, who meets my gaze over his shoulder and smiles and then nods to me, which makes Freddie turn around.

Finally.

"Hi," I say again.

He laughs and runs a shaky hand through his hair. "Hi."

"Can, uh, we talk?"

"Yeah," he says, dropping his hand and reaching out for mine, but then stopping halfway, like he's not sure he has the right. I don't let his hand get far. I take it and twine our fingers together, like I wanted to for every moment we were walking along the Seine.

"This way," I say, and lead him away from the group that's staring at our retreat, nonplussed. I find the door to the room off the lobby that I went through earlier with Dad and Elisa. Maybe I'll have fonder memories of it in a few minutes.

I lean back on the door, making sure it's closed to the prying eyes behind it and Freddie wanders into the room, suddenly pacing back and forth.

Then he turns to me, bouncing on his toes like he might spring away at the first sign of rejection.

"You read the letter?"

"I did."

"And . . ."

"You said a look or a word would be enough? Is . . . this not enough?" I ask, looking at him with all the love and want I can muster from within me. As I talk he walks closer to me, slowly. "I've been working on my expressions for years now and that's at least fifteen words, more if we count the number of times we've said hi—"

He doesn't let me finish.

This is how I've always wanted to kiss him. Without a care in the world except how long I can keep my mouth against his. His body is pressed to mine, and I wind my arms around his shoulders, pulling him in, burying a hand in his hair to keep us as close as possible. I deepen the kiss, my mouth opening under his, and a groan rumbles up from his throat. He wraps his arms around my waist, hauling me against his chest. And when I pull away to breathe, he shifts his focus to the line of my jaw and blazes a path over my skin, leaving a fire in his wake with just a gentle brush of his lips.

"Can I?" he murmurs against my neck, his nose against the soft skin at my pulse point.

"Yes," I manage to rasp, and then I'm almost lost again to the sensation. "Wait, no."

"No?" His brow furrows, pulling back with clear concern in his eyes.

"I mean, yes, but I need to say something first."

Reaching up, he brushes a stray curl off my forehead, his eyes running over my face like he can't choose where to look. "Okay."

"I love you," I say, and that pulls his gaze straight back to mine. "You said you were fighting against it all this time, and I was too. Nothing ever changed. I tried to pretend like it all didn't come roaring back again when you walked through the door at Kellynch, but it did, and it scared the hell out of me. I'm sorry if I sent you mixed messages or made you think that I . . . that I wanted someone else. I don't want anyone else."

"But Brayden?"

"We're not together. We were never together and that's a messy complicated story that I promise to tell you soon and hope you don't change your mind completely after I tell you the truth."

"I'm not going to change my mind," he says, but I just talk over him.

"And it was all such a mess and I was worried that Riley—"

"Riley?" he asks, tilting his head in clear confusion.

And that's when I realize he really was oblivious to it. This whole time he had no idea how Riley felt and there's no way I'm going to betray that, not even for him. We're a hell of a pair, both completely oblivious that our partners had feelings for us.

"You guy are partners and that's important. I didn't want to get in the way," I say vaguely.

"You won't," he says softly. "And anyway, Riley's with Ben now. He's been into her for a while, since Nationals, I think. It's hard to tell with Ben, because he keeps everything inside, but he finally worked up the guts to say something. If she can date my best friend, I think you and I should be okay."

"Yeah, she just told me about Ben."

"Is that why you needed to talk?"

I shrug. "Something like that."

He leans down, resting his forehead against mine. "You said you love me."

"I do."

"I love you too."

"That's what you said in your letter."

"But I wanted to say it out loud after *not* saying it out loud for so long."

"Freddie?"

"Yeah?"

"Kiss me again."

Chapter 23

"AND YOU'RE SURE you don't mind?" I ask Brayden as I straighten my costume for tonight's gala.

"Mind? No. Wish you'd said something a little bit sooner? Yeah."

I raise my hands in surrender. "No more secrets, I promise. You really think people aren't going to melt down about this?"

"Are you kidding? Of course they are. People love a love triangle. Just, you know, maybe stay out of your mentions for a few days."

I snort. My social apps have been a mess for weeks now. I'm a pro at ignoring them.

"Okay, as long as you're sure you don't mind."

"I don't mind. I actually think it's really sweet and that's what I'll tell any reporters that ask about it. If Nike doesn't give a shit, they won't either."

"You really are my favorite partner."

"Go," Brayden says, "before I change my mind." He's laughing, but there's a tension around his mouth that says maybe he's pretending a little.

I kind of want to give him a hug and press a kiss to his cheek, but I think maybe that would just make it worse, so I send him a tight smile.

I leave the locker room and head toward the ice, and that's

where I meet Freddie, who is racing down the tunnel toward me.

"Are you okay?" he asks, breathless. "Georgia said you had an emergency and you needed me here right away."

Shaking my head, I laugh, taking his hand and squeezing. "Not *that* kind of emergency. Breathe."

He takes a deep breath and then shakes his head. "What's going on?"

I hold out a bag. "Your skates are in here and the costume you were supposed to wear for the rhythm dance. It's not *exactly* right, but it's close."

"Adriana, what are you talking about?"

"You and me, we're going to skate 'Time of My Life' in the gala. In about ten minutes, so go get changed," I say, nodding toward the door to the men's room.

"You're crazy! How?"

"You missed your first World Championships, so I thought you should get to skate at least once, even if it doesn't count. And I'll probably regret this soon enough when you and Riley hit the ice again when she gets back, but you should get to know what it feels like out there in front of a packed house. It's . . . beyond description."

"You," he says, shaking his head, a sweet kind of awe washing over his face. "You are beyond everything."

"I know! Now go get changed."

He's back a few minutes later.

"We're cutting the big lift, right?" he asks, running a hand over the back of his neck. He's nervous. It's adorable.

"Uh, yeah, but we can probably do the others still, like the other night."

We walk together hand in hand toward the ice.

"Mesdames et Messieurs, nous avons une surprise pour vous ce soir. Malheureusement, l'une de nos équipes, Freddie O'Connell et Riley Monroe, n'a pas pu concourir cette semaine après une blessure à Miss Monroe." The spotlight in the arena shines on Riley, who waves to the crowd while they cheer. "Adriana Russo, leur bonne amie, patinera Freddie en hommage à leur coéquipier blessé. Veuillez accueillir Adriana Russo et Freddie O'Connell."

The lights go down as we skate out to a spotlight at the center and wait, only feet apart. And then the music starts, and the crowd makes the same delighted sound as the people did in front of the Eiffel Tower. An awed, collective gasp of excitement.

I smile as he crooks his finger at me, beckoning me toward him as he closes in himself, before he slings an arm around my waist and dips me low as his leg slides between mine. Then we spin together and I stand, my back to his front as my arm reaches up and around his neck, and he trails his hand down my arm, along the line of my body, before our hands meet and grip firmly and he spins me out into the dance.

The crowd is clapping along with every beat of the music.

And then I barely hear them and it's like we're back at that outdoor rink a few blocks away from the Eiffel Tower and we're skating for no one but ourselves, somehow even able to twizzle over the ice in perfect sync like we did two years ago, and then the music slows and it fades to a close and the crowd applauds for us.

We join our hands together and take a bow, one last time.

"Thank you," Freddie says as we skate off the ice, hands still entwined. "Thank you so much."

"I love you," I say simply, and that makes him stop. Instead of leading me off the ice, he's spinning me toward him and kissing me for the entire arena to see, and the crowd goes from polite applause to full-out shrieking.

When he pulls away, he's smiling. "If this is the last time we skate together, I wanted to make sure it was memorable."

Biting my lip, I shake my head. "Oh, I am *so* going to kick your ass at the Olympics."

"Bring it on."

Epilogue

Three years, eleven months, and thirteen days later . . .

"ADRIANA RUSSO E Brayden Elliot degli Stati Uniti d'America!" the announcer calls out to the crowd in the Mediolanum Forum, and like always, our fans shower us with shrieks of love and adoration, along with a downpour of stuffed animals we'll sign and then donate to young fans.

I can barely catch my breath and I'm not sure I'll ever be able to again. Brayden's hand is grasping mine tightly as we take our bows to the crowd.

Was it enough?

It's impossible to know.

We didn't give an inch, but then neither had our competition. Coming into tonight, the margins were so small, the tiniest error might be the thing that makes the difference. We skate to the edge of the rink and Camille is waiting for us, a wide smile on her face, and she pulls us both in for massive hugs, but her expression is tense, like she's as unsure as we are.

It's been back and forth for two and a half years now. Literally.

Ever since Riley's knee healed, we've flip-flopped with her and

Freddie for first and second place in every single ice dance competition we've entered. We won Nationals. They won Skate America. We won Worlds. Then they won it the next year.

And now, nearly four years removed from the Junior Figure Skating World Championships, where most of the media traces back our intense, but friendly (and in one way, more than friendly) rivalry, it's time to name an Olympic Champion.

We promised that it'll be okay between us, no matter what. That's what we decided four years ago on the ice in Paris. That no matter what happened on the ice, we'd always love each other, and nothing could change that.

It hasn't been easy and there's been more than one fight, more than one time when we've taken our frustrations out on each other, but mostly it's been everything I could ever imagine. I've been able to have it all. A great partner on the ice and a guy I love off it, and mostly it's worked out fine, especially after Brayden found a girl he wanted to go on a second date with, that student at MIT, studying brain and cognitive science, who calls him on his bullshit but loves him in spite of it. Turns out they were right to let her in after all.

The cameras in front of us are beaming our images up to the screen high above the crowd and to audiences back home, so I talk to them, sending Maria and Charlie my love. They're up in the stands, newly minted Olympic bronze medalists, with Dad and Elisa, who made another Olympics but isn't going home empty-handed this time. As a team, we secured a gold medal, like Freddie said we would, four years ago back at Kellynch House. There's no justice more poetic in the world, at least in the figure skating world, than my older sister getting her Olympic gold but having to share it, not only with her sisters, but with Brayden and Freddie and the rest of Team USA.

"I punteggi, per favore," the announcer says, and it brings me back to this moment. Brayden holding one hand, Camille the other. My eyes flick up to the scoreboard where Riley and Freddie sit in first place with a 227.52, a huge total score.

This is going to be so close.

Off to the side of the Kiss and Cry, Freddie and Riley are standing with Georgia, holding hands and staring at the scoreboard, but Freddie must feel my eyes on him because he looks down and we make eye contact.

I love you, I mouth silently.

I *love you,* he mouths back.

"Adriana Russo e Brayden Elliot hanno guadagnato nella danza libera, 139.2, il meglio di una nuova stagione per un punteggio totale di 227.46. Adesso sono al secondo posto."

There's a shriek of unrepressed joy from outside the Kiss and Cry. Brayden's hand tightens on mine, and my shoulders deflate.

It's not gold. It's silver.

Disappointment barely has a chance to fully settle in my chest before Camille pulls me into a tight hug and when she releases me, Brayden holds me against his chest. There aren't any words to say, nothing that will make it better. There will be time to deal with it in the days and weeks to come, but right now, I need to congratulate the new Olympic Champions.

Then the others converge, the bronze medalists from Canada along with Freddie and Riley. Brayden and Freddie shake hands.

They've developed something of a friendship in the last four years, and while I wouldn't call them close, there's definitely a certain level of respect between them.

Riley leaps at me, tear tracks lining her cheeks, and I catch her easily, the girl who has become more than a friend and competitor, but another sister. She came all the way back from a blown-out ACL to the top of the Olympic podium. "I'm so proud of you."

She hugs me tight, still sobbing, unable to speak. I finally release her to let Brayden give her a hug and I move over to the love of my life.

I rise up on the toe picks of my skates to wrap my arms around him. His forehead rests against my shoulder, his body practically vibrating with unbridled happiness.

I smile into the curve of his neck, the pain of the loss not gone, just eased the tiniest bit. "Next one's mine."

He huffs a laugh and holds me tighter. "Bring it on."

Acknowledgments

PUBLISHING A BOOK is hard. Publishing a book in the midst of a pandemic is . . . well, I'm at a loss for words, and that doesn't happen often. It always takes a village to bring a book into the world, but that was especially true this year.

First and foremost, to my editor, Julie Rosenberg, whose keen eye and instincts never fail to make me a better writer. You always know exactly what questions to ask, what buttons to push to gently guide my work into what I envisioned in my head. Thank you to the entire team at Razorbill and Penguin Young Readers: Marinda Valenti, Alison Dotson, Abigail Powers, Esther Reisberg, Tessa Meischeid, and Felicity Vallence. I am so lucky to have you all in my corner. Most especially, thanks to Simone Roberts-Payne and Casey McIntyre for holding my hand all the way through this one! And to Vanessa Han for taking my words and creating a gorgeous cover to wrap around them!

To Alice Sutherland-Hawes, for whom I am grateful on an hourly basis, for always having my back, believing in me and my books, and routinely making my dreams come true. I'm so proud to be a part of ASH Literary and cannot wait to see you do your thing for years to come. Thank you to the team Alice has assembled,

Alice Natali and Clementine Gaisman at ILA, and Tara Timinsky at the Gotham Group, for taking my stories to places I never even thought to dream about!

Writing can be isolating and that is even more true when you're writing in lockdown, but my writing community never failed to have my back through the chaos.

To my Writerly Crew: Mark Benson, Tabitha Martin, Jean Malone, Krista Walsh, Christian Berkey, Megan Paasch, Angi Griffee-Black, Trisha Leigh, Sarah Blair, and Jennie Davenport. You are a constant source of support and inspiration. To the most unlikely of sisterhoods: the phenomenal Katarina O'Dette, Jenni Rosal, Taryn Lentes, Ela G., and Dani Laver, for keeping me calm in a crisis and helping me let my muse wander where it likes. To my early readers: Jessica Swann, Brett Werst, Rachel Simon, and Natalie Crown, your insights and thoughtful feedback were everything I needed and more. To my work family: Michelle Heaney, Victor Correa, Bonnie Rubin, Colleen Korte, and Linda Wygonik, for always having my back. To the people who I can always vent to: Cindy Otis, Lisa Lin, Isabel Sterling, Sarah Henning, and Diana Urban, you keep me sane in this wildly insane industry. And to Hannah Stuart, for taking pity on a girl who didn't quite know where to start with this one! I, quite literally, couldn't do this without you all.

And, finally, thank you to my family, for being the reason any of this matters in the first place.